THE MISSING PIECE

Parul Sharma is the author of *Bringing Up Vasu*, *By the Watercooler*, *Tuki's Grand Salon Chase*, and *17, Morris Road*. She grew up in the small towns of India, absorbing their rhythms, contradictions, and social codes. She later spent two decades in qualitative research, listening to how people narrate their lived experiences. These twin apprenticeships in place and in people inform her fiction, which explores memory, belonging, and the evolving idea of home. Parul lives in Singapore with her family.

THE MISSING PIECE

PARUL SHARMA

hachette
INDIA

First published in paperback in 2026 by Hachette India
(Registered name: Hachette Book Publishing India Pvt. Ltd)
An Hachette UK company
www.hachetteindia.com

1

Print ISBN 978-93-5731-854-9
Ebook ISBN 978-93-5731-968-3

Hachette Book Publishing India Pvt. Ltd
4th & 5th Floors, Corporate Centre,
Plot No. 94, Sector 44, Gurugram 122003, India

Typeset in Ibara Real Nova 11.5/16 by R. Ajith Kumar, New Delhi

Printed and bound in India
by Manipal Technologies Limited

FSC www.fsc.org
MIX
Paper | Supporting responsible forestry
FSC™ C043100

For those who wonder where home lies.

1.

London, 1988 – Shiladitya

Shiladitya's daughter arrived in the world on a freezing night in London. Freezing nights in London were not something he was overtly fond of.

'People appreciate winter when they have enjoyed a full run of summer,' he would often say to the other homesick Indians in his neighbourhood at their monthly get-togethers. Dull evenings overloaded with Jameson whiskey and masala peanuts; everyone looking to get drunk quickly so that they could begin to forget and remember. 'How can we look forward to winter here when it's not been hot enough?'

How indeed! Before a chilly dusk could fall early, with an indefinable, smoky mist in the air, before they could gather around a small fire to eat moongphalis, making a veritable mound of brown shells at their feet, before they could warm their feet beneath the razai listening to Tai's stories about deadly chudails and covetous dayans, before they could rub their hands together to tease out some warmth, before all of this, something else had to come first: an endless summer.

A summer which would come blazing with unrelenting, oppressive heat, hot gusts of loo winds, power cuts, and scorched earth, but also gujhiyas, gulaal and thandai at Holi, the mango journey from Dussehri to Langda to Chausa, and nights spent sleeping under the night skies, a net massehri the only thing between them and the stars. This summer made it impossible to hurry for anything, forcing certain languorousness upon everyone, slowing everything down to a drowsy, laid-back pace.

'Bhai, we like our seasons four in number and well defined,' Shila would laugh, as he had done all these years.

Like back home, though that always remained unsaid.

Not once had he been back, not once.

All these years had passed and yet, the dream had remained unchanged. Bade Papa playing his harmonium and singing in his deep, sweet voice, 'Mera joota hai Japani, yeh patloon Englishtaani, sar pe laal topi roosi, phir bhi dil hai Hindustani.' Sometimes, he would wake with a jolt in the middle of the night, the strains of the song still in the air, having made their way from his dreams to the place where he tried to forget things.

Sometimes, he would sit at the table to eat and find himself suddenly and brutally ravenous for something that only Badi Mummy could make, aloo ka halwa perhaps, something that couldn't be bought, the memory of the flavours burning on his parched tongue. Sometimes, unexpectedly, he would think of Rajni Mausi sitting at her sewing machine and churning out blouse after blouse to put her three royal princes through school as they struggled to move their academic careers beyond eighth class. Sometimes, he would find himself sitting on a charpai in Bibi's courtyard, listening to all the gossip of the mohalla he called home. Whenever this happened, Shila tried to think of it as a wave of nausea. He just needed to sit still for some time, take a few deep breaths, and with time, it would pass. All of this, people, songs, home, was left behind in another space-time. And now he, like the man in the song, was only Hindustani at heart.

All this for Api. No regrets there, not ever. In which world did someone like Aparajita Dugar notice Shila, the 'scholarship boy'? That was all he had going for him back then, his college scholarship, established by a wealthy seth, in the memory of his young son, hard-fought and hard-won through years and years of swotting and slogging, in his room next to the terrace. The terrace itself was always boiling hot, always smelling of the pigeons that Natwar tamed and kept nearby. To get out, to leave, to get away from that small town, that was Shila's rosary. To not get trapped in the house-town-life of his father.

Though on that winter night, the night when his child arrived, he forgot all about the home he had left behind. Here she was, his flesh and blood, his firstborn, his only born. The cold, impersonal hospital and the interminable wait that he had spent pacing the hallways while his wife went through the pain of childbirth melted away as he held his child. He peered at her tiny, scrunched-up, perfect face, awed and delighted by her newfound presence in the way only new parents can be.

'Sukanya,' he said, a smile lighting up his own even features, the features that the little girl would assume before too long. 'Beautiful girl. Isn't that a perfect name for her, Api? She is pretty at birth, surely a rarity? Look at her, perfect as a rose. Someone has spent a lot of time on her, don't you think?'

Aparajita did not reply. Tired and overwhelmed, her desperation gave way to tears, making their way out quietly from the corners of her large eyes. Everything hurt.

'What is this, Api?' Shiladitya hastily handed over the baby to the six-foot tall maternity ward nurse who had been watching the new father inexpertly handle the newborn. The nurse discreetly made her way outside, taking the infant with her.

'Why are you crying, darling? Are you in pain? What happened?' Shiladitya asked again, gently pushing away the black strands from her forehead that had escaped the blue hospital cap, and sat on the steel stool next to her bed.

In response, Aparajita shook her head and said nothing. Shiladitya didn't probe any further. He knew Api's thoughts mirrored his own. On a day like this, they didn't know what they were supposed to do with all the unfinished business they were left holding. Who were they supposed to call? Who was supposed to come looking for them? What was to happen next?

2.

London, 1988 – Aparajita

Aparajita looked at her husband, holding her hand absently, lost in thoughts of his own. The newborn baby with the perfect face, her daughter, *her daughter*, was still with the nurse. The well of despair that she normally kept guarded rose once again. Had they been at home, her daughter would not be welcomed by the father alone. In the seventh month of her pregnancy, her mother would have arrived, bearing gifts for the godh-bharai. Songs would be sung in her honour as a mother-to-be and exhortations to be careful whispered as she did the simplest of things – walk, climb up steps and water the plants. And then, when the baby would arrive, there would be celebrations, songs would be sung, sweets would be sent to the neighbours' homes, the servants would be given money as they blessed the baby, protecting her from nazar again and again, cracking their knuckles on the floor.

Sukanya would not be named like this, by her father in a bare, impersonal hospital room where a picture of a smiling, plump, blue-eyed Caucasian baby on the wall was its only decor. The naamkaran itself would be an elaborate ceremony. Relatives from all over would come to their home and after due consultation with the stars and constellations in the skies above, the family pundit would announce the single auspicious letter with which the child's name must begin. Of course, Gulshan would dismiss pundits and their affectations in her inimitable way.

'These priests, they know how to ruin a baby's life. Listen to me, last winter, when Gaura had her son, the pundit said the name had to start with "jh". Gaura's father-in-law named his grandson Jhamroo. Now you tell me, is that a good name for a boy or a dancing bear?'

Gulshan, her beautiful, brilliant cousin, who could tell the most offensive jokes with a perfectly straight face, was now beginning to fade in Api's memory, becoming a relic in the secret heart where she kept Delhi alive. Gulshan, the only sister she had ever had. Gulshan, the one she had grown up with, had shared a room and clothes and toys with, the one who would sit with her every evening to solve tricky mathematical theorems and help her learn Keats and Frost, and write her essays. Gulshan, the one with that beautiful mind that got everything twice as fast as anyone else, the one that lapped up complex concepts and spat them out, making it simplified for a six-year-old. Gulshan who played Bach on the piano, had taught herself Spanish and Italian just for fun, whose stories were regularly published in the local newspaper.

Everything else was fading too. The sprawling, white-washed, garden bungalow in North Delhi with its wrought-iron gate, the lawns lush with daisies, pansies, tulips, the breathtaking Nathdwara pichwai made with real gold in the living room, a tribute to the Rajasthani roots of her father, the beautiful brass elephant that stood at the door, the stuffed cotton quilts with the kalamkari and leheriya covers that her mother would make and discreetly sell – all this was fading and soon would be gone.

Gone also would be the memory of her family. The stern, handsome father whose face would soften at the sight of Api. Her quiet, elegant mother, her head always covered with the pallu of her chiffon sari, besotted with Indian textiles, stately like a queen of some princely state. Api's widowed aunt, Kanta Bua, always in white, cooking this and that for her beloved niece. Api had become the child that Kanta Bua never got to have. The never-ending visitors, the retinue of loyal, ageless servants. The games of rummy that were played on the expansive terrace of their beautiful home on cool evenings would disappear next. The Lohri celebrations that their neighbours, the Malhotras, invited them to every year, would vanish too.

Api clung to the memories of the years she had spent in India. She did not regret her decision to marry

Shiladitya. Not ever. But her homesickness, cruelly and steadfastly ignored for a couple of years, a painful sore that had to be kept covered and cushioned, had reared its head ever since she conceived Sukanya, bringing bits and pieces of India to her in weird, senseless, vivid dreams of her own. She didn't know it yet, but she had passed on this strange homesickness to the baby.

Everything was fading. If you don't remember things, do they still exist?

3.

Delhi, 1981 – Small Towns, Big Cities

Every great city inspires and imagines its own version of a beautiful girl. Aparajita Dugar was one such girl from Delhi, her crisp chikankari kurtis and silver baalis drawing admiring glances and besotted gazes wherever she stepped. And yet, disturbingly enough, the tall, khadi kurta–clad Shiladitya Pandey, the scholar from some small town in the back of beyond would march past her without as much as a look. Shila hid his fears well and carried himself as if he really couldn't be bothered with anyone.

In her first year at the University, Aparajita relentlessly tracked this intriguing boy, saying nothing but always on the lookout for him, following his movements as he made his way from the college hostel to the classrooms to the library, his head always held high, never looking anywhere except where he was going.

Who was Shila back then, she would smile as she sometimes remembered those days to herself. He was superlatively sharp, that much was immediately apparent, more well-read than anybody she knew, save Gulshan perhaps. He had a masterful command over any topic he chose to declaim over. His English was sometimes suspect, learnt as it was from books, but it seemed absurd to make fun of someone so erudite. Api, raised in large parts by Gulshan, knew intelligence when she saw it and found it irresistible.

'Api, it baffles me, this infatuation of yours,' Charu Sinha, Aparajita's friend often said as she saw Api stare longingly at the oblivious Shila. 'Why anyone would pine over a boy who reads books that can serve as weights in a gym is beyond me. Look at him, that kurta is at least three sizes too big, though those silver buttons are pretty. And when was the last time he got a haircut? So dehaati, my God.'

Api would only laugh in response. The truth was that she herself did not know why she liked to look at the brooding and inordinately shy Shiladitya over the other attractive specimens doing the rounds of the college. These others were good-looking and well-groomed, scented with perfumes bought in the duty-free shops of airports around the world, careless with their money, generous in their disdain for anyone not like them. They were articulate and well-spoken, having been brought up in the company of accomplished men and women since they were children. They could talk about musical theatre and jazz clubs, and they were willing to take her to either, for Api had the self-assuredness of a much older person, like very attractive people often do.

Aparajita persisted with her silent devotion to Shila probably because she knew that there was no risk of this, this *thing*, going anywhere. Like most students attending college with the aid of scholarships, Shila stayed completely focused on his grades, always topping each course and leaving no doubt in the minds of the authorities that he really deserved to be there. Only later would Api come to know of his nightmarish anxiety over losing his place in the hostel if his grades slipped. He lived an austere life, always dressed in old khadi kurtas, a pair of tiny silver buttons connected with a chain – the only reminder of the ancestral jeweller's shop that Bade Papa had so carelessly lost. He spent every spare minute in the library, his sights now set on UPSC. A career in diplomacy. See the world a little bit. Count for something.

Shiladitya's grandfather had been a successful jeweller, owner of a large store in Meerut's Sarafa Bazaar. His son, Shiladitya's father, known in their mohalla only as Bade Papa, turned out to be a poet at heart, a man of bazms and mushairas, and therefore, with very little sense for business. The poor, beleaguered shop had to be sold soon after he took charge. Bade Papa was relieved; it was not for him: sitting at the galla, showing beautiful baazubands and chaandbaalis to unshapely women who didn't do them justice.

After saying a relieved, if untimely, goodbye to the longstanding family business, Bade Papa started teaching literature in a small local college. The modest salary he earned there was supplemented by the tuitions he gave to college boys particularly challenged in English. It was a hand-to-mouth existence but it was enough for Shila's father. His true passions were poetry and literature, and he spent most of his days rocking in an old, worn-out chair that had known better times, one leg draped over its arm, reading and re-reading *Anna Karenina*, *Rashmirathi* or *Of Human Bondage* with his myopic eyes, still a handsome man despite the receding hairline and the worn-out clothes.

'Wait till Shila grows up and becomes an IAS officer,' Shila's mother, predictably known as Badi Mummy, would say. 'He is not like his father. He'll go really far in life. My Shila is different.'

Shiladitya was different. Not only was he exceptionally bright, but from an early age, he also knew that the narrow gullies of Meerut and the 150-year-old ancestral Pandey house couldn't contain his ambitions and his plans. It was something that he never spoke of, but he never forgave Bade Papa for ruining things in such a spectacular fashion – selling the jewellery shop, allowing poverty and all its accompanying hardships to creep into their lives. Poverty, Shila would remind himself, was a parasite that was difficult to shake off, and he was determined not to follow in Bade Papa's footsteps.

At eighteen, Shiladitya was one of those rare men who knew, with an unwavering certainty, that destiny had something wonderful waiting for them just around the corner – it was only a matter of time before they would meet. His confidence in his future was so immense that sometimes Bade Papa couldn't help but feel that the cheap cotton kurta draped on his son's slender frame was melting away, replaced by a Brooks Brothers suit – the kind accomplished men wore in books. The boy had inherited his mother's graceful carriage, that much was certain.

Shiladitya's mother did not keep too well, suffering for as long as he could remember, but even that hadn't dulled the flawless lines of her beautiful face. She had been so lovely at sixteen that Shiladitya's father had been completely enamoured by her at first sight, immediately sending his mother that very evening to ask for her hand. Now after a lifetime of financial struggles, everyday compromises, and years spent with a particularly unambitious companion, she sometimes forgot to check her once-perfect reflection in the only mirror in the house.

When Shiladitya topped the district in his board examinations, Bade Papa tried to make a case for him to stay back but Shiladitya wouldn't hear of it. And when St. Theresa offered him a scholarship, it became even clearer that his future lay outside of the confines of Meerut. This was the small-town dream – to escape it at all costs, until they did, and then spent their lives being homesick for it.

'This is what I've waited for so long, Bade Papa,' he had said, pulling out the only suitcase the family owned – likely a relic of his mother's meagre dowry from her wedding. 'I need to step out, see the world. There is no competition for me here anymore. Everything is waiting for me out there.' The determination in his voice left no room for the weak arguments his father might have made. After bidding a series of curt goodbyes to the life he had known, and inflicting this first wound on his parents, Shiladitya left for Delhi, carrying with him large steel katordaans filled with mathris and laddus, tearfully made that night by Rajni Mausi and stoically packed by Badi Mummy.

Dhiren Chaudhary, Shila's unlikely best friend since childhood, made regular visits to him in Delhi. Dhiren's family owned vast tracts of farmland in the state, had in fact made a considerable fortune off sugar but wrapped in a chaadar and reeking of cigarettes, the stubble-covered Dhiren never gave away the slightest hint of his affluence. He had systematically failed every public exam he'd ever taken, only to promptly organize fraudulent certificates for each one, finding them perfectly acceptable. Fiercely loyal to Shila, Dhiren became the bridge between Delhi and Meerut, the old and the new, carrying news back and forth. Meanwhile, Shila avoided returning home even for holidays, preferring to stay in Delhi and study in the library, quiet and cool even in the most brutal of Delhi summers.

4.

Delhi, 1970s – Gulshan

It was because of the Gulshan Fiasco that Api was even allowed to attend the college of her choice, considering how the Dugar girls didn't study in co-educational institutes.

Gulshan, fair-skinned, long-haired, kohl-eyed, had been sent to live with Api's family after finishing high school at fifteen. Older than Api by a few years, she had been allowed to move to Delhi because high school was as far as her small town in Rajasthan went, at least for girls. High school and no more. The Dugar patriarch, Dada Saheb, fancied himself a progressive man, balancing his role as the head of both the family business and the household in equal measures. Under his watch, newborn girls were allowed to survive, were raised well in the family mansion, and given an education at the town's lone all-girls' school. This was enough.

Gulshan, being who she was, needed more. She had what one of her college professors would later call 'a once-in-a-generation kind of brain'. Even at the small school of her hometown, her exceptional sharpness didn't go unnoticed. Two of her teachers even went so far as to visit Dada Saheb, advocating on her behalf. *Send her away*, they urged, *let her study a bit more, give her a few more years*. The local MLA joined the chorus, it made the town look good if the girls were educated. And Dada Saheb, feeling very magnanimous, granted Gulshan this largesse.

This is how Gulshan came to live in her Chacha's sprawling bungalow at 101, Shankar Marg, in the leafy Civil Lines area of north Delhi. The house, surrounded by large, blooming gardens complete with fountains, servant quarters, and a small room by the gate for the guard, had been built by the British. 'It has good bones,' Chacha ji always said, with a touch of reverence for the colonizers. Chacha ji owned a large departmental store in South Extension, a business that spat out enough money to buy a bungalow like this. At first, Gulshan was a little awed by this new grandeur, but she soon proved that even Delhi was no match for her.

Api, just a young girl at the time, was thrilled to have Gulshan around. They went to the same convent school, and Api proudly boasted to everyone about her older sister, who seemed to collect every trophy the stern Catholic nuns could give out.

At home, Gulshan helped her Chachi with the quilts. The entrepreneurial gene had transferred effortlessly to her; she was the one who first thought of selling them from the house, with the living-room serving as the perfect display for the beautiful, hand-stitched quilts. 'Another step forward for the Dugar women,' she told her Chachi when the first payment came in from a handloom-sari clad Triveni Kala Sangam culture-vulture. Chachi shushed her, but the joy that poured out of her – as it only does when earning your own money for the first time – was undeniable.

Mrs Dugar's Traditional Quilts quickly grew into a thriving business, becoming a staple in well-to-do Delhi homes, de rigueur for a certain kind of Delhi winter, their warmth and beauty sought year after year, long after Gulshan was banished from the house.

School ended on a high note for Gulshan, right at the top, as expected. She shed her convent uniform, its hem precisely measured two inches above the knee and slipped into ikat and sanganeri print salwar-kameez seemingly overnight. Soon, she was attending an elite women's college in South Delhi. Chacha ji, of course, wouldn't hear of her taking local buses, so every morning Gulshan was duly packed off in the family car, silently reading *The Economic Times* on the way. As long as she didn't meet any boys and maintained her vestal virgin status, no one seemed to mind that Gulshan had now exceeded the educational expectations of a good Dugar beti.

There were whispers about her impending marriage, but Chacha, Chachi and Dada Saheb stood firm in defending her education. Everything seemed to be going well.

College was a delight for Gulshan. Here it was at last, the freedom she longed for, the women who thought like she did, and the library filled with works that gave shape to the thoughts that had been a confused jumble in her mind. Here were the professors draped in Bhagalpuri saris, their undyed hair worn in loose buns, referencing Marx and Foucault, smoking openly, and laughing with the abandon of freedom. Gulshan joined the theatre club and had the most wonderful time staging productions of *Waiting for Godot* and *Yayati*. She befriended exchange students from places like Barnard, Bryn Mawr and Fukuoka, became part of the quiz team that won the University Cup thrice in a row, and participated in fierce debate competitions. All of this strictly within college hours, of course.

Gulshan had finally arrived at the place she was meant to be all along. Every evening, she would come home and tell Api about college – where all good things happened, where women were equal to men.

Of course, she was careful. She knew that one misstep could cost her everything, unravelling the life she had meticulously crafted for herself, far away from the small town that destiny had once assigned her. She avoided boys like the plague – none of them was worth the risk. She didn't go out for late-night parties, or concerts. *Careful, careful.* And yet, there were nights she would stay awake, anxious about what the future held. College was drawing to a close. Her fellow students were preparing for competitive exams, with some planning to pursue a master's degree. Everyone was eager to see what their star student would do next, but Gulshan kept her plans to herself.

IIM Ahmedabad had been admitting women since 1966. She could combine her innate sense of money with a solid management education, later she could join a public sector company – iron and steel, perhaps – and then who knew what the future held? Times would change, evolve, and after enough time had passed, she could be the first woman so-and-so. She would drift off to sleep with these dreams every night, as a young woman of her intelligence and stature must, where things always unfolded in her favour.

When the time came, Gulshan went for the moonshot. She had saved enough money for the application forms, and Chachi blindly signed everything that Gulshan presented, so there was no obstacle there. She secretly sat for the admission test and found it as easy as she had anticipated. The group discussion and the interview also went smoothly. So far things were unfolding according to plan.

But Gulshan hadn't yet figured out what she would do once the admission letter arrived. An MBA – what would Dada Saheb say? Would he make an exception for her, allowing her to study alongside men? What sort of chastity promises would she have to make? How would she pull this off? She didn't have any answers. All she envisioned were plush corner offices, glowing balance sheets, and successful turnarounds for struggling companies. Admiration, success, and wealth – all hers by right. It was a vision she clung to.

The admission letter arrived. Chacha ji got to it before she did. As he opened it, Gulshan stood nearby, her heart sinking with each word that he read. The acceptance letter, inviting Miss Gulshan Dugar to join the incoming class of 1979, seemed to hang in the air, and then everything exploded in a spectacular fashion.

Chacha ji dragged her back to their hometown, cursing all the way. Dada Saheb slipped into one of his brooding moods and emerged from it carrying that old formula for keeping errant women in check – marriage, marriage, marriage. And not to some Prince Charming, but to someone, anyone, willing to marry her that very week.

Api heard about all this from afar, stricken and silent, realizing that they may live in Delhi, but the old ways were far closer than she had imagined.

Gulshan didn't even come back to collect the university gold medal.

5.

Delhi, 1981–84 – The India–Pakistan Issue

After swiftly putting all of Gulshan's promise to rest, Api's father and grandfather likely felt a sense of pride in upholding the family's conventional feudal values. There were murmurs of discontent – the town's Mahila Morcha had a few sharp words for Dada Saheb. At home, Api often found her father staring blankly at all the spots where Gulshan used to be – the swing in the garden, the small stool where she would sit and read, the dining chair opposite his.

Api's mother retreated even further into quilts, emerging only at meal times to arrange the dal, sabzi, papads, and chutneys for the family, as a good homemaker was expected to. Her mother's murky silence and her father's viscous regret became the defining motifs of the house with the Nathdwara pichwai.

News about Gulshan was sporadic, sketchy at best in the years after her marriage to a shopkeeper. Api heard that the newlyweds had moved to a different town, and that there were no children. A few years passed, and it was time for Aparajita to begin college.

'I was shocked to see you here, in St. Theresa's,' Charu would often laugh. 'Won't you get polluted by the mere presence of men? You're even drinking water from the same fountain!' Charu knew all about Gulshan, but she could never really understand how the seemingly modern Dugars of Shankar Marg had allowed such a thing to happen. Her own mother had been one of Gulshan's professors. Those people, that poor girl, her mother would mutter, shaking her head. Not that anyone ever lifted a finger to help *that poor girl*.

Things would have gone according to destiny's plan. Shiladitya would have graduated with a gold medal on his lapel, and over time, Api would have swallowed her silent admiration for him had it not been for the India–Pakistan issue.

The annual inter-college debate at St. Theresa's College was a prestigious event. Shiladitya, a consummate orator in any setting, needed the prize money and had prepared meticulously. Like many college debate topics, this one, too, was vague – something about the possibility of a plebiscite in Kashmir, leaving ample room for argument on either side. Shiladitya had combed through every book in the college library on the subject, examining the issue from every angle. He wasn't overly concerned. There was no one who could rival his expertise in these matters.

On the morning of the debate, he was confident, a little smug even. Little did he know that in just a few hours, the course of his life was to be altered forever.

The stage was set. A mix of intellectuals and pseudo-intellectuals graced the dais that day, their faces masked in feigned contemplation as college students presented impossible and creative solutions to a problem that had long divided nations. A hush fell over the crowd when Shiladitya stood to speak.

It was true that Shila spoke bookish English and could never have the fluency that students from first-rate schools had, but in the tight-knit debating community of Delhi University, he was something of a legend. Fellow competitors often conceded the first prize as soon as he entered the fray. That day, he roared about the topic for about five minutes, dissecting it from every conceivable argument and confronting the myriads of complexities that made the issue a political minefield for both India and Pakistan.

He spoke with a confidence rooted in his extensive knowledge of the subject, aware that he likely knew more than the esteemed judges.

As he concluded, he sent the applauding crowd an arrogant half-smile. His teammate greeted him with a doting look as he returned to his place. They shook hands, confident that the prize was as good as theirs.

The next team to compete comprised a couple of girls Shiladitya didn't recognize. Were they enrolled in his course? They didn't seem nervous at all. What was the short, curly-haired one saying? Oh, those were some impressive points. She certainly didn't seem like a novice. And what a polished accent! He leaned forward slightly, intrigued. She was on fire. And the crowd seemed to love her, applauding loudly every now and then.

And now the other girl, the one with the lovely eyes and a blue college sweatshirt, was taking her turn. She didn't have the same commanding charisma as her teammate, but there was something truly captivating about her. She was incisive and sharp, and everything she said had her personal quality to it.

He couldn't look away. Where had these girls suddenly emerged from? How had they mastered the topic so much better than he had? Why was the audience responding so fervently to them, as if they hadn't heard anything this profound before? He felt a prickle of discomfort.

'It doesn't look good,' muttered Shila's teammate in a whisper.

'No shit, Sherlock,' snapped Shiladitya, feeling nervous. 'Don't worry. We will bring it home in the rebuttals.'

The rebuttal round came, but the tables didn't turn. The two girls in the other team were clearly enjoying themselves very much, widening the lead with every question that came their way and smiling as if they did this every day. Who were they?

'And now we have a question for Shiladitya Pandey,'

the voice of the moderator cut through his thoughts, and Shila snapped to attention at the sound of his name. The girl in the blue sweatshirt was now standing and smiling at him, asking a question of him. Shila felt his heart race.

He had never noticed this girl in college, did not even know that she studied in the same course, had no inkling that she had tracked him like a hawk from afar for almost three months. Who did she remind him of? Some yesteryear Hindi film actress, the ones who look beautiful in sepia pictures, with ringlets and saris and all? Her smile deepened her eyes and lit up her face. Yes, she was definitely worth a second look, and a third, and many more, he found himself thinking and then realized with horror that she had finished speaking and everyone was looking at him expectantly. He had no idea what she had asked him.

Shiladitya took hold of himself and then spoke the words that he had never before had to speak in all his years of public speaking. He blinked, and the fog lifted.

'Could you repeat your question, please?' he said.

'Of course,' she said, smooth and poised, ignoring the sniggers that rose from the gathering, looking straight at him as if they were the only two people in the room and had all the time in the world. She repeated her question, slowly, deliberately. He knew how to answer her; this was not a question that he wasn't prepared for. He cleared his throat unnecessarily. She was still smiling, he noticed, and her eyes were crinkling at the corners as she did so. Waiting patiently for Shila to speak, she rocked slightly on her heels as she dug her hands in the pockets of her jeans.

'You are right,' he finally managed, trying his hardest to ignore his dry mouth and the sweat that was making its way on his skin. He seemed incapable of saying another word and the moderator realized that, quickly moving to the next question after shooting a puzzled glance at Shiladitya. Shiladitya did not notice. His eyes were still fastened on the girl, who raised one eyebrow at him, and with her smile still in place, took her seat. *Bewitching*, yes, that was the word for her, he thought.

Shiladitya spotted her again outside the auditorium, holding the winner's big trophy, standing with a group of girls and laughing at some joke. He wanted to go and talk to her, ask her name, tell her more about himself, and convince her somehow that the tongue-tied version that she had seen inside during the debate was an unfortunate aberration, no more. But before he could do any of this, she caught sight of him and detached herself from the group to walk to him.

'Congratulations,' she said, looking at his second-place trophy and certificate, 'though it was just too bad about you losing the first place.'

'All thanks to you,' he replied, the words getting stuck in his throat.

She laughed, and suddenly, stray phrases from books that he had grown up reading began to swirl in his mind.

She was Elizabeth Bennet of course, lively and light-hearted; but also Daisy Buchanan whose voice was full of money; and Anna Karenina, melancholic and complex. Before he could proceed to Catherine Earnshaw and Jane Eyre, he realized she was speaking again.

'Oh come on,' she said, 'I never thought I could impact anyone quite like that, least of all you, Shiladitya Pandey, topper extraordinaire.'

He looked away, surprised that she knew about his academic standing, surprised that she knew anything about him at all. How had she even noticed him?

'But tell me, Mr Pandey,' she continued, still teasing him, 'exactly what happened in there?'

'You did,' he said, and for a fleeting moment, he saw the self-assured smile on her face falter. Then she laughed again, quickly reclaiming her composure.

'If only I had known earlier how easy this would be,' she said. 'I wouldn't have waited this long. Anyway, now will you lock this money up like you always do or is there an ice-cream waiting for me somewhere?'

Shiladitya wanted to buy all the ice-cream parlours in the world and place them at the lotus feet of this diva who had surfaced out of nowhere into his life.

'Out of nowhere!' She would scoff in the later years when he would remind her of that fateful day, 'I had been under your nose all along, but it would have needed you to look up from your books.'

Much like everything else in his life, Shiladitya's love

for Aparajita Dugar was deep and lasting and had no room for frivolity. He could not see beyond her. He saw her every day and followed her around unashamedly, worshipping her every move, painfully devoted.

They sat next to each other in the library, their one sanctuary, where they held hands and stole kisses, their whispered words echoing in the silent halls. She laughed at all his jokes. He adored her laughter. They walked all over the university campus like the couples before them, feeling that the smoky evening of that famed Delhi winter had been created especially for them.

But that was the extent to which the romance could progress. There were no rickshaw-rides to go and eat chhole-bhature at the market nearby. There were no spontaneous matinee shows at the cinema halls of north Delhi. There were no Sunday afternoons at Janpath to buy her cheap silver trinkets. All of this was denied to them.

It was a wonder that someone like Api, so confident, so well-spoken in college, shrank into a nobody when she went back home. It was Gulshan who had once noticed the fresh green grass blades growing out of the thin cracks between the bricks on the pavement and said with a loud laugh, that's us alright, the Dugar girls.

For Aparajita, meeting Shila was like stepping into a dream, a dream where the Dugars from Shankar Marg did not feature.

'Dada Sahab is an absolute terror, thundering around the haveli like some film patriarch. He has written a role for himself and performs it like a method actor.' Aparajita told him very early in their relationship, 'He married Gulshan off to some obnoxious man in a week's time. He threw a right royal fit even about my joining St. Theresa's, it happened only because Papa is so guilty about what they did to Gulshan. As he should be. But Shila, let's not fool ourselves; he would rather disown me than have me marry someone outside the caste. They are very old-school in that way.'

Dada Sahab's horror stories often kept Shiladitya up in his hostel bed at night. In fact, in the later years when he thought about that time, he recollected worrying so much for Aparajita and what his decision would mean to her that he almost forgot to think about his own family, about his father's inability to stay in the real world, about his mother's towering ambitions for him. In his mind, there was never any doubt about spending his life with her, but he knew that despite all her dissatisfaction with her family ways, she was deeply attached to them. This was true. While Gulshan had appeared to think of the Dugars purely as academic specimens to be studied under a microscope, Api had deep ties with the idea of family, contained within a home.

He was still mulling over this, no solution in sight, when placement season kicked off in college. A British pharmaceutical company, known for its tempting offers, was one among the many that came to recruit fresh graduates. Shiladitya, with his characteristic nonchalance, applied.

'I didn't know you were planning to flee the shores of our sacred land, Shila,' said Api, when she saw the form that he was diligently filling out, trying her best to keep the panic out of her voice.

'Just for the experience, Api, just to see if I can clear the interview,' said Shila with a laugh. 'I'm not going anywhere. I'll stay right here in Delhi with you. My race will begin at Kashmere Gate and end at Hauz Khas, no more.'

He cleared the interview, though, and they were very keen on taking him. When he looked back at those days, everything seemed to have assumed a dreamlike fluidity; there was no knowing what would happen next.

They wrote their final year examinations and arranged to have letters delivered to Charu's house during the summer break.

'Of course the letters can come to my place,' Charu said, comfortable in the intellectual coziness of her own family, with their wood-panelled library and cerebral dinner parties. 'Goodness, but what an archaic family you come from, Api. Just please be careful. I don't want you to go Gulshan's way. So brilliant, so articulate, so all-around perfect, and now married to some bhondu. What I am saying is the Dugars need to chill. Anyway, I need to run. Who asked me to be the president of this blasted deb soc, please remind me. Now I am running around organizing the food like some shaadi wala caterer.'

6.

Delhi, 1984 – The Elopement

The end of college had arrived. Shiladitya had to vacate his hostel room. He spent the morning packing his meagre belongings and taking timetables and posters off the walls. Aparajita would be at home today, her family sitting around for an improbably elaborate Sunday lunch, he thought to himself with a smile, used to teasing her about these lavish weekend feasts.

He was to return to Meerut the next day for the summer break, and then, they would have to see how they could make a future together. He would write the dreaded UPSC prelims during the summer. Aparajita had said that she could wrangle permission for post-graduate studies – two more years in the sheltered sanctuary of the university campus. Somehow they needed to last till he made it into the civil service. After that, they could try to break some boundaries. Shila weaved these dreams, these plans, almost unconsciously all day long, turning them over and over in his mind.

He stepped out of the hostel, looking for someone to

eat lunch with, when he saw an auto-rickshaw pulling up at the gate. Aparajita got out and paid the driver. Something made her look up and catch Shila's eyes. In that instant, Shila felt his plans, so carefully constructed, unravelling right before him.

Aparajita couldn't stop crying. 'They will marry me off, Shila,' she kept repeating in between sobs. 'It's going to happen, and it's going to happen soon. Apparently, the talks have been going on for some time now. I...I didn't even notice, I was so busy with...everything else. Do you think someone tipped them off? They'd never stay quiet if they knew about us though. Oh my god, what am I going to do now?'

'I will talk to them,' Shiladitya said quietly, taking her hand.

'What makes you think that talking to them will change anything?' she snapped, yanking her hand away. 'What is this, some bilateral negotiation? If anything, it'll just spur them on to move faster.'

Shiladitya paused. 'Let me think for a moment,' he told her, his voice calm.

She nodded and sat down on a stone bench, watching him as he worked through the situation in his meticulous, logical way. Only once did he turn around to look at her, as if making up his mind about something.

'Let's go,' he said after about ten minutes.

'Where?' Api asked, her voice hoarse with the crying.

'It's over now, Api,' he said, as if discussing what he planned to have for lunch.

'What? What's over?' she asked, panic rising in her chest. Was he letting go of her? Would she have to go home where her wedding preparations would soon start?

'The secret courtship,' he said, hauling her to her feet with an ironic smile. He tugged off the pair of silver buttons from his kurta – the only thing of value he had on him – and handed them to her. 'I don't have a ring for you, Api, but keep this. Will you marry me? I am sorry to rush you, but I need an answer right now.'

'Marriage?' she spluttered, the words hanging in the hot summer air of that Delhi afternoon. *Marriage*. Things moved at lightning-fast pace after that. Shiladitya called Dhiren, and Aparajita was stunned at how deviously they planned everything, as if they had orchestrated a thousand elopements before this one. Shila would accept the job offer from the British firm. They would wed in secret, no one the wiser. Afterward, they would return to their ordinary lives, slipping back into the patterns of home and family as if nothing had changed, till it was time to leave.

'There is only one thing you need to do,' Shila told her softly as she stared blankly at him, 'get your passport out. That's it, I will take care of everything.'

It sounded ridiculous, it was ridiculous. Of course they would be caught. Gulshan had tried to keep a secret and had failed. How could they pull off something like this? To run away from India, their homes, their families?

Within the next month, Api became thinner and

thinner, dark half-moons appearing under her eyes, each and every moment bringing with it the terror of discovery. Each time the door to her room opened, she would expect to see her father barge in, furious, some damning token of her hidden plan in his hands. She had no way of knowing it then, but she would continue to get nightmares about being discovered thus for the rest of her life, tear-soaked dreams from which she would wake up completely panicked, her heart racing.

Not knowing what else to do and exhausted from holding everything within her for so long, she called Gulshan. As soon as Gulshan answered, all the closely guarded secrets spilled out of her like a torrent. Gulshan didn't interrupt. She didn't ask a single question at first, just listened closely.

'I know they will find out,' Api finally said. 'What will happen then?'

'They won't find out,' said Gulshan, calmly. 'Not if you are careful.'

'What do you mean, Gulshan?' Api asked. 'They found you out, didn't they?'

'Yes, because I didn't plan well enough. I've thought about it a lot, Api. I just hoped for the best and went along. That is the only reason things fell apart. They are not that intelligent. If I had saved some money and applied to a different address...anyway, let's not talk about all that for now. There is no time to waste. I'll help you plan. Just be very, very careful. It will work out, I promise.'

It did work out. In fact, in the end, it was shockingly simple. Gulshan guided Api every step of the way, with her trademark precision. Api's parents had to go to Rajasthan for a wedding of some impossibly distant relative, the invitation carefully crafted by Gulshan. Only Kanta Bua remained at home and whether by accident or by design, seemed to be completely oblivious of Api's plans.

On the day of her flight to freedom, Api walked out of the house at Shankar Marg and made her way to the airport. Nobody stopped her. Shila, Dhiren, and Charu stood waiting for her. Api would never forget the look on Charu's face as she waved goodbye, a mixture of pride, pity, and affection – so much happened in so brief a time. And then there was the flight to London, the plane soaring above the city of Delhi. Aparajita finally leaned back and closed her eyes. A silent tear escaped from the corner of her eye and trailed down her face. She felt Shiladitya wipe it off and take her hand. She opened her eyes.

'We will be very happy, I promise you,' he said. 'Now, are you hungry?'

She smiled through her tears and nodded. As she watched him casually ask the air hostess for some snacks, not betraying for a second that this was his first flight, she knew that she would never truly understand what it had cost him to abandon his family, his home without as much as a goodbye. What did it mean to let go of a dream that had lived with him long enough to become a phantom limb? Where would all that he'd aspired for – the positions of power and prestige, the important assignments, his name in the papers – go to die?

He was right; he did make her very happy. As the days passed, it became clear that no one would come looking for them, not in London. Charu was visited by Aparajita's family soon after the elopement. She had played the part of the innocent bystander, claiming complete ignorance in the whole affair, her stern-faced mother standing behind her in support while she was interviewed. It was obvious that the Dugars did not believe her for a second, but despite that, they chose not to pursue the matter further.

'A runaway,' her father had said, equal parts disbelief, rage, and hurt. 'Even if we found her, she won't find a match anywhere in our community. Let her be. We don't want to have anything to do with her.'

When Shiladitya learned of this exchange, he chose to edit it carefully before sharing it with Aparajita. In what was quite typical, his own parents responded to the elopement with complete silence. There were no tears, no recriminations, just a deep, dark, oppressive silence. He could see Bade Papa in his mind's eye, seeking echoes of his own disappointments in the verses of Ghalib, Faiz and closer home in Bashir Badr, but never openly confronting his son's betrayal, of his silent disappearance from their lives. Only a long, lonely silence.

It seemed there would be no way back home.

7.

London, 1984–2006 – The Days Are Short, But the Years Are Long

The early morning mist of London caught Aparajita just right and she found herself desperately longing for a hot, steaming bhutta at India Gate. It was happening more and more these days. But as she had done all these years, she swallowed that feeling, wrapped her green scarf around her neck, and stepped out with a smile, chiding herself for letting Delhi creep in through the cracks of her heart. She hoped that by the time she reached work, the weight of India Gate would have lifted, replaced by the sight of Westminster Abbey, foreign and distant. She was no longer a Dilliwaali, she reminded herself.

In the tube, Api thought back to when she'd first come to the city that had become her home. What were those first few London years like? At first, there was disbelief and exhilaration, Api remembered, lulled into a daydream by the steady hum of the train. They had made it! That had slowly given way to the business of life, to the daily grind. Shila had begun work as a trainee at the pharmaceutical company, a small step in a long journey. Aparajita had found work as a retail assistant in a large store, and they were truly pitch-poor to begin with, often too tired by the end of the day to think of much else except sleep. Yet, as happens with truly blessed unions, things improved steadily with every passing year. At the end of four years, they were no longer counting every penny and were able to afford an occasional night out or a holiday. Both of them recognized the unhealed wounds of homesickness they carried and tried not to talk about it.

Nobody from home ever reached out to Shila and Api in those strange years, but their friends stood in for family. Charu Sinha, now working with the United Nations and brimming with words like 'multilateralism' and 'consensus-building' would visit them when her work brought her to London, but her visits always left Api feeling unsettled and regretful for days on end. Dhiren came by only once. No more the intense, chaadar-clad, brooding man, he had now become quite portly. His elder brother had been murdered in a dispute over their sprawling sugarcane fields, and Dhiren, now the reluctant heir to the family's fortunes, responded to this new surge of responsibility by drinking heavily, cultivating the deadly cirrhosis that would eventually claim him at the ripe old age of forty-five. Gulshan kept in touch with Api now and then, but the conversations were almost always brief and hurried. She still hadn't had any children, but beyond that, she didn't share much.

The bhutta craving refused to die out, and Api suspected something was up. On her way back home, she bought a pregnancy test from Boots. Once at home, she dithered over it, holding it in her hands while she sat in the dark living room, trying to gather the courage to use it. She already knew what it would tell her. The cravings, the bouts of crying, the strange foretelling dreams that came to her every night – they could mean only one thing. She rose to her feet resolutely, and before she could lose her nerve, went inside the small bathroom.

The result was undeniable. Two lines. Strong and clear, a message from her future.

At first she didn't know how to feel. She didn't know whether she ought to celebrate or not. It felt wrong to be carrying her parents' grandchild while they remained half a world away, oblivious to all of *this*. She found herself apologizing to them in her mind, guilty, ashamed. She hadn't planned for the estrangement to last this long. She hadn't accounted for the cruelty of her parents, for their ability to carry their silence all these years.

Shiladitya, on the other hand, had no such misgivings. He was utterly delighted.

'Sure, it has happened a bit early, Api, but I wanted this all along. And to be honest...' he paused, drying a dish with a towel, his eyes softening as he watched her, tears streaming down her cheeks as she stood by the kitchen sink, washing up after dinner, '...everything happened so quickly that I've always felt that it wasn't real. That one day, I would wake up one morning and you would be gone. The baby will make it all...true.'

The days after Sukanya's birth passed in the sort of tired, aching blur that most new parents recall with dread. Late one night, as she rocked the baby to sleep, Api realized with a jolt that she hadn't heard from Gulshan in months. The next morning, she tried calling, but Gulshan's number had changed. Worried, she called the landlord of the house where Gulshan had once lived with her husband, only to be curtly told that she had moved. It seemed that Gulshan too had disappeared from Api's life without a forwarding address.

Api couldn't stop thinking about her cousin. What could have happened to Gulshan? It wasn't like her to float away like this. Why hadn't she let Api know where she was moving to? Finally, after weeks of seeing this endless worry chafe at Api, Shila suggested that they reach out to their families back home. They wrote identical letters, each word carefully chosen, speaking of having been in love, and of being scared, and of not wishing to cause hurt, and of the new baby, and if it would be possible to visit them.

Predictably, no replies came by returning post.

Months rolled into years, and slowly, Shiladitya and Aparajita let go of the hope of ever reconciling with their families. Their lives, once shaped by longing and guilt, now centred around the long task of creating a comfortable, stable life for their daughter – Sukanya – in a foreign country. Shiladitya, ever driven, rose steadily through the ranks of the pharmaceutical firm, his ambition and intellect carrying him effortlessly to the top. Aparajita completed her master's degree and began teaching Textiles and Materials at an arts university, in some way tethered to the threads of Mrs Dugar's Traditional Quilts. They lived in a small house on the peaceful, tree-lined streets of Hampton Close. And they had Sukanya.

Shila was besotted with his little daughter, now at that age where she needed more than just feeding and changing. Now she demanded games and stories, complete with sound effects and play-acting, which her doting father was ever-willing to supply. He didn't really know when he started telling her the stories of home. Holding her close at bedtime in her small nursery, the bed redolent with her baby smell, he started talking to her of his old mohalla of Bulandwada. Shila always had a way with words, and he was able to spin Bulandwada out of thin air for his baby every night, complete with its worn-out old buildings, its old-world smells, the sounds of temple bells and azaans, the hawkers that walked its cobbled streets – gubbarewala, chaatwala, budhiya-ke-baal wala, the interconnected terraces that spread for miles, and its funny, flawed characters, people that he had known all his life before they forgot all about him. Bibi and Natwar and Munto and so many others.

Shila wove in impromptu songs and poems into the stories, making young Sukanya laugh in delight.

Ghantaghar mein chaar ghadi
Chaaron mein zanjeer padi
Jab ghantaghar bajta tha
Khada musafir hansta tha

Perhaps it was a way for him to keep his home alive, to keep connected with the memories that were already fading. Every night, when he didn't need to be strong for Api anymore, already in bed and exhausted by the day, he could talk about home to his child.

Shila realized that he'd probably told the stories a little too well when Sukanya started refusing to even consider any other story.

'Which story do you want today, Suku?' he would ask.

'Bulandwada.' Sukanya would answer, throwing her chubby fists in the air.

'Again? How about something else today? *The Gruffalo? We're Going on a Bear Hunt? The Very Hungry Caterpillar?*'

'No! Bulandwada!' Sukanya would shout, crawling into the nook of her father's arm, knowing fully well that he couldn't refuse her, that she had him wrapped around her tiny little finger.

It was difficult for Shila to remember when his daughter finally outgrew the Bulandwada stories, probably around the time she started reading on her own. But by then the stories had done their magic, and imprinted themselves deep into Sukanya's psyche, never to be forgotten and always just a dream away.

The stories brought their own consequences. Even as a young child, Sukanya's sharp mind quickly began to notice that there was something amiss in her family, that there was no real-world equivalent of the people and the places from the stories about her ancestral home. Every time she expressed a desire to visit Bulandwada, she was told that there was no access to that realm. The older she got, the more pronounced the absence of these markers of childhood became. While her brown-skinned friends in school shared stories of long summer holidays spent in bustling homes in India, filled with the chatter of uncles, aunts, and cousins, her own world was quiet. There were no trips to India, no streams of buas and chachas and mamas showing up at the door for weeks on end, no stories of family reunions or weddings to attend.

There were many pieces missing in the puzzle, and they tormented her endlessly, creating an ache that she couldn't quite place. She would ask her mother about it, only to be met with a flash of sudden tears in her eyes – quickly masked, but unmistakable.

Shiladitya believed Sukanya deserved an explanation and would try to untangle the knots of his past as best as he could. He'd speak of the circumstances that had pushed them away from their families and the choices that had left them estranged, but Sukanya couldn't even begin to wrap her head around it, to fathom a reality where her parents had been forced to cut ties, to live with that kind of distance and loss. All she wanted with a childlike insistence was to be in the Bulandwada of the stories.

Thanks to this unresolved quest, Sukanya's teen years were particularly eventful. Gone was the sweet, plump, dimpled child in the dolphin-patterned pajamas. Shila would sigh to himself as he thought of that memory, to be replaced by a perpetually grumpy, confused teenager. Those years required infinite patience but they got through those too. But even after the stormy tantrums, sulks, and slammed doors had passed, and Sukanya was nearly eighteen, Shila could see that she felt unanchored in an inexplicable way.

'How can one miss people that one has never even seen?' he would wonder to himself, not wanting to upset Api if he could help it but nonetheless worried about his daughter and her unresolved dilemma about the absent family. At these moments, he couldn't help but feel a pang of guilt for the choices he'd made so long ago.

8.

London, 2006 – The Troubling Question of The Gap Year

Sukanya and Angelina walked side by side down a sidewalk towards school, as they had done countless times over their shared lives. They wore similar clothes – band t-shirts, denim jackets, and the ever-present combat boots clicking purposefully on the street, but that is where the resemblance ended. Angie's hair was dyed black, having rejected its flaming ginger origins a few years back, making her green eyes and pale skin pop. Sukanya, on the other hand, was brown-skinned and sharp-featured. Her long, unruly curls snaked down her back, dark against the cold morning. Much against Api's wishes, she had pierced her nose and wore a gold nose pin to match the multiple earrings in her ears.

At the age of nearly eighteen, Sukanya looked a lot like Shiladitya and had none of her mother's soft grace. Tall and lithe, she walked the same way as Shila, her patrician nose up in the air, deadlocked on where she was going. She took after Shila in more than just looks.

Like him, she was sharp-minded and projected the same self-confidence that seemed to border on arrogance, an effective way to hide her insecurities and confusion.

In many ways, Sukanya – Suki to her friends – was a fairly typical Londoner, with a steady wit and a politeness that became more evident when she was upset. She smoked Marlboro Lights with Angie when she could, drank furtively out of beer cans, and tried to fake ID her way into clubs and pubs. She was ardently devoted to Green Day and My Chemical Romance and followed their lives closely. She was also what Angie called a book nerd. With parents whose romance had blossomed in a library, it was a given that she was a voracious reader, a yellowing copy of *Trainspotting* wedged somewhere in her bag at all times, a literary talisman of sorts.

But the Indian part of her, the part that was brought up on Bollywood films, the part that spoke in Hindi at home (albeit with a decidedly clipped accent), the part that had imagined and reimagined the myth of Bulandwada through the years was restless. She wondered incessantly about who she was and where she was headed, a background hum that just wouldn't quieten down. But she wasn't a garden-variety Britain-Born Confused Desi either, given that she'd never even taken a flight to India. Her parents didn't insist on salwar-kameez and saris, festivals and fasts and feasts, but she still wanted to get to know her Indian story.

In only one way were Shila and Api typical desi

parents – they wanted to see straight A's and Sukanya didn't disappoint. Given her academic prowess, they had set their sights on the likes of Oxford and Cambridge for Sukanya, the meccas of learning from where their daughter would emerge a success, an achiever who could prove to the world and their absent families that they had done something right, that their running away from home hadn't destroyed everything.

Nothing had prepared them for Sukanya's reaction when they first brought up the topic.

'What do you mean – you don't want to go to university?' Shila had asked, bewildered as Api watched in stunned silence.

'You heard me, Daddy. I don't want to study further, at least not till I've had some time to myself to think things through.'

'But, Sukanya, what do you want to think about?' Shila was flailing about in confusion, the ground slipping from beneath his feet.

'I want to explore the world on my own. This readymade script that you've written for me doesn't work, Daddy.'

'There is no script, beta, I've no idea what you mean by that. Do you honestly think this is our bid for validation for our own choices, Sukanya?'

Sukanya kept silent. Shila saw her face and turned away.

'Please, just let it go, Daddy,' Sukanya called after him. 'I'll let you know when I'm ready.'

Soon, this became a bone of contention in the household and led to heated exchanges nearly every day. Shila would try to reason with her, Api would cry despite herself, and Sukanya would declare ever-more heatedly that she wouldn't even think about university.

On that morning, as she walked to school with Angie, she was seething, still stinging from yet another argument with her parents that morning about her future plans.

'It's all we ever talk about these days. I don't know why they have this need to pack me off to uni as soon as possible,' she muttered, kicking the pavement. 'Fact is – I don't know what I want to do yet. I need this gap year to figure things out, Angie.'

'Lots of people take gap years. What do you want to do? Travel? Work?' Angie asked.

'Nothing. I want to do nothing,' Sukanya said, her tone militant.

Angie raised an eyebrow. 'Now I see what the problem is.'

Sukanya let out a long sigh and rolled her eyes. 'Daddy just wants me to have everything planned out and sorted. I think he is shocked that I don't want to go to uni right away. Sometimes I feel I don't get them at all.'

Angie gave her a look – kind, but sharp. She understood. Sukanya caught the look and sighed.

'I know, I know! I don't blame him, but all this elopement stuff, with their families still back in India.

Who are these people out there in Bulandwada, Angie? I *need* to know! It's like there is a missing piece of me just floating out there somewhere. And I don't like that I haven't seen it for myself. I want to meet them, Angie, I want to make up my own mind about them.'

'Oh, yeah, that sounds about right,' said Angie, wryly, well aware of Sukanya's need to see things for herself. Sukanya laughed at her tone and linked her arm in Angie's as they crossed the street, her mood lifting.

'Listen to me, Suki,' Angie said, watching out for traffic. 'All this missing piece business is cool and all, but you've to still study, yeah?'

'I get that, and I will get to it eventually, though I honestly can't tell how a degree is meant to sort me out.'

'Oh trust me, you will need a lot more than a degree for that!'

As Sukanya and Angie walked to school, Shiladitya made his way to work, a lone figure walking along the riverbank in the kind of suit that his father had wanted to see him in. Now in his early forties, he was a quieter version of his younger self; the sharp pangs had given way to a dull, familiar ache. The years had been kind to him; he still looked the same, a little thinner, a little greyer around the edges, and 'infinitely better dressed' in Api's words. No more oversized kurtas with the silver buttons.

The city hummed around him, cars rushing by; the remnants of last night's rain still glistening in the puddles on the street. The little tiff with Sukanya that morning had left him feeling restless, unsettled, unsure. He didn't like being the source of confusion for her. Shila was very proud of his fiery daughter, with all of her stubborn will and her strange fascination with her imagined homeland of Bulandwada, a place she had conjured only in her mind. He often ached to show her to his parents and quickly stifled this desire just as he had so many others.

He couldn't shake the question that had plagued him since Sukanya announced her decision to not apply for colleges. What should he do next? Let her take the gap year? What if after a year, she decided not to go to university at all? Lots of kids did that, going adrift after letting go of the structure of school. What would that mean? That he had failed in raising her right?

He had reached the lobby of his office building without even realizing it. He looked up at the chrome and glass structure he had been coming to for the last two decades. Here was something that was familiar and controllable. As he stepped inside, he let out a deep breath that he had been holding for what felt like hours.

9.

London, June 2006 – The Letter

The letter arrived at work, and Shila's thin-faced assistant brought it in, sensing the weight of its handwritten significance. Shila looked at it and immediately recognized Bade Papa's spidery, angular handwriting. He took it from the assistant with a nonchalant nod but his heart was pounding like it wanted to jump out of his chest. He ripped it open, looking with surprise at his own hands, trembling with urgency and something that resembled panic.

The words inside were sparse but heavy.

Shiladitya,

I never thought I would write to you again. But now, I find myself compelled to bow down to your mother's wish, it is probably her last. It is said that the aatma gets no peace if the dying person's last wish is not fulfilled. I would've thought that with a son like you, her soul would never have any peace anyway but still...

Your mother wants to see her granddaughter before

she leaves us forever. I know that we have no control over your life, but it is my duty to let you know. Send Sukanya to Meerut if you want your mother to die in peace and if she still means something to you. There is no need for you or your wife to accompany her.

Diwakar Pandey

Shiladitya sat motionless and silent for a long time, the letter gripped tightly in his clenched fist, as if it were his mother's hand. His mother's dying hand. Then he walked out of his office, completely forgetting about the meetings he was supposed to run, the people he was supposed to meet. London and the past twenty-two years spent in it vanished, and he was chasing kites in the gullies of Bulandwada once again, looking up at the serpentine sky.

Shila walked and walked, the hours melting by, thoughts whirring in his mind. At some point, his assistant called, worried about him and told him that he had cancelled all his appointments. Finally, as the sun began to set, Shila made his way home. Aparajita was already there. Without a word, he handed the letter to her. She read it and looked askance at him, trying to read his expressions. Shila paced up and down the house, trying to reason with himself and against himself.

'How do I send her there? I don't know what they might tell her. All that anger...I know he's still simmering at me,' he said, as much to himself as to her. 'But also, I can't let Badi Mummy not see her. What if something were to happen to her? Sukanya should visit them, shouldn't she, Api?'

'It is as much Sukanya's wish as it is yours, Shila,' Aparajita pointed out quietly as she took his clammy hand in hers, gently guiding him to sit down. 'She is not a child anymore. And we both know she's been wondering about that missing part of her life for years. She needs to know she is being called to it.'

Shiladitya nodded. His precious Sukanya. What was he thinking? How could he send her into the midst of strangers – people who were completely unknown to her? It seemed unfair, reckless. No, he couldn't do it. He'd have to write to Bade Papa and ask if it would be acceptable for him to accompany Sukanya. If not, he wouldn't send her at all.

But then he thought of Sukanya's endless questions about India through the years, the endless curiosity, the confusion about the absence of an extended family. Api was right, Sukanya was her own person, and she would make her own decision. She had to.

That evening, Shiladitya handed the letter to Sukanya, watching her face closely. She glanced at him, brows furrowed in confusion, before turning her attention to the letter. She read slowly because Bade Papa's formal Hindi wasn't easy for her, despite years of regular Hindi lessons.

After she read the letter, she sat still for a long moment,

even as her parents exchanged anxious glances. She had always known something like this would happen, had practically willed it into happening.

Finally, the missing piece. After an entire lifetime of waiting and wondering.

'Of course I'll go, Daddy,' she finally looked up at her father, her face softening into a smile. 'Don't look so worried. I want to see them. I've always wanted to see them. You know that. I'll go. It will be fine.'

'Not so fast, beta,' said Shiladitya, helplessly looking at Aparajita who only half-smiled in response, fully aware that conversations were all good and well, but Sukanya's mind was already made up. 'Bade Papa doesn't want to see me. Or your Mama. That means that we cannot accompany you and that you'll be all alone there. How will you manage? I mean, for God's sake, it's Meerut! Crime is second nature for half the population, and third for everyone else. Everyone walks around with fat egos. The water is dirty and unfit for drinking. There will be power cuts and mosquitoes. The food will be really spicy. And they might say strange things to you. Oh, the list is endless.'

'I know, Daddy, I know. I'll get the culture shock of my life. But I've been waiting for this my whole life,' said Sukanya, getting up to sit next to her father, her clear, large eyes so much like his. 'School ends in two weeks. This couldn't have come at a better time. I'll tell Brent I won't be able to work at the store. Angie can cover for me.' Sukanya worked part-time at a neighbourhood store that sold second-hand books. It was one of the highlights of her life.

'Let me call Angie right now,' said Sukanya, ready to go upstairs, before turning around again. 'See, Daddy? I told you a gap year was a good idea.'

'Yes, beta, but please remember your grandmother is very unwell. You need to be careful and quiet and sensitive around her,' said Shiladitya, going towards her and holding her close.

'Of course, Daddy, though I doubt she will feel poorly once she sees her beautiful granddaughter in the flesh,' said Sukanya, making her parents laugh. Soon Shiladitya found himself dismissing his misgivings. Maybe she was right, this bull-headed girl of his. Maybe she would be fine. Shila knew that Natwar would be a bulldog when it came to Sukanya's safety but there was so much else to worry about.

What would it be like? Would they find her strange, this girl from London with her dry wit and easy smile and long, loping strides? Would they talk to her about her parents, her father who had been a mere boy when he left them forever, her lovely mother who had been a stranger to them all these years? Would she just serve as a painful reminder of his betrayal, or would they look past all of that to see her for who she was?

The weeks passed. Sukanya bade goodbye to school with final exams and the various rituals of leavers' assembly and Senior Ball and many, many prank days. She signed yearbooks and shirts, posed for pictures, gave thank you cards to her teachers, some of whom she had known since kindergarten. And through it all, she kept thinking of her impending trip with ever-growing excitement. *Soon, soon.*

The town, the gullies, the mohalla where her father grew up. The world that she had imagined all these years, blurry visions with no real shape or form that swirled in and out of focus. The scents and sights, music and poetry, the bazaars and bazms, gazals and guldaudi, the thin zari in Badi Mummy's sari, the aunts holding pooja thalis climbing the steps of their family temple, the street dogs wagging their tails as she approached, the ill-tempered, red-beaked parrots in Bibi's courtyard, holding sharp chillies in their claws, all of this that had beckoned to her from behind the seven veils of time for as long as she could remember.

All of this was about to leave the world of her dreams and become a thing of her present.

And she couldn't wait.

10.

Meerut, September 2006 – Shikanji and Tharra

Bade Papa had sent his trusted aide, Natwar, goonda extraordinaire and Rajni Mausi's eldest son and heir to pick up Sukanya from the Delhi Airport.

'Arrey, bitiya, you look exactly like Shila Bhaiyya,' Natwar exclaimed, spotting her as she emerged from the Arrivals lounge, still a little dazed, and scanned the crowds. Sukanya had done her best to keep up with Shila's efforts to educate her about the sprawling family tree. Rajni Mausi was Badi Mummy's sister, married to Bade Papa's cousin. Their union had produced three mustandas, Shila's words, each more nikamma than the other, also Shila's words. Two of these fine men were from the bloodline and one was adopted.

'Namaste, Chacha ji,' said Sukanya, folding her hands and taking in Natwar's appearance. He looked freshly washed and suitably dressed and appeared uncomfortable with both, far more used to being dishevelled. 'I was wondering how I'd find you.'

'Ha-ha-ha, Natwar is always prepared,' he boomed,

proudly holding up a crumpled piece of paper with her name scribbled on it. 'Here is the placard that I was carrying, just in case. I asked Bade Papa to write your name for me, but you know, I knew there'd be no need. You're my flesh and blood, bitiya, how could I not recognize you?'

Sukanya did not question Natwar's unwavering faith in the science of genetics and followed him as he wheeled her luggage trolley towards the parking lot. Sukanya looked around, everything around her seemed at once familiar and strange, like a half-remembered fever dream. This wasn't the second-hand version of India she'd heard in her parents' stories, night after night. She was truly here, in the flesh!

The light felt different, as if a veil had lifted, and the colours rushed at her – vivid and sharp, the grey patina of London left far behind. Everywhere she looked, there were people, too many people. The air was thick and warm, dusty and muggy, and the trapped heat in the ground beneath her feet seemed to have been recently released by the rain. She stopped for a moment and closed her eyes, letting it all wash over her, capturing this first snapshot of India in her mind's eye. A thought drifted up at her, as yet, undefined.

Home.

Natwar was in a hurry to get to the car, a sturdy, white Ambassador in which a tall and well-built Haryanvi driver snoozed, wrapped in a blanket. After kicking at the driver's door to wake him up, Natwar put Sukanya's luggage in the spacious boot of the car.

'Air-conditioned, bitiya, just for you,' Natwar declared proudly, opening the door with a flourish. 'Waise, you have escaped the worst of the summer, but still.'

Sukanya slid into the backseat of the car. The air inside was cool, but the smell was a mix of musty, old cloth and faint smoke – oddly comforting and not at all unpleasant.

'He-he-he, a little smoky, hain?' Natwar asked apologetically, as she sniffed the air. 'I had resolved not to smoke beedis in here, but what to do, beta? I've been smoking since I was seven. Now I need it more than air. Don't mind, haan, beta, and don't tell Bade Papa.'

Sukanya, who had also been sneaking cigarettes since her teens in London, didn't mind it at all but carefully refrained from saying anything.

'It's okay, Chacha ji,' she said generously, and left him to smoke in peace while she looked outside the window at the city of Delhi rushing past, its wide lanes choked with traffic.

'Waise, we could have taken a shorter route and reached Meerut faster,' Natwar said. 'But I thought you should at least get a glimpse of what Delhi looks like.'

Sukanya was already bewitched, unable to keep up with the just-washed montage rushing past. She had seen Delhi framed in the countless Hindi movies her father loved, glimpsed it in snippets on the BBC, but nothing could have prepared her for the chaotic beauty unfolding before her eyes. What *was* this place?

Flyovers arched above, framing ancient Mughal monuments standing by serenely, oblivious to the frenzy of cars and motorcycles and buses surging below. The rage of the drivers was palpable even to her, the air thick with fumes and gaalis flying fast and furious. On the roadside, vendors peddled every kind of delicious-looking street food possible, while sleek, modern malls flashed past.

Sukanya realized she was holding her breath. It was impossible to take it all in. Shila always said that there were seven Dillis, but he hadn't told her that they existed simultaneously, a tangled mass of ruins and echoes. It was lovely and forbidding, charming and anarchic all at once, and Sukanya felt an aching desire to step outside, climb inside its belly, and to see it all.

'We have metro now,' Natwar announced with a hint of pride, pointing toward a station. 'And look, look, that's Teen Murti Bhavan, and over there – that's Rashtrapati Bhavan. Grand, huh? They say it has hundreds of rooms inside. I brought your chachi here right after we got married to see the roses in bloom. Every year they open the Mughal Gardens to the public. Ha-ha-ha, those were good days, bitto. Now your chachi just raises hell all day long with our three ugly brats. What to do, they all take after me.'

He gestured toward another landmark. 'See that? That's the Old Fort. Beautiful, hain?'

Natwar's running commentary on Delhi's landmarks, woven together with snippets of his own life story, continued unabated. But Sukanya was only half-listening. Her eyes were fixed on the city outside, absorbing it all.

Her phone rang, cutting through the hum of the car and Natwar's voice.

'Hi, Daddy,' Sukanya answered the call. 'Yes, I have reached. Yes, Natwar Chacha is here with me. We're on our way. I'll get a local number soon. Don't worry, Daddy. I'll be fine. Everything will be fine. Give my love to Mama.'

She hung up, and for a moment the quiet in the car felt heavy. Natwar had fallen uncharacteristically silent and was looking at her with a mix of pity and concern.

'Yes, Chacha ji, you were saying?' she prompted him.

'Shila Bhaiyya must be worried about you,' Natwar said quietly, almost to himself. 'Bade Papa can be so stubborn...so...but what can one do? So many years... twenty perhaps, I have lost count. When Badi Mummy... when the doctors said...anyway...'

Sukanya realized that Natwar, ever an optimist, was loath to articulate any unpleasant thought. At least, not fully.

'I told him – if you are calling Sukanya, you might as well call Bhaiyya and Bhabhi too. He wouldn't listen... "over my dead body" and all that, you know, ha-ha-ha. But Shila Bhaiyya also na...' Natwar shook his head. 'Marrying outside the caste has to be done a certain way.

He should have taken my help. I would have smoothed things out. What's this business of disappearing overnight and all that...so much trouble. Chalo, such is the way of the world.' This philosophical speech seemed to unsettle Natwar. He quickly reached for another beedi to collect himself. *Special Sher Beedi*, Sukanya noted the brand name. *Purely academic, of course.*

'But Daddy tried contacting him. He even tried sending them money, several times,' Sukanya said, feeling compelled to defend Shila. 'He may not have become an Indian civil servant, I know that's what Bade Papa wanted, but he has done well for himself, I think.'

'Arrey, beta, it's very complicated, and very sad... anyway, let it go.' Natwar replied, waving a hand. 'Now that you're here, there will be much fun. Look, there is the famous shikanji shop. Will you have some? Bade Papa said I wasn't to feed you off the road. Your stomach will get upset, he said, but this is Jain Shikanji. We'll ask him to make it with Bisleri water, haan? And don't tell Bade Papa.'

He called out to the driver. 'Oye, Balvinder, stop the car.'

Clearly, with Natwar, there would be many events that needed to be kept from Bade Papa. Soon, Sukanya found herself, somewhat bemused, standing outside what appeared to be a lemonade stall, except that it was unlike any lemonade stall that she had ever seen.

It was packed to the rafters, filled with a noise that

she couldn't place before realizing it was just people, throngs and throngs of people. She couldn't shake off the feeling that like Dorothy, she had left the sepia-toned world of her old life behind and stepped into the technicolour world of Oz.

Plastic tables and chairs were scattered all around, and everywhere she looked, people were deeply immersed in ingesting deep-fried samosas, paneer pakodas, and other delights, all washed down with cold, tangy shikanji. Natwar, unfazed by the madness around him, placed the orders for three glasses of shikanji.

'Here you go,' said Natwar proudly as he handed her a very large, very chilled glass of shikanji. 'Drink up.'

Sukanya took a sip. It was delicious, sweeter, saltier, and tangier than any lemonade that she had ever had.

'Mama makes shikanji at home sometimes,' she told Natwar, taking another appreciative sip. 'But honestly, this is way better. This is shikanji on steroids.'

'Ha-ha-ha, shabaash, my child,' said Natwar and gave Sukanya a hearty clap on her back, making her yowl in alarm. Natwar was disappointed.

'Arrey, you cannot be hurt by this,' he said. 'We will feed you sweetened milk every morning, strengthen you up in no time. Then when you go back, you will be able to lift two-two angrez women with one-one arm.'

'Yes, Chacha ji, but why would I want to do that?' Sukanya wondered aloud.

'Oho, now don't ask too many questions.' Natwar

waved it off. 'We should be on our way. Balvinder, stop sipping delicately and drink up like a man. Pretend that it's tharra, ha-ha-ha.'

Balvinder sniggered, finished his drink, and made his way back to the car.

'What's tharra?' Sukanya asked when they were back on the road.

'Hmmm? Nothing, nothing,' said Natwar, clearly uncomfortable. It was clear that tharra was something completely forbidden and immensely desirable. Must be some kind of drug, Sukanya made another note to herself. Natwar Chacha had to be on something potent to be this wired.

Jet lag was beginning to catch up with her, and she found her eyelids growing heavy as the car continued along the endless road. Soon, she drifted into a short dream in which she was a small child again, chasing butterflies with Angie. Small, delicate butterflies that always seemed to be out of reach.

She stayed asleep for most of the way, only waking up as the car entered the town. Shila called it a chhota sheher – a small town – but more than a million people lived there. It hit her all at once, with its cacophony of sounds – the shrill clamour of rickshaws, the honking of bicycles, cars, and trucks, all battling for space on the narrow streets pocked with potholes. Around her, grimy auto repair shops, Ayurvedic medicine stores and tuition classes flashed by. So many tuition classes. For Physics,

Chemistry, Maths, and Accounting. For UPSC, Bank, Railways. All run by bespectacled, respectable teachers with names like *Khanna Sir, Ansari Sir, Vidya Ma'am*.

Sukanya looked around, disoriented by this scene. A light rain was falling again, but it was different from the steady drizzle of London. This was intense, dramatic, making a statement.

'Ah good, good, you are up,' Natwar Chacha's voice broke through the silence. 'We're almost home. Must be a shock to you after London, hain? Now what to say about this town, beta...it could have been like Lucknow, or Banaras, or Allahabad. God knows we had the virasat and the siyasat – the heritage and the politics, you see. If only they did not have the ego and the flaming tempers, me included! Anyway, whatever it is, here it is.'

He waved his hand to encompass the town.

11.

Meerut, September 2006 – Bulandwada, At Long Last

The car was inching its way down the narrowest gully Sukanya had ever seen. The street outside was dirty, dirtier than she could have imagined possible, as if the grime and filth of ages was embedded in the ground. The cobbled streets, paved with ancient-looking bricks, looked weathered and worn. They had seen too much.

On either side of the gully stood houses – two or three storeys high, some better kept than others but all with the same time-scarred façades, forming a complex mosaic, sharing walls and secrets. The windows, barred with thin iron rods, revealed glimpses of what lay inside. Some had delicate, flowery curtains hanging on their edges, but in most, it was easy to look inside – past the curtains, past the grime, and into homes that were impeccably clean and freshly washed, a stark contrast to the world outside.

Some doors stood ajar, revealing a narrow passage that led to an open courtyard, with rooms stretching off to either side. The houses themselves were set higher than the road, built on raised platforms that required a few steps to reach the door. This raised level served as an additional pedestrian way, and children of all shapes and sizes, in various stages of dress or undress, ran across the length of the street with disquieting speed.

'We are almost there, bitiya,' Natwar said with a nod, and the car lurched to a stop, right on cue. 'The car cannot go beyond this point; the gully is too narrow, built long before motor cars came around, right, Balvinder? Bring the child's things inside. Let's go.'

Mercifully, the rain had stopped, leaving behind damp, sticky air. Sukanya stepped out of the car, her sneakers meeting the ground with an unpleasant squelch. She nearly lost her balance as the soles slid on the slimy floor, slick with muddy rainwater. *This will take some getting used to*, she muttered to herself as she slowly walked with Natwar towards her grandparents' house, looking around, bewildered despite all the mental preparation of the past weeks. She couldn't have imagined anything like this, let alone expected it.

'The lanes are very narrow,' Natwar repeated apologetically, glancing over his shoulder to monitor Sukanya's slow progress. 'It must be so strange for you, hain? But this is it – Bulandwada, the mohalla where your father grew up. And his parents before that, and well, who knows how far back our family history goes, huh? Very long, very long indeed.'

Sukanya made a non-committal sound. She noticed that the small children were now staring at her with open curiosity. She was dressed conservatively, in her opinion, in jeans and an oversized t-shirt. Still, she probably stuck out a mile.

'Arrey bhaago,' scolded Natwar, catching sight of Sukanya staring at the children. Most of the children scattered, laughing. Only a couple of older boys remained, their eyes fixed on Sukanya.

'Bade Papa's granddaughter,' one of them whispered to the other. 'She has come from *foreign*. She won't speak any Hindi, only English, and that too very fast, like they show on TV.'

'No, I won't,' said Sukanya to the boy in Hindi with a smile. The boy gawked at her and then broke into a wide smile.

'Arrey saala, she speaks first-class Hindi,' Sukanya heard him exclaim to his friend as she walked away.

'And here we are,' said Natwar, as they stopped in front of a heavy, thick wooden door that seemed to have been there since the dawn of time, old, time-weathered, and beautiful. *Must have taken an entire tree to build this thing*, Sukanya thought to herself, trying to steady her racing heart.

There was a circular, iron knocker attached to the door, but it looked like it hadn't been used in years. Natwar rang the bell, and almost immediately, the heavy door creaked open, its weathered hinges groaning. For a brief moment, in the dim light of the rainy afternoon, Sukanya had an uncanny feeling that she was looking at her father. Older, greying but unmistakably him. The same frame. The same large, thick-lashed eyes that danced in her own face. The same straight-backed demeanour. The same quiet desire to not follow the world's expectations.

'Here you go, Bade Papa,' Natwar laughed, breaking the spell. 'Your precious granddaughter, delivered safely at your doorstep. Doesn't she look like Shila Bhaiyya?'

The old man's face crumpled, everything in it sagging, as he took in the girl in front of him. His eyes crinkled, his mouth drooped a little, his shoulders slumped. Then he spread his arms wide, Sukanya walked into that embrace and was enveloped in a fragrance that was tobacco and talc and incense and leather, a scent that was her father's but not quite.

'Namaste, Bade Papa,' she mumbled, trying to recall the words she had rehearsed, still engulfed in his embrace. She felt him tremble and weep.

'Oho, Bade Papa, enough, enough,' said Natwar, patting him on the back. 'She needs to meet everyone, no? Let her go.'

Suddenly a conch blew right behind Bade Papa, making him jump and let out a loud curse.

'Uff, this Sunita. Always making me jump out of my skin,' he grumbled, before stepping aside to reveal a pretty, plump, fair-skinned woman in a bright, vibrant sari. A large bindi shone between her brows, and her head was covered with her pallu. She wore an impish grin on her round, moon-like face, her eyes twinkling.

She handed the conch to a small girl who seemed to appear out of nowhere. The girl took it away, and the woman took charge of a plate full of aarti offerings – with a large lit diya, camphor sticks, incense, flowers, mishri and dhoop, all arranged with care.

'Sukanya, this is your Chachi, beta,' said Bade Papa, as he introduced the woman to Sukanya.

Sukanya folded her hands again, as taught by her mother. Everyone was Chacha or Chachi, she had been told. Just how many relatives did she have in this place?

'Natwar Chacha was talking about you on our way here,' she said politely.

'No, no, this is not *that* Chachi,' Natwar interrupted hastily, realizing what she meant. 'Not that I would mind, ha-ha-ha, but it's too late for that. This is another Chachi. You will meet many, many Chachis, beta.'

'Haan ji, but there is only one Sunita Chachi,' the pretty woman said with a warm laugh, her fleshy cheeks forming two deep dimples that made Sukanya like her almost instantly.

'Chalo ji, now you stand here and let me do the aarti,' Sunita said, and Sukanya stood while she expertly moved the heavy plate in large, graceful circles around her, all the while smiling. Bade Papa and Natwar stood to the side and watched. Sunita broke a coconut at Sukanya's feet and offered her some mishri.

'Now we have welcomed you properly,' she said. 'Come, meet Badi Mummy.'

Sukanya stepped inside the house and found herself in a small enclosure. She looked around, a little disconcerted. Just how old was this place? The thick brick walls shone in the dim light, their surface rough and weathered to the touch. As her eyes adjusted to the space, Sukanya noticed a niche in the wall directly in front of her. Two small idols sat within it, as they had probably done for the last hundred years. The soft flicker of a clay lamp bathed the sooty niche in its glow.

To the left of this niche was a small room, its door thick and wooden, set at a higher level than the rest of the house. The door was closed; Bade Papa opened it and looked inside.

'Sukanya is here,' he said quietly, and took Sukanya's hand to guide her in. 'Come, beta.'

Sukanya stepped into the small baithak, her eyes immediately drawn to the bed where her grandmother lay. Her first thoughts were how lovely and faded she looked, like an old Renaissance masterpiece in need of urgent restoration. Her frail, thin frame looked shrunken against the bed, and her skin had assumed a transparent quality, as if about to powder into nothingness and fade away altogether.

But it was clear that she'd taken care over her appearance. Her salt and pepper hair was oiled and plaited, and her thin, printed, cotton sari with little lavender blooms was starched. Semi-sitting in her bed, propped by pillows, she looked for all the world a resplendent queen waiting to receive her subjects. As if to complete the image, a plump, disdainful cat sat at the foot of her bed, grooming itself with a superior air.

'How to meet God without meeting you, child,' said Badi Mummy and smiled, spreading out her wafer-thin arms, her bangles easily sliding past her elbows.

'Goodness, Badi Mummy, no one told me you were this gorgeous.' Sukanya blurted out before she could stop herself, making everyone burst into laughter, lifting the pall almost immediately. Badi Mummy laughed too, her face streaked with tears.

'So what did your father tell you? Arrey, bitiya, we never had any beauty contests in our times. Otherwise, I would have been Miss Universe, no?'

'Sure thing, Badi Mummy. Miss Universe and Miss World, in the same year,' Sukanya laughed, a clear sound that went and settled into the corners of that old room.

'The same laugh,' said Badi Mummy, almost to herself, thinking of the son that she hadn't seen in decades. Then she looked at Sukanya and smiled again. *How much like Shila she looks*, she kept repeating to Bade Papa who sat across from her, nodding in agreement. *Yes, yes, she does.*

Sukanya sat next to her grandmother, taking her small hands into her own, peering at the blue veins under the paper-thin skin, the half-moons of her nails, the frail knuckles. How tiny she was, how feeble. How had her father stayed away from her all these years?

Bade Papa sat quietly on the other bed, his gaze never leaving Sukanya. Every now and then, he would reach out and touch her, as if to make sure she was really there, sitting in front of him. Sukanya felt her bewilderment melt away. These people were no strangers. She felt their need to hear her voice, and fell into an easy conversational rhythm, telling them about her flight, her co-passengers, the tasteless food she had been served, the things she had seen on the way. Hours passed this way, till finally Sunita came back.

'Badi Mummy, should I show Sukanya to her room?' she asked, hoping to break the waves of grief and joy that seemed to be flooding the room by turns.

'Yes, yes, give her some tea and something to eat. Look at me, I cannot even cook anything for my granddaughter,' said Badi Mummy, her words tinged with sadness.

'Oh, Badi Mummy, plenty of time for that,' said Sukanya encouragingly, and got up. 'I've the appetite of a horse, you'll see. I'll eat everything. You must get better first. Now, you rest, and I'll be back in no time.'

'Well, this is the house,' said Sunita as she led the way out of the baithak. 'There are a few rooms on the ground floor and this small courtyard. The kitchen is here too, though it's hardly used anymore. The toilet is through here; it now has indoor plumbing, thank goodness. Come, gudiya.'

Gudiya, bitiya, bitto, rani. Those tender terms of endearment, all hers by right.

Sukanya followed Sunita through the house, looking around, her eyes drinking in the details. The whole house had a derelict quality about it, the thick walls sighing with age and discontent. Modern appliances had been fitted, but they seemed to not quite belong. The rooms were all very small and tunnelled into one another with their low ceilings and heavy doors. It was clean, but clearly no maintenance work had been done in decades. A little like living in the ruins of some bygone era, Sukanya thought to herself. Everywhere she looked, there was evidence of a thousand lives that had been lived here already. Large steel trunks sat in corners alongside old wooden beds with creaking frames, armchairs with faded upholstery, an old television set, piles of newspapers, magazines, and old books. Lives connected to hers, she knew not how.

'Let's go upstairs. Balvinder has kept your things in your room already,' said Sunita as she led the way up the steep staircase. Exposed bricks peeked through the walls on both sides, some of them disintegrating under the weight of their years. Sukanya ran her fingers over them, and the touch left a trail of powdery dust in the air, a reminder of how much time had passed since they were first put together. 'I will help you unpack.'

The room upstairs was larger than she had expected. The furniture was old but sturdy. An old wooden bed sat in the centre, its frame carved with intricate patterns. Next to the bed stood a very old-fashioned dressing table, the glass of the heavy mirror warped with age. A cupboard, built right into the wall, stood on the far side. It was painted a garish hospital green, the colour peeling in places. A small, attached bathroom was tucked away to the side.

Sukanya wondered if this had been her father's room, the one that had featured in all those bedtime stories, where all manners of misadventures had unfolded. She noticed the narrow door that led out to the small balcony, its wooden, latticed railing faded and worn-out. She pushed open the door to the balcony, and a rush of fresh, rain-washed breeze swept into the room, clearing its stifling, musty air almost immediately.

'Oh this is nice,' said Sukanya and stepped out on the balcony that opened out on the gully. The sky above had turned a soft grey, the rain had reduced to a very light drizzle. She could see the gully below. The rooftops of nearby houses rose up in a jagged line, with an assortment of tulsi pots, makeshift laundry lines, and the occasional weathered satellite dish, standing in sharp contrast to the timeless, weathered brick walls.

'Keep the door shut,' Sunita warned, glancing up at the balcony. 'There are monkeys everywhere, and they are very mischievous and completely fearless. One snatched my new sunglasses right off my face! But what can you do? Hanuman ji only they are. We must not harm them.' Evidently the pain of the robbed sunglasses was struggling with the piety in Sunita's heart. She sighed loudly.

'Which one is your room, Chachi?' asked Sukanya as Sunita turned to go downstairs to get tea for her. Sunita looked puzzled for a moment. Then she realized what the girl meant and laughed.

'Oh, I don't live here, beta. I am just your neighbour. That house there, right across the gully is ours. I come over every day for some time to take care of things and to spend time with Badi Mummy. They have no one here, na.' Sunita suddenly realized that she had said too much and muttering something about getting snacks ready for Sukanya, she hurried back downstairs.

Sukanya, alone in the room, kicked off her shoes and lay on the bed – much firmer than the one she had at home – not knowing how to feel about this whole new chapter that she had kickstarted. Poor Bade Papa and Badi Mummy, living all alone in this dilapidated, ramshackle, ageing house. Too proud to call their son back, too frail to manage on their own. What a strange, sad life. And now they had her, someone who had been a stranger to them all these years. What did they think of her?

When Sunita returned with a tray of tea and samosas, she found Sukanya fast asleep on the bed, her mouth slightly open as she dreamt of London, lemonade stalls hidden in its foggy depths.

12.

Meerut, October 2006 – Bibi's Chowk

A few weeks went by. Sukanya, who had not known any family outside of her parents in her nearly eighteen years, now found herself thrust into a bustling microcosm where everyone – by blood or by association – was her chachi, or bua, or mausi, or tai. The families of both her grandparents had lived in this mohalla for generations. Everybody was in everybody else's business. Every house bled into the other, sharing walls and family legends, and looping into an endless daisy chain that ran alongside the narrow, paved gully.

Everyone in this neighbourhood knew of Sukanya, Shila's daughter. Shila, who had abandoned his ageing parents to run off with some pretty Dugar girl. Shila, who had been the most prodigious talent the town had ever seen. Shila, who had been forbidden from returning home all these years. Still, they didn't let their disapproval of Shiladitya dull their affection for Sukanya. For the first couple of days, it was bemusing to find herself being dragged inside the house of some pallu-covered chachi or tai for a cup of tea, asking after her father, about her life in London, about her pretty mother, nobody bothering to hide their warmth or their curiosity in the least.

Shiladitya and Aparajita called her every four hours for the first two days until she finally told them to ease off, and even then there were frequent calls. Angie called too, but she did not want to know if she had eaten or if the bathroom facilities were acceptable. No, Angie wanted to know if the culture shock had hit yet and if Sukanya's hair was standing on end.

'I wouldn't call it a culture shock, Angie,' Sukanya told her friend, sitting on the small balcony outside her room. 'More like an other-world shock, really. It's nothing like anything that I've ever seen before, but also a part of me that feels like I've always known it – without knowing it. Do I sound bonkers? Must be all those stories Daddy used to tell me when I was little. It looks strange but feels familiar somehow.'

There was a pause, and then Angie's laughter came through.

'The place sounds proper weird, to be honest,' she said. 'No wonder your folks are so worried about you. I saw them yesterday.'

'I know, but oh, Angie, you should've seen the look on my grandparents' faces. It's like I've knocked years off overnight. No one's ever been this chuffed to see me!'

'Glad it's working out, mate, but be careful anyway.

I've been reading up on this place, it has got a few stories, that's for sure. That place is exactly where your lot decided to kick us out, y'know, and before it was time 'cause they got impatient or something. And don't go getting involved with Indian men, y'know?'

'That's the last thing you need to worry about, Angie. Indian men and me, not going to happen!'

'Good! Just keep your wits about you, yeah? And come back soon.'

Sukanya found herself getting slowly drawn into the rhythm of life in Bulandwada. She would wake up early and help her grandfather prepare tea, the only bit of cooking that took place in the old, soot-streaked kitchen. After tea, a nurse would arrive to tend to Badi Mummy. Tinku, the indoor–outdoor cat, would keep a watch on the proceedings, his amber eyes taking in everything. In the weeks that Sukanya had been there, some colour seemed to be returning to her drained-looking face. Just an illusion, Bade Papa had dismissed with a sigh, a common red herring in her kind of illness.

After tea, it would be time for breakfast. Sukanya had blanched the first time she saw the towering pile of deep-fried kachauris with aloo sabzi which looked like it contained half a kilo of red chillies. All of this served first thing in the morning, fresh from the karahi of the nearest obliging halwai.

'Bade Papa,' said Sukanya, looking at the spread and realizing for the first time just how different food must have been for her father when he moved away. 'I don't think I can eat that.'

'Of course, you can! Arrey, your father used to have breakfast at home, and then he'd go and have six of these before school, with one paav of jalebis, and top it with some milk. He could eat, that boy,' said Bade Papa, remembering the days when Shila was still around.

'Anyway,' he continued, 'here, I also bought this bread and butter. You must be eating this in London, nahin?'

Actually the truth was that Aparajita, consumed by her own version of mothering guilt and anxiety, made hot Indian breakfasts almost every day, but Sukanya had quickly learnt that the mention of her mother caused a sudden, uncomfortable hush around her grandparents. So she skirted these topics whenever she could. Even when Aparajita called, Sukanya would make an excuse, take her phone into her room upstairs and shut the door behind her.

After breakfast, which was a compromise between deep-fried delicacies and dry bread, she would dress quickly and make the five-minute walk to get to her great-grandmother's house, learning to step around the open drains of Bulandwada without even thinking about them anymore.

Badi Mummy's mother, Bibi, was a force of nature, a sprightly eighty-year-old who woke up at five every morning without fail, starting her day by washing her entire house twice with bucketfuls of water she would carry herself. Bibi had seen too much to be impressed by anything and delivered judgement quickly and mercilessly on most things.

She had been unsurprised by Sukanya's arrival, quickly making place for her in her days and her heart and her much-washed house, as if she'd always been around.

Bibi's courtyard, or chowk, was the sunlit hub of activity in the neighbourhood, hosting anything of import in Bulandwada. A place of charpais under the winter sun, or massehris under the moonlight during summer, of community worship, and wedding shamianas and everyday huddles of women sitting together to shell peas or cut mounds of mustard leaves for a winter pot of saag, or grate kilos and kilos of carrots for gaajar ka halwa.

Mithu and Mishri, Bibi's two parrots, kept a vigilant eye on the goings-on in the chowk from their brass cages, squawking occasionally to demand pieces of carrot or beetroot. The chowk was bordered on two sides by tightly packed houses, some of them three stories high, their terraces spilling into one another, their windows gazing out onto the chowk, from where one could catch framed glimpses of ordinary lives.

And on the third side of the chowk, very unexpectedly, was the back façade of an intriguing building called Nawabon Ki Haveli, built sometime around the first war of independence.

Nawabon Ki Haveli. Sukanya had been utterly charmed by the name.

Nobody in Bulandwada seemed quite able to tell Sukanya about its history, so she had looked it up online, sensing that its clean lines and neglected exterior held some significance. Her feelings were well founded. The haveli had been built by a Bangash Nawab, a man of great influence and culture, in the memory of his father, a renowned Urdu poet and nationalist. In the early days of the freedom struggle, the haveli had served as a gathering place for freedom fighters who would meet in its dimly lit, high-ceilinged rooms, plotting the country's liberation from colonial rule.

However, after the partition of India in 1947, the Nawab's family had been torn apart. Most of them moved to Lahore, but one of the Nawab's sons stayed back in India to look after the haveli and its treasures. The family still owned the haveli after all these years, and distant relatives came and went, living in it for short periods before moving on to other places.

Bibi had told Sukanya that the haveli had seen a long parade of transient relatives over the years, each one quirkier than the other. A few years ago a woman called Roshni had moved in. It was unclear how Roshni was related to the Nawabs but her crisp, simple, cotton saris, her perpetually covered head, aquiline nose, and indisputable air of arrogance forbade any questions. She taught in the same local college as Bade Papa had before retiring and did not mingle with anyone except Bibi. She did not receive any guests either, except occasionally her nephew, who was studying medicine at Lala Lajpat Rai Medical College in town and would come by on weekends.

Sukanya, starved of family connections for so long, loved the chowk and all of its idiosyncrasies. Someone was always willing to sit with her and tell her juicy stories of the mohalla. She would spend the better part of the afternoon there, savouring Bibi's warm, salty parathas dipped in comforting curries.

Bibi's only son, Hari Prasad, stayed with her. After a crippling accident during a pilgrimage years ago, Hari Prasad walked with a painful limp and had been unable to work since. Now he was a general do-gooder, taking his creaky cycle out every morning to mind babies, run errands, or accompany old relatives to the hospital. People both needed and ridiculed his services, treating him like a necessary nuisance. Sukanya once overheard Nandi, Bibi's next-door neighbour laughing openly as Hari Prasad limped to deliver a crying toddler to his mother, his back hunched under the weight, even as the child unexpectedly relieved himself all over him.

Sukanya complained about this to Bibi.

'Nandi Chachi laughed at poor Hari Mama today,' she said with a frown, as Bibi put away fruit in a wicker kandi and placed it on the counter of her spotless kitchen. Bibi did not believe in the science of refrigeration. She made fresh meals three times a day, not to mention countless cups of chai.

'Ignore her,' said Bibi, uncharacteristically, for she never ignored anything. 'Nandi is a thoroughly frustrated woman. She was only fourteen when she got married and came here, much younger than you, bitto. Her mother-in-law – may she burn in hell for all eternity – was a complete tyrant. She was a giant of a woman, weighed a hundred kilos or more, and she would chase Nandi all over the courtyard with a jhaadu. God help Nandi if she was ever caught. That monster would pin her down and pummel her mercilessly. No daya-maya.'

'How could Nandi Chachi's husband let this happen? Why didn't he stop his mother?' asked Sukanya, horrified at the terrors of Nandi's past.

'Ha-ha, that stick figure Atma Ram at seventeen? Not a chance!' laughed Bibi. 'His mother held the purse strings, bitiya, and that is what makes the world go round, nahi? He was completely hopeless with studies, and anyway, this is a Baniya family – whatever they study, the boys have to join the family business. So her husband tolerated all this nonsense in his youth, and now, as a reward, he is selling women's panties and bras in that disgraceful shop of his in the bazaar.'

Sukanya could not understand Bibi's objection to Atma Ram's hosiery store. It was true that Bibi, like most women of her generation, had little use for artificial support for their breasts, going as far as to claim that wearing a bra caused cancer. But surely, she thought, they knew that most women did not share those views. Bibi could be funny in these ways, often quite silly and sometimes downright bigoted. Sukanya often found herself getting exasperated at times. Still, she was growing quite fond of her legendary great-grandmother, fearsome temper and all. After the whole Hari Mama incident, Sukanya overheard Bibi giving Nandi a good talking-to in no uncertain terms.

'Laugh as much as you like at my poor son, Nandi, but remember that you will die a dog's death if I curse you in the morning after my bath and before I eat. Be careful, if you don't want maggots crawling in your flesh.' All this was said with eerie calm as Bibi cooked in her kitchen and Nandi in hers. Bibi felt superior because of the strict dietary restrictions that governed her life and was not above using them to her advantage.

'You are a tyrant, Bibi,' said Sukanya, a little in disbelief as she heard the exchange. People certainly got away with a lot out here.

'Hmm,' said Bibi, unbothered, her hands busy in the kitchen.

'What are you working on now? I never see you rest.'

'Arrey, that boy's fallen ill again – Roshni's nephew. Kaahe ka doctor, when he gets sick like this? I promised her I'd make him this tulsi tea. Nobody else in this mohalla even speaks to her, you know that. Anyway, be a good girl, bitto, go and take this thermos to the haveli. You know how to get there, right? That Hari Prasad helps everyone except his own mother.'

13.

Meerut, October 2006 – Nawabon Ki Haveli

Sukanya felt a thrill at the thought of finally seeing the interior of the fascinating Nawabon Ki Haveli, having only caught tantalizing glimpses of it so far. She took the flask from Bibi's hands, and made her way through the narrow, cobbled alleys that wound their way towards the haveli. As she walked, her eyes wandered up to the decaying buildings and decrepit façades that lined the street, smiling down at the girl they'd been waiting for.

These remnants of the city's past appealed to the history buff in Sukanya. She had spent hours poring over old books from Bade Papa's collection, each dog-eared page deepening her fascination with the city's layered story. She had learned that Meerut had once been a walled city with nine gates, though most of the fortifications had been lost over the centuries. The thought of those scattered ruins, the lost entry points into the city was enough to make her itch to explore them. Soon, soon, she told herself.

For now, though, Nawabon Ki Haveli was her destination.

Rubbing her arms against the slight chill of the October air, Sukanya finally reached the haveli. A massive wooden gate, studded with iron nails, loomed in front of her, bolted shut. Embedded within it was a smaller window gate, a practical addition for daily comings and goings.

She scanned the gate for a bell or knocker but found neither. She had been in the mohalla long enough to know that it wasn't unusual for guests to let themselves in. With a quick bend, she pushed on the smaller door. It creaked open as she stepped inside, her senses alert to the silence stretching in the mansion.

She found herself standing in a marbled courtyard, its centre dominated by a large floral design typical of the region. A verandah with decorative pillars stood right in front of her, leading into the rooms within. Faded, stuffed sofas were arranged there, flanked by intricately carved wooden end tables. A pair of distinctive Chinese blue-and-white porcelain stools stood next to one of the sofas. The simple coffee-table seemed to be a new addition, its ordinariness accentuated by the beauty of the threadbare Kashmiri carpet beneath it. A niche in the wall held a collection of old books, the glass door cracked but still dutifully protecting its treasures. The walls were covered with old portraits in gilded frames and hunting trophies. To Sukanya's untrained eyes, the haveli seemed to be a fusion of architectural styles – there was a touch of Europe to be sure, but something distinctly Awadhi as well.

The haveli was clearly not very well-maintained. In places, the paint had peeled off the walls and pillars, and minor repairs appeared to have been done haphazardly over the years – patches of cement stood out like eyesores against the beautiful pillars. A chandelier hung from the ceiling, though it wasn't switched on. Doors led to other rooms, inviting her to explore, but Sukanya now could not bring herself to go any further. In London, she never even visited a neighbour without calling first – and yet here she was, standing in a stranger's palatial residence.

Sukanya looked around. No one in sight.

'Roshni ji...Aunty,' she called, surprised by how feebly her voice emerged. The place was deathly quiet, and in such eerie surroundings, she half-expected the ghost of the old poet Nawab, believed to be haunting the mohalla a hundred and fifty years after his demise, to jump out and seize her by the throat. Consequently she nearly jumped out of her skin when a low voice behind her said, 'Hello, how can I help you?'

Turning around, she found herself face to face with a young man – tall, bespectacled, with long hair falling over his eyes, wearing a sweatshirt that hung loosely from his lean frame. This must be the budding doctor. Sukanya cleared her throat and tried to get her racing heart to calm down.

'Hello, I'm Sukanya. Bibi is my great-grandmother.'

'I see.'

'You're not well,' she said, her words coming out like an accusation, making the boy smile.

'What I mean is, your aunt asked us to bring you this tea,' she added, holding out the flask.

He took it from her with a smile. He had nice teeth. He could have been called handsome, but the rigours of medical school had clearly taken their toll on his face and body.

'Yes, my aunt doesn't believe in the wonders of paracetamol. Baithiye na,' he said, plopping himself down on one of the carved Louis XVI chairs. 'Where did you get that accent from? Very Jeeves and Wooster.'

Sukanya bristled. Everyone had always complimented her on her perfect Hindi, despite being born and brought up in Ing-LAND. What a rude, dismissive boy.

'Well, I'm from London so I suppose you could find it in your heart to forgive me,' she said, turning to go, her nose in the air.

The doctor-to-be laughed loudly and lit a cigarette. So much so for a bad throat, Sukaya thought to herself, but said nothing.

'Sensitive, are we? Arrey, come na, sit down. Look, I can't beg – my throat really hurts,' he said, making a piteous face. Sukanya reluctantly sat down on the faded sofa and looked around.

'What's your name?' she asked as he opened the flask and looked around for a cup.

'Aman,' he replied. 'A hot favourite for Hindu–Muslim couples. Like Kabeer. And Sameer.'

Sukanya didn't know how to respond to that so she changed the subject.

'Have you been here long?' she asked, waving her hand around.

'In Meerut? Oh gosh no, I was accepted to the medical college here – nobody was more surprised than me, honestly. Before this, I was in Dehradun for school.'

'And which school was that, Aman?' asked Sukanya, leaning back on the sofa.

'Doon,' he said and watched her face for a reaction. She remembered that it was supposed to be very elite and said so.

'Isn't that really posh? So, the Nawabi riches are still very much in evidence?' asked Sukanya, regretting it immediately as she saw Aman's face shutter.

'I got a scholarship,' he said, looking down at his tea. 'Though of course the family connections helped.'

'What luck! So why aren't you kicking back and chilling or whatever, instead of slogging it out in med school?' Sukanya asked, trying to lighten the mood though she was genuinely surprised.

He sighed dramatically.

'You'll laugh,' he said.

'I won't,' Sukanya insisted, taking the bait, prepared to be disarmed. 'Go ahead, tell me.'

'Too much brains,' he said, smiling as he tapped his forehead. Sukanya laughed.

'See, I knew you'd laugh. There's no point telling the truth,' he clutched a cushion to himself.

'Boy, aren't you full of yourself?' she said, getting up. Aman hastily followed suit and rose to his feet. Where was she going already, just as he was switching on the charm?

'Hey, maybe we should hang out. How long are you here for?' he asked.

'Not long enough, not long enough,' Sukanya replied, picking up Bibi's flask. Aman followed her outside, wishing she would just slow down for a second so he could talk to her. But Sukanya wasn't having any of it. He watched helplessly as she strode purposefully out of the haveli, taking great pleasure at not even turning around for a goodbye wave.

Bibi was napping when she got back so she slipped out quietly and headed home. By now, the college boys must have shown up, she thought with a sigh. Bade Papa, though retired, still gave private lessons to some absolute duds. Whenever Sukanya was home during those sessions, she could hear him growing more and more frustrated as he tried to hammer the rules of English grammar and the beauty of Shakespeare's works into their unreceptive skulls.

She didn't like these boys. Not having interacted with too many girls in their lives – certainly none who wore combat boots and spoke with that clipped accent – they were all quite captivated by her and stared lustfully whenever she walked by, though nobody had the nerve to actually strike up a conversation. All said and done, the fearsome Natwar lived next door.

But Aman hadn't stared at her, she thought to herself; in fact, he was nothing like these boys. Rude and self-satisfied, sure, but not lecherous. She didn't inspire any awe in him, at least not in the same way as she'd seen in the others. In fact, he seemed to be so in love with himself that he probably hadn't noticed she was a girl. Or maybe he had. Either way, he was interesting. Perhaps she shouldn't have brushed him off with such vigour. Then she remembered Angie's warning words about Indian men and gave herself a chiding shake. No sir, that wouldn't do.

Before she could ponder this further, her phone rang. It was Aparajita. Sukanya went inside to take the call and when her mother asked how she was finding her new life in a mohalla, she truthfully replied, 'Very interesting, indeed.'

14.

Meerut, October 2006 – Enter: Gumbi

'Do you have any traditional clothes to wear to a wedding?' Badi Mummy asked a couple of days later, as Sukanya sat on the bed beside hers, flipping through one of the old *Reader's Digest* magazines that Bade Papa had collected for decades. This particular issue was dated 1972 and had likely survived a couple of baths in its time, so yellowed and brittle were the pages.

'Err, no, I wasn't expecting to be invited to any,' replied Sukanya, sitting up and setting the magazine aside. 'Who is getting married, Badi Mummy?'

'That Gumbi – Nandi's daughter. The wedding card hasn't arrived yet, but that doesn't matter. We'll need to attend. At least, you and Bade Papa will. I cannot go anywhere these days,' said Badi Mummy, turning to face the wall. Sukanya knew that Badi Mummy longed to be out and about.

'I know Gumbi. She's very pretty!' said Sukanya, trying to lift the mood and to pull her grandmother out of her melancholy. 'Well, so who's she marrying?'

'Some landowner; the family is well-off, but the boy doesn't do much,' Badi Mummy replied without turning back to face her. 'I guess we can't complain. No dowry to speak of. But still, like you said, Gumbi is a very pretty girl, and she means well.'

Sukanya had seen Gumbi around Bibi's chowk – a small, slender girl with long, black hair, always caught up in some household chore or another, very much dominated by her tyrannical mother.

'Well, I'm excited! Oh, and about the clothes. I could wear a salwar-kameez, I suppose, but I doubt it will be as festive as you'd like, Badi Mummy.'

Badi Mummy cheered up at the thought of new clothes. 'I have some lovely dress material saved up. I'll give it to Rajni, and she can make a sharara for you. You can wear it for the sagai. We'll figure out the other dresses later. Now, take these keys and get it from that cupboard.'

Soon, Sukanya found herself armed with a shiny olive-green dress material and headed straight to Rajni Mausi's house with strict instructions to tell that good lady to add some golden gota at the edge of the sharara and not to charge extra for it.

'I'd prefer if the gota weren't too thick, Rajni Mausi,' said Sukanya, her voice tinged with concern as she sat beside her grand-aunt in the small, makeshift space outside her house where Rajni Mausi sat all day, her sewing machine steadily churning out kurtas and sari blouses until the fading light made it impossible to see the tiny buttonholes her deft fingers created.

Rajni Mausi didn't reply but smiled sadly. She went inside to fetch the gota samples for Sukanya to choose from, and Sukanya glanced into the house.

The frustrations of poverty were evident everywhere. No wonder Rajni Mausi always looked so weary and glum. Badi Mummy, though older, had still managed to hold on to the last vestiges of her graceful beauty, even as her health rapidly declined. In contrast, Rajni Mausi seemed broken and spent.

Like Nirupa Rai, the poor widow toiling at the sewing machine struggling to keep her family afloat, thought Sukanya, brought up on a steady diet of Hindi films by Shiladitya in an effort to keep her Hindi sharp.

Rajni Mausi had three strapping sons, each with questionable life choices. There was Natwar of course, infamous for his violent temper and his uncanny ability to profit off it, sometimes working as a hired goonda when the need arose. So far he had managed to stay out of prison, but nobody had any doubt about where his life was headed. Natwar was fiercely loyal to Bade Papa, who had treated him like a wayward son over the years. He'd slapped and scolded him frequently during his decidedly delinquent teenage years, but now he had accepted him as he was, abandoning any hopes for reform. Much of this shift had to do with Shiladitya's departure. An absent son, no matter how brilliant, was as good as none. After Shila left for London, Natwar had stepped in to take on many of the responsibilities that should have fallen to a son.

After Natwar came Munto, certainly not named after the famed writer; that much was certain. Munto had followed in his older brother's footsteps, proving the Indian education system completely ineffectual. After failing to clear class eight three times, Munto ran away to Banaras, embracing the life of an ascetic. He joined a band of Gorakhnathi sadhus. He had supposedly severed all family ties, but Sukanya had heard that he still made an occasional appearance, reappearing as Munto Baba, no less.

Rajni Mausi's third son was not her biological son. No one knew exactly how he came to live with her, but he had been hers since infancy. It was no secret in the mohalla – everyone knew that Rajni Mausi, who could barely scrape together a square meal for her own family, had taken in that sickly baby without a second thought, even while she was still nursing Munto. She had named him Paresh, but now he went by the infinitely more homely Puru.

Puru was no academic disaster like his two older brothers. He made it through college and even earned a degree, though in the less-than-glamorous third division. Puru belonged to the school of thought that advocated turning one's passion into a career. Leveraging his ardent love of Hindi films to his advantage, he worked as an assistant and general dogsbody at a local DVD rental shop, where he happily offered free advice and film recommendations to anyone who'd listen. He wasn't bad to look at either – tall, slim, bushy-haired, and with an easy, affable charm that made him easy to like.

'Arrey, Sukanya, getting clothes stitched already?' Puru teased as he stepped out of the house, twirling the keys to his moped. 'It's a little early for Nauchandi, nahin?'

Sukanya knew all about the famed Nauchandi fair, held every year in honour of the Chandi Devi temple and Hazrat Bale Mian's dargah – the high point of the city's cultural calendar. She remembered her father's words.

'It's a reminder of how Hindus and Muslim have lived here for ages,' he would say. 'Not that there isn't tension. Plenty of that, too.'

'Not Nauchandi, Puru Chacha,' Sukanya replied as she sifted through the box of gota samples that Rajni Mausi had placed in her lap. 'This is for Gumbi's engagement. It's in a few weeks, but Badi Mummy says I need to get my clothes made right away. Will you come too?'

There was no response from Puru. Sukanya glanced up. He looked a little pale, she thought, his eyes fixed on her with a look she couldn't quite place. Then, without a word, he turned and walked off, leaving her feeling puzzled.

'I think this one should work, don't you, Mausi?' she said, picking out a sample and handing it to Rajni.

'You can pick up the sharara next week, bitiya,' Rajni Mausi replied, smiling. 'How much like Shila you sometimes look.'

The next day, Sukanya spent the afternoon at Bibi's house where housework was carried out with the kind of military precision that usually ends in a coup. After lunch, she stretched out on one of the two high, wooden beds that dominated Bibi's peaceful home, gazing at the posters of various bhagwans that adorned the walls. There was Hanuman, carrying the Sanjeevani Mountain; there was Bharat Milaap, and here Lord Ram sat serenely with Sita and Laxman. The prints were undeniably of a very high quality, and Sukanya vaguely wondered if they might be lithographs by Raja Ravi Varma.

That evening, a jaagran was planned, and Bibi had been asked to prepare prasad. Sukanya listened to the sounds of her great-grandmother bustling around in the kitchen – pounding almonds, roasting flour – until the rhythmic sounds lulled her into sleep.

When she woke, the house was quiet. It was almost evening, and Bibi was nowhere to be seen. She had probably gone to the jaagran. Sukanya folded the woven cotton khes that Bibi must have covered her with before leaving, then decided to step onto the terrace, which offered an uninterrupted view of the neighbourhood stretching out below.

On the terrace, dusk was settling in, and the October wind had picked up, biting at her skin. The rooftops of Bulandwada stretched out in every direction, a tangle of terraces crammed together, so close that you could leap from one to the other. She had often seen children do it – darting across the gaps with fearless abandon, making her own heart leap into her mouth. In the distance, the lights of the mandir shimmered, and the soft, muted hum of the aarti drifted up to her. Sukanya put her cold hands on the sun-warmed wall and leaned forward, stretching her back.

'Ah, you couldn't leave me alone after all,' a voice suddenly spoke from a shadowed corner, making her startle. She spun around to peer at the corner, as someone stepped out from it.

Aman, of course. He had startled her twice in as many days.

'Ah, the young Nawab himself. What are you doing here on Bibi's terrace?' she now demanded of him, pretending that she hadn't felt unsettled by his sudden appearance at all. Aman lit a cigarette and inhaled deeply, channelling some deeply admired rock star.

'All the terraces are interconnected. I saw you from the haveli's terrace and jumped a few boundaries to get here. You didn't even see me coming. That's me, lithe as a cat.'

Sukanya rolled her eyes and was about to open her mouth to tell him off when he suddenly pulled her into the dark corner and placed an admonitory finger on his lips. He pointed to the adjoining terrace. Sukanya followed his gaze and saw two shadowy figures creeping towards each other.

She held her breath as the two figures gravitated towards each other, their silhouettes visible against the dimming sky, before melting together in an embrace. The wind carried their voices towards her and Aman with eerie clarity – low, urgent words that mingled with the evening breeze, speaking of love, passion and something darker, something close to panic. Sukanya strained to hear their words.

'Why didn't you say anything, Gumbi?' asked the male voice. Sukanya recognized the deep baritone in an instant. Yes, there was no doubt about it. It was her uncle Puru.

'What could I say? What could I do?' replied Gumbi in a piteous whisper.

'I could have asked your mother. She would have agreed.'

'Never. You know that. It is not just the difference in caste, Puru. My father has borrowed money from them. We are indebted to them. I could not refuse.'

'Your mother must have asked for your choice, Gumbi. She wouldn't have tied you up and thrown you into a well like this.'

'So what am I supposed to do now?'

'There is no option. We have to run away before the wedding.'

'Run away? No!'

'Yes, it's the only way. I'll put some money together before next month. We'll leave after that.'

'I...I need time to think, Puru.'

'There is no time to think. Don't you love me?'

'I do. You know I do. But this is too sudden, too dangerous. What if they find out?'

'Nothing will happen. Leave it to me. Now, leave. Go straight home. Some people are coming back from the jaagran.'

Suddenly the loudspeakers installed in the temple crackled to life, and the gentle sounds of the aarti gave way to the distorted beat of a Hindi film song, remixed to praise the lord. Puru and Gumbi slipped back down the stairs the way they had come. In the dark corner of the terrace, Sukanya's racing heartbeat slowly began to return to normal. She sank to the floor, feeling the weight of the moment.

'Phew, that was quite something. They almost saw us,' Aman said a few minutes after Puru and Gumbi had disappeared. He sat down heavily, his breath still a little shaky. Sukanya's heart was still racing.

'So, Puru and Gumbi, huh? What do you make of it?' Aman asked, leaning back against the brick wall, his eyes narrowed.

'I met Puru Chacha just yesterday. No wonder he was so upset at the thought of Gumbi's wedding. Turns out, she is his girlfriend.' Sukanya shook her head in disbelief.

Aman raised an eyebrow, intrigued. He pulled a pack of cigarettes from his pocket and offered it to Sukanya. 'Here, want one?'

'Like never before, but I'd better not. Badi Mummy has the nose of a hound – she can usually tell what's cooking five houses away.'

'Yes, must keep up appearances,' said Aman with mock seriousness, making her bristle exactly as he'd intended. 'Anyway, what did you make of the love-birds?'

'Gumbi and Puru Chacha, I didn't see that coming,' she said, her voice trailing off. 'Her wedding has been fixed.'

Aman shrugged, unfazed.

'There is always stuff going on behind closed doors out here. Or on terraces, in some cases. Anyway, things are about to get interesting,' he said, the glee coming through in his voice.

He paused, then added, 'Maybe we should leave an anonymous note at Gumbi's house. Tell her mother the bird's about to fly the coop.'

'That's really wicked,' said Sukanya, thinking of the defenceless Gumbi and her harridan of a mother. 'Nandi Chachi will skin her alive. You really just want to stir up trouble, don't you?'

'Only kidding,' said Aman, flicking his cigarette to the ground. 'I don't even like that busybody Nandi. But seriously, what should we do? Are you planning to tell your family about this little rendezvous?'

Sukanya paused, considered. Should she tell Bibi or Badi Mummy about the conversation that she'd inadvertently overheard? Wouldn't that just complicate things for the pitiful Puru and Gumbi, clutching at love in an impossible setting?

'No,' she finally said. 'We are just observers. Let's just see how the play unfolds.'

'Ah, ha-ha, a stoic at heart,' laughed Aman. 'Well, so be it. We will keep this secret to ourselves. So, Madam, what's on for the evening? Care to join me at good old Nawabon Ki Haveli?'

'No, thanks. I've to go,' said Sukanya, lifting her nose in the air, her tone dismissive. Aman chuckled again and raised his hands in surrender as she turned and began walking down the stairs, making it clear she was done with the exchange.

Later that night, after Badi Mummy had gone to bed, Sukanya found that she couldn't sleep. Her thoughts kept drifting to the exchange between Gumbi and Puru. How helpless they both sounded. Sukanya wondered if her own parents had been similarly desperate in their youth, wondering how to build a life together in the face of such opposition. On a whim, Sukanya picked up the phone and dialled her mother. Aparajita answered on the first ring and as always, started the conversation with first stating her offer to get Sukanya back to London.

'Are you all right? Do you want to come back? You can say so, you know. I'll organize your flight.'

Sukanya laughed. 'Mama, stop it! I'm having a good

time. I need to do this. You've got to stop worrying so much.'

'It's just that we all miss you. I ran into Angie and a bunch of your other friends at the mall over the weekend. I feel bad that you are missing out on your holidays.'

'I am not missing out on anything. I've spent years with my friends in London. Now I need to get to know my other family. Please relax, Mama? I am fine, really.'

'Yes, all right.' Aparajita paused, her voice faltering. 'Suku, did they...I mean, how do they feel about us now? About Daddy and me, I mean.'

'Mama,' Sukanya hesitated, not knowing how to frame the words hanging between them. 'The thing is, Mama, they don't talk about you at all. I've tried to bring you up, but they just...glaze over, y'know? They aren't ready, Mama, I'm sorry.'

Aparajita went silent at this. Even Sukanya's presence was not enough to soften Shila's parents. What would it take?

Sukanya lay in bed that night, the steady whirr of the fan filling the silence. She thought back to the nights in London, when she would lie awake, thinking about the people from the stories that her father had told her at bedtime. Now she was in the midst of these very characters, but she was far from the dynamic force she had imagined herself to be, changing the course of things. She was, at best, an observer, conflicted that she needed the love of the very people that refused to reconcile with her parents.

15.

Meerut, October 2006: Sudhir Tyagi Makes an Appearance

Power cuts were a way of life that the people of Meerut accepted with a certain stoic resignation, all the while cussing loudly. They were unbearable in the summer months, but even on cold evenings such as that one, they could slow things down, and the darkness would stretch for hours, relieved only by emergency lights. On one such stifling evening, when the power had been missing for hours, Sukanya lay on the bed next to Badi Mummy as she slept, wrapped in a thick blanket from Gandhi Ashram. Outside, Bade Papa sat hunched over in the *dalaan*, taking a class by the flickering light of a candle, a woollen cap pulled low over his head, shivering a little. The weary students struggled bravely to keep up as Bade Papa explained the difference between heroic couplets and Spenserian stanzas, but clearly it was a slow day, made worse by the dark. Bade Papa was fast losing patience, his temper flaring at the slightest provocation. Finally, unable to take any more, he dismissed the students early.

'Go away, go away, all of you,' Sukanya heard him shout. 'Do the work. And you, Sudhir Tyagi, why you want to spend your life firing desi kattas when you could have studied like a real scholar is beyond me. This town will take a poet and turn him into a ruffian.'

Whoever Sudhir Tyagi was, he only laughed in response, a low, throaty laugh, easily amused.

Once the boys had left, Bade Papa poured himself a drink and moved to his harmonium. Soon he was singing an Urdu ghazal that Sukanya found sweet, though she could not understand it at all. It sounded familiar and distant all at once; perhaps she had heard Shila hum it to himself on a cold evening as he prepared dinner?

yūñhī be-sabab na phirā karo koī shaam ghar meñ rahā karo
vo ġhazal kī sachchī kitāb hai use chupke chupke paDhā karo

Bade Papa was definitely a poet, she thought and smiled to herself. It was now about eight and completely dark. Badi Mummy was still asleep; the pain medication often made her sleep like this at odd hours.

'Kaun hai, kaun hai?' Bade Papa suddenly shouted, his voice ringing in the quiet. Badi Mummy woke up with a start. Sukanya's heart gave a lurch; she shot out of bed to check on the cause for excitement, switching on the flashlight that lay on the side table just for these emergencies. From the dim light, she saw a figure, Natwar's wife, her face covered by her *ghunghat*. She had been raised in a village and believed in covering her face and head with the pallu of her sari whenever faced with an elder.

'He-he, Bade Papa, it's me,' she said, her voice muffled. 'I was only touching your feet.'

'In the dark? I thought it was a rat! What do you want now?' Clearly Bade Papa had not taken this display of respect in a good spirit, having spilled a little of his drink.

'Amma ji said that I should give this to Sukanya bitiya,' said the poor woman, clutching a small packet to her chest. 'She said it's important.'

'Humph,' grumbled Bade Papa, his face scrunching into a scowl. 'Sukanya, come here. Take a look at this.'

'Thanks, Chachi,' said Sukanya, taking the package. 'Could you tell Rajni Mausi I will come by tomorrow if I need any alterations? Bade Papa, it's my dress, for Gumbi's engagement.'

Natwar's wife nodded and dived at Bade Papa's feet again.

'Jeete raho, khush raho,' grumbled Bade Papa and moved away, going back to the kitchen to refill his glass.

'Arrey, show it to me,' said Badi Mummy after

shouting out a few earfuls at Natwar's wife for startling people in the darkness. Sukanya duly handed over the garment.

'Hmmm,' Badi Mummy muttered, as she stretched the dress this way and that in the feeble light. 'Chalo, theek hi hai, but tell Rajni she will have to fix it if there is any problem once you try it out. She has limited skill. She spoils my sari blouses all the time.'

'She's okay, Badi Mummy, this looks gorgeous, and she made it in record time. This is the first time I have a custom-made outfit! Let me try it on,' said Sukanya and went to her room to change, stumbling in the dark. It fit well, a beautiful gota-laden sharara, a far cry from the muted tones of the Zara and TopShop outfits she wore in London. The bright green suited this new Indian Sukanya, she decided, and maybe Badi Mummy would lend her some jewellery to complete the look. She came back downstairs to model her new look for Badi Mummy and twirled around in the dalaan to show her the beautiful skirt, holding the flashlight to illuminate herself, while Badi Mummy watched approvingly from her bed in the baithak, offering remarks on the fit and the colour and declaring her the most beautiful girl in the world.

With a sudden flicker, the lights returned, flooding the room with sudden brightness. Sukanya blinked, disoriented by the change. Right then, someone barged through the door, and she found herself facing a young man, dressed in a kurta-pajama that accentuated his broad frame. He paused awkwardly in the doorway as soon as he saw Sukanya, momentarily transfixed, not knowing whether to stay or leave. He couldn't have been more than nineteen or twenty, with a stubbled face that seemed more an attempt to look more mature than anything else. Sukanya stopped twirling at once and lowered her arms, still holding the flashlight, embarrassed, and looked at him quizzically.

'I forgot my bag,' he finally found his voice and gestured at a black bag lying in the corner. Sukanya picked it up and handed it to him, not looking him in the face.

Bade Papa came back to check who was at the door.

'Ah, Sudhir Tyagi, back again like a bad penny,' he said, on spotting the visitor. 'What have you forgotten this time?'

'Ji, Master ji, bag,' said Sudhir and held the bag up with both hands.

'Off with you, then, and I hope you have stopped all that netagiri nonsense,' said Bade Papa, chattier now that he had had a drink. Sudhir sensed his pliancy and grinned, his gruff appearance melting into something charming. Sukanya stood by and watched him. He looked like the stock of the earth but interesting nonetheless and a bit rough-hewn. Someone to be careful of, to be wary around, an unstable compound. Sudhir quickly touched Bade Papa's feet, who only sighed at all this blessing-taking, and dashed off, casting another look at Sukanya, glittering in her green, gota-laden sharara.

'Who was that, Bade Papa?' she asked, a bit unsettled, when the young man had left.

'The youngest Tyagi boy,' sighed Bade Papa, clearly dissatisfied with the Tyagi progeny. 'This one is a little complicated. He is a goonda; of course he is, through and through. Or a rebel, depending on how you define it. How could he not be, with that family.'

'What sort of family is that?' asked Sukanya, now intrigued.

'They come from a village nearby, a place called Asauda. Affluent zamindars, but patriots. I've been told his family gave a lot of money to Bahadur Shah Zafar to fight the British back in the day. And during the freedom struggle, Gandhi ji would stay in their family mansion whenever he came to this part of the country; there are pictures of his meetings there. Now the mansion has gone to ruin, of course. Nobody lives there. I used to know Sudhir's father; I taught him too. Tall, proud man, Sudhir looks like him. Died young in a family feud, shot through the chest. Mother died when Sudhir was little. The boy has no family left to speak of, and that is a bad thing for someone like him.'

Sukanya blinked; she hadn't expected the boy to have such a storied past. Bade Papa paused for a moment, lost in his thoughts and memories of Sudhir's father. 'He's some kind of a chhatra neta in the university. But he does have a real passion for literature, if you ask me. The university doesn't hold any regular classes, of course, so he comes here to study. Likes to keep it quiet. It doesn't do him any favours, to come across as studious. The boy has charisma, though. Matter of time before he gets taken out by a rival gang or gets kicked up into city politics, if you ask me.'

'A student leader? But why is that such a bad thing?' asked Sukanya, mystified.

'Oho, out here that is a complicated thing, bitiya,' said Bade Papa, wondering how to start explaining the intricacies of politics in UP to his London-bred granddaughter. 'Suffice it to say that the boy will head into only murkier waters from here on. Marxist ideals, Meerut genes, Ram milayi jodi.'

Bade Papa sighed, shook his head, and downed his drink. A chill ran up Sukanya's spine. Away from the Meerut of tehzeeb and adab, of music and poetry, of endless affection and ties that had reached out to her across the oceans and had pulled her to its gullies, was that other Meerut. Caste politics, violence, crime – all of this she knew nothing of.

Bade Papa spoke again, now chuckling. 'I've heard Sudhir is quite the politico in the university. Has a room of his own in the hostel where he holds meetings and so on. Much drinking and whatnot too. The boy is sharp; otherwise, I wouldn't let him come home. He's just focused on all this political nonsense. My task is to teach him, for his dead father's sake. Khair, let's see what he makes of his life.'

Bade Papa and Sukanya were up till late that night, discussing many things. After Badi Mummy took some medicines and the pain became bearable, she lay down, and Bade Papa too went to bed. Sukanya grabbed an Agatha Christie book from Bade Papa's collection and retired to her room, but she found she could not get past the first chapter, quite unusual given that she was a third-generation Poirot aficionado. Much to her annoyance, she found herself dwelling on chhatra neta Sudhir Tyagi and his strange life.

16.

Meerut, October 2006: Badi Mummy Wanes Further

Sukanya had just drifted off to sleep when loud voices from downstairs woke her up. She fumbled for the light switch, her heart pounding. Hearing Bade Papa's panicked voice from downstairs, she leapt out of bed and rushed down the stairs, taking two at a time. The clock said it was three in the morning.

When she reached the baithak, Bade Papa was trying to keep Badi Mummy in bed, who seemed to be in complete agony, her body twisting violently, her breath coming in shallow gasps. Her eyes were closed, but she was whimpering, clutching at her stomach, her face contorted. Sukanya's heart skipped a beat.

'What is it, Bade Papa, what happened to Badi Mummy?' her voice came out in sobs, panic rising in her throat. *She's dying, she's dying.*

'Go and call Natwar, Sukanya; wake him up. Hurry, hurry,' shouted Bade Papa and Sukanya ran to obey. She unlocked the door with trembling hands and rushed outside, the cold air hitting her face, to fetch Natwar from the house next door. She banged at his door with clammy hands, shouting at the top of her voice. Natwar took only two minutes to open the door; his eyes were alert, despite being woken up from deep sleep. Without a word, he rushed off on Puru's moped to fetch the doctor who lived a few houses away. A couple of lights came on in the houses nearby. Some of the neighbours emerged from their houses, wrapping shawls and mufflers around themselves as they came out to check on the sounds they'd heard. Sukanya made her way back to the house, her heart sinking like a heavy stone, feeling as though there was no ground beneath her feet.

Badi Mummy, Badi Mummy, don't die, please. A small child's plea, sent into the great void.

Badi Mummy was still thrashing about, deliriously calling for Shiladitya, the son who had been absent for twenty-two years.

'Shila, where are you? Stop this zidd. Come down this instant. No more hiding! I need you home. Come down and eat, I have made your favourite halwa – why won't you come? Shila, I won't ask again. Don't make me come there. Shila, Shila, Shila.' She was shaking, her brow covered with a feverish sweat.

Bade Papa sat next to her, helpless tears streaming down his face, trying to hold her back but she continued to writhe, her cries becoming more animal-like, the creatures from the otherworld asking for her hand in death.

Mercifully, Natwar returned with the doctor, a plump woman in a crumpled salwar-kameez, who shooed everyone out of the room with authority. Once outside, Sukanya realized that her cheeks were wet with tears. Not wishing to speak to the neighbours crowding outside the small baithak, she made her way outside the house and sat down heavily on its steps. The night air was very cold now. As expected, she wouldn't be alone for more than a moment. Sunita Chachi spotted her almost immediately, and made her way towards her, wearing a voluminous patterned nightie, a dupatta draped modestly over the loose garment.

'Arrey, don't cry, lalli,' she said affectionately, placing a warm hand on Sukanya's shoulder. 'Badi Mummy will be all right. The doctor has come now. Have faith in Bhagwan.'

A few other people were looking outside their doors and asking each other what had happened. Sukanya suddenly felt very young and out of place and furious with her parents for letting her go so far away from them and her home, conveniently forgetting that it had been her choice, her decision to leave London and come here. They were supposed to handle these grown-up things, not her.

'Come, let's go to my house, Sukanya,' said Sunita, gently pulling the young girl to her feet. 'You look pale, beta. You need some tea.'

Sukanya obeyed and stepped inside Sunita's house,

barely four steps away from her own, right across the gully, vaguely recognizing that this was the first time that she was doing so. The room that she sat in was tiny and crowded with furniture – a diwan, a wooden settee with hand-embroidered cushions on it, a ubiquitous sofa set, something that Sunita must have got as part of her dowry, small tables and stools. Oil paint landscapes, made by someone with more enthusiasm than talent, lined the whitewashed walls, as did a calendar that exhorted, 'Visit! Hong Kong!' There was a niche in the wall that had been repurposed into a showcase. For some reason, it was now stuffed with soft toys, their eyes permanently unblinking.

Sunita went inside to make tea, that panacea for all of life's problems. Sukanya clasped her head in her hands, defiantly disobeying her father's admonitions to never give in to despondency. Sukanya thought of Shiladitya who never gave in. Not once, despite the burdens he had carried since he was young. Sukanya felt the familiar weight of grief for all that happened in her fractured family, much of it unfolding even before she was born. She shook her head to clear it, telling herself that she ought to see if Bade Papa needed any help instead of going to pieces like this.

Sunita came inside with the tea. Sukanya did not want it but after a few sips realized that she needed it.

'Badi Mummy will get better, bitiya,' said Sunita Chachi once again, sitting next to her and patting her head gently like one does to a very young child. 'Don't worry. You don't know how happy she is that she got to see you.'

'Chachi, does she...does she miss Daddy a lot?' Sukanya asked before she could stop herself.

Sunita sighed and bowed her head.

'How could she not miss him, beta? She has never said a word to me, or to anyone else, but he's her only son. He left so suddenly. All these years...it's enough to break a mother's heart.'

'Not that I would know,' Sunita added, quietly. Her childlessness had been openly discussed at Bibi's chowk. Sukanya kept silent, not knowing how to offer comfort.

Sunita spoke again. 'Maybe they feel that they didn't deserve this treatment. The fact is – Shila Bhaiyya did choose your mother over them. That is how it is. At first there is anger, and then there is petulance, and then we just get used to being estranged.'

'And the years go by,' said Sukanya. 'Do you think they will ever come around to reconciling, Chachi?'

'Dekho, gudiya, in my experience, the struggle is in remaining estranged. The natural thing is to make up, get back together, fight again. The important thing is – you've made Badi Mummy very happy by deciding to come here, Sukanya.'

Sukanya glanced out of the window and said, 'Oh, look, Chachi, the doctor seems to be leaving. I'll just have a quick word with her.'

The doctor stood at the doorstep, talking to Bade Papa, who seemed to have aged more in the last couple of hours. Natwar stood next to him, nodding attentively. Puru hovered in the background, fiddling with the blanket that covered Badi Mummy – finally asleep, her face grey and lined. Beneath her bed, Tinku's amber eyes glinted in the dark, watching everything carefully. The doctor advised some more tests and left with Natwar and Puru, asking them to call in case Badi Mummy took another turn.

Sukanya quietly watched Badi Mummy's face, beautiful and faded in repose. No, she was not asleep. She was unconscious, slipping away to an infinitely more comfortable place where she would not be a stranger to her only son. It was clear even to Sukanya's inexperienced eyes that she didn't have much longer left. She took Badi Mummy's thin, bony hand in her own, drawing courage from it, all the while wondering how to say what she had to.

Outside, dawn was breaking, the first, feeble rays of the sun struggling against the winter sky. Sukanya lay on the bed next to her. Bade Papa was sitting in his customary place outside in the dalaan. She could hear the creak of his rocking-chair.

A half-forgotten piece of poetry rose in her mind.

Night wanes-the vapours around the mountain curl'd,
Melt into morn, and Light awakes the world.
Man has another day to swell the past,
And lead him near to little, but his last.

Badi Mummy too had another day to swell the past, she thought to herself, even as she got closer to her last.

'Bade Papa,' she called out tentatively, her voice coming out in a whisper.

'Yes?' his tired voice floated towards her. She could see his silhouette framed in the light-dark, his shoulders slumped, his head bent.

Sukanya cleared her throat, the words taking their own time to form. She hesitated for a second, but her natural courage came forth, and she spoke in a clear voice.

'Do you think we should call Daddy and Mummy to visit? I feel...I think Badi Mummy would like to see them; I'm sure of it. She needs to see them, Bade Papa. And I know they are just waiting for your call. Should I call them?'

There was complete silence for almost a minute. Sukanya felt the air in the small baithak become thick and heavy with her own hope, with Badi Mummy's fading breath, and with her grandfather's silent rage. Her words hung in the room, waiting for an answer.

'Sukanya,' he finally spoke, his voice cracking slightly, turning his face away. 'I cannot allow him to return. And if Badi Mummy and I mean something to you, you will never broach this topic again.'

17.

Meerut, November 2006: The Pleasures of the Chaat Shop

Ever since the night Badi Mummy took a turn for the worse, Sukanya was loath to be away from her, a superstition taking hold that her presence could stave off the inevitable. She would sit with Badi Mummy even while she slept, watching her quietly, and refuse to go even to Bibi's chowk. Finally, one evening, worried about her, Bade Papa pushed her out of the house.

'Go and eat chaat at Lachho's,' he said, thrusting some money in her hands. 'Shila used to love eating... anyway, you go and try it for yourself. See what the fuss is all about.'

Sukanya hesitated but seeing Bade Papa's drawn face, she nodded slowly and stuffed the crumpled notes in the pocket of her jeans. She stepped out into the narrow gully, taking in its sharp, old-spice smell that now felt familiar, and looked around at the chajjas overhead, decorated with pots of wilting plants, and at the chabutras jutting out of the walls, worn smooth with years of use. Pigeons sat high up on the walls. At the sight of these familiar, comforting sights, she felt some of the weight lifting from her shoulders. Yes, it was a good idea to come out of the house.

She didn't know the way to the chaat shop, but that didn't matter. It was enough to know that the next child she passed – a boy with a patang and manjha – would lead her all the way without hesitation.

She reached Lachho's shop and looked at it, a little bewildered. It was a small, unassuming shop without a sign, there was no need for one. Inside the shop sat two worn-out benches and rickety tables that looked like they would crumble under the weight of the patrons at any moment. The air smelt of hot oil and pungent, smoky spices. The walls were blackened with years of smoke from the karahi that was undoubtedly older than even Bibi. Lachho himself presided behind the karahi, an old and slow man in a vest and pajamas that must have once been white. His hands shook slightly as he stirred the contents of his pots and pans. He looked up leisurely when he saw the girl come in and smiled with his milky, cataract-infested eyes, an ageing symbol of the mohalla who had been dispensing chaat in the same spot for decades.

'Golgappe first?' he asked in a soft voice. Sukanya nodded, feeling warmed by the old man's voice, wondering if her father had stood in the same spot, pressing coins in Lachho's weathered hands, demanding to be fed. Lachho didn't know it but he had featured strongly in the Bulandwada stories of her childhood.

The golgappe started making their way from the chaatwala's deft hands, each one sending a burst of strong, delicious flavours through her, making her eyes water. For a moment the world outside faded, all that remained was the crunch and heat of each bite, dulling the heaviness in her chest, lifting the sadness. What was this glorious food? Why had she waited so long to taste it?

'As they say in these parts, akele, akele?' asked a familiar voice. The words, light and teasing, broke the reverie. She turned around to see Aman standing next to her, half-smiling, his eyes amused. A small backpack slung from his shoulder. His medical college sweatshirt and jeans – everything too big for his lean, spare frame – seemed to swallow him whole. His dishevelled hair and the dark circles under his glasses spoke of the exhaustion that clung to him, alongside the familiar smell of cigarettes.

Sukanya wiped the spicy water from her lips. 'Ah, doc-boy,' she said as another golgappa was thrust into her sakora. Aman grabbed it from her bowl and popped it into his mouth.

'What is this? No heat, no spice!' he scoffed. 'Surely, we can do better than this? Lachho, come on, let's up the game!'

'Give him a bowl, Bhaiyya,' Sukanya told the chaatwala. 'He deserves his own ulcer.'

'Ten points if you can guess who she is, Lachho,' said Aman to the shopkeeper, nodding at Sukanya, with a grin. 'And give us two plates of tikkis while you deliberate over it.'

'This is Shiladitya's daughter,' said Lachho without missing a beat, and without as much as a second glance. 'She looks like him. Kyon, bitiya, does Shiladitya ever talk about me? That boy, he could eat chaat like nobody's business!'

'He talks about you often, Lachho,' said Sukanya in a light tone. She wasn't sparing the old halwai's feelings – her father's eyes would grow distant when he reminisced about Lachho's chaat, a strange longing flickering behind them. She was beginning to understand why. This was heavenly, food fit for the gods! Each bite of the steaming aloo tikkis, liberally doused with cold dahi, a magical tamarind chutney and another green one seemed to answer some unspoken need within her. This was food that could, should endure for generations. She took one bite, then another, each pushing her into a blissful reverie. The ghost of the boy Shiladitya sat next to her, watching her eat, a reminder of the life he had left behind.

'This may be the best food I have ever eaten,' she said after she had taken her last bite and seriously contemplated putting the plate to her mouth and licking it clean. Lachho reappeared with hot gulab jamuns, smiling widely. Sukanya looked up at the old man and felt a deep affection for him for giving her a taste and glimpse of her father's past.

'Thank you,' she said, quietly. 'I'd like one more, please,' she added, making Aman and Lachho laugh.

'Just like her father,' muttered Lachho as he went back to his perch behind the karahi to fix her another plate of gulab jamun.

'English food is a bit bland for your taste, eh?' asked Aman. Sukanya noticed that he'd barely touched his food. How could anyone refuse this fare?

'I could just live in this shop for this food,' she sighed, looking around the sooty walls with affectionate eyes.

'Oh no, my dear, that won't be possible,' drawled Aman. 'Soon you'll be back in the land of jam and tea. Let me pay for this?'

'Very Nawabi of you, but there is really no need,' said Sukanya, reaching for the money that Bade Papa had given her.

'Ah, another hope dashed. Can we at least walk back home together or even that is not acceptable?'

Sukanya laughed and paid Lachho, who watched sadly as he saw her walk away, thinking of all the times her father had walked away with that same loping stride, looking over his shoulder, promising to be back soon.

They made their way towards Nawabon Ki Haveli. There were many curious glances shot at them along the way, but Aman seemed oblivious to the attention, talking easily about his study load and the multitudes of pressure it had heaped upon him. Once they reached the haveli, Aman sat down on the marble steps that led up to the gate, leaning against one of the twin elephant statues that guarded the gate on either side. Sukanya joined him. He lit a cigarette, the glow of the tip illuminating his face for a brief moment.

'Is your aunt inside?' asked Sukanya, curious about the invisible Roshni. Aman's face immediately shuttered.

'I don't think so,' he said, shrugging a bit. 'Anyway, how is your cultural excursion to India coming along?'

'Well, my grandmother has been very unwell, so I haven't exactly been partying wild and hard.' She tried to be light-hearted, but her eyes moistened of their own accord, as they always did these days when she spoke of Badi Mummy. How much longer did she have left with her grandmother, exactly how many days? What if she knew? What would she do with the weight of that knowledge?

Aman did not say anything for a few moments, her sadness settling between them like a third friend. He knew all about Sukanya's situation, the fractured history of her family. How could he not? There were no secrets in this ageless neighbourhood, just whispers in the gully and gossip in the chowk.

'How is she now?' he asked. She had had the time to force back the tears that wanted to leak out of the corners of her eyes.

'She's better than she was the other day. She just took ill so suddenly. I mean, she had seemed all right in the evening when Sudhir Tyagi and the other boys had come for their class, but then she just took a turn.' At the mention of Sudhir Tyagi, Aman seemed to forget about everything else.

'Sudhir Tyagi?' he asked in a sudden, sharp voice. 'Gajender Tyagi's youngest? How do you know him?

'Like I said, Bade Papa teaches him,' Sukanya replied, puzzled. 'Why do you ask?'

Aman shook his head, laughed, finished his cigarette, and rose, dusting the ash off his jeans. He pulled Sukanya to her feet, holding her hand a little longer than necessary.

'Someone or the other from Sudhir's gang is always being brought to the medical college for injuries, sometimes even gunshot wounds. He's trouble, that fellow. I am just surprised your family knows them. He isn't...he is...I mean, well...he's hardly your type.'

'Well, Bade Papa knew Sudhir's father and now he teaches him, and that is all there is to it.' She waved her hand and said, trying to change the topic. 'Anyway, where are we on our little secret regarding Gumbi and Puru Chacha? Any more sightings? Are the lovers still trysting, would you know?'

Aman grinned, accepting that she didn't want to talk of Sudhir anymore.

'Nothing since the last time. I am quite looking

forward to some fireworks, come the time for the wedding. In the meanwhile, of course, we keep mum.'

'My lips are sealed. Even Lachho's chaat will not unseal them.'

Aman laughed again and waved goodbye. Sukanya walked back home, realizing that she had shed the heavy sadness of the past few days. She closed the zipper of her jacket against the cold evening and felt warmer than she had in days.

18.

Meerut, November 2006 – The Sagai

'All set for Gumbi's sagai?' Badi Mummy asked Sukanya that morning as she came down from her room.

'I think so, Badi Mummy. I'm not a complete novice, you know? I've been to an Indian wedding in London, a family from our neighbourhood had invited us; their daughter had married a boy from Mumbai. Angie and I had danced all night!'

'Yes, but I have a feeling this function will be different from the one in London,' laughed Badi Mummy, a rare sound that Sukanya had grown to love. She reached out and took her grandmother's hand, the veins so clearly visible through that transparent skin.

'I wish you could attend all these things, Badi Mummy,' she said, her voice thick with wishfulness. 'And I wish I could take you back with me to London and show you everything.'

'Let me get better, bitiya; I will try to come for the wedding. Cheer up; I don't like to see you mope. You have to attend all the functions and see them with my eyes.'

'Like Dhanteras!' exclaimed Sukanya.

'You mean Dhritarashtra,' Badi Mummy laughed till tears came to her eyes.

That evening, Sukanya assessed herself in the mirror. She had worn Indian attire a couple of times before – at the Indian Council's annual gala dinner and at her school's Origins theme party – but this felt different. The yards of unfamiliar sharara fabric billowed about her legs. Her ears hurt a little bit already, her mother's jadau jhumkas, made by some talented chiterias and gharias long since gone, dangled from either side of her oval face. Gone was the wing-tipped eyeliner, replaced today by kohl that seemed to deepen her eyes. Everything felt uncomfortable and resplendent, all at once. She drew the line at the flowers that Badi Mummy wanted her to wear in her hair, but other than that she was making the cut.

Beauty takes work, beauty takes work, she muttered to herself and, armed with Badi Mummy's approval, she walked out of the house and made her way to Bibi's chowk, tottering a bit.

Bibi's courtyard had been transformed. A colourful shamiana stretched above the space, and it was abuzz with the chatter and laughter of women and children. Everyone looked busy, laughing, working, preparing for the evening ahead. Nandi sat at the centre of a small crowd of women, merrily drumming on a dholak, her voice rising in a cheeky song that tossed playful insults at Gumbi's new family. Sukanya was told that it was a time-tested, passive-aggressive way to let off steam and vent unsaid frustrations. Soon, one of the women who sat surrounding Nandi tired of the banter, stood up, and started dancing, her arms moving in graceful arcs. The women clapped enthusiastically; some of them joined the dancer.

As the women twirled and danced, a man entered, balancing a tray laden with small glasses of tea, fragrant with ginger and cardamom. Behind him, a boy followed, carefully carrying a large tray of motichoor laddus, colour like marigolds. The sight of the treats made everyone pause.

Nandi stopped mid-song, her eyes lighting up at the arrival of food. 'Chalo, enough singing for now. Arrey bhai, Compounderni, where is your gaane-waali? She needs to take over.' Compounderni, forever christened thus for being married to a compounder in the hospital, looked up and shook her head.

'Nahin, nahin, Nandi jeeji, you sing better than the professional gaane-waali. Don't stop. Sing, sing!'

Nandi blossomed under the attention, gulping down her tea in one swift swig before slapping the dholak with renewed vigour. The women clapped and cheered her on.

Bibi came into the courtyard and spotted Sukanya

standing in the corner and watching the celebrations. Her face softened as she took in the Indian attire and came forward to take a closer look. 'Sabse sundar, the most beautiful ever,' she said, without a shred of doubt. Sukanya basked in the affectionate compliment and then was reminded of the gift she had carried.

'I got something for Gumbi, Bibi,' said Sukanya, reaching into the batua that Badi Mummy had lent her. She carefully pulled out the MAC cosmetic pack from London, oddly foreign in this setting.

'Hmm, looks expensive,' said Bibi. Sukanya knew that it was probably a hundred times more expensive than Bibi's imagination was letting on but did not confirm it.

'Well, all right then, you better go and give it to her,' said Bibi. 'Nandi is busy singing. Gumbi will be alone in her room right now.'

Sukanya made her way out of the shamiana, out of the courtyard and to Nandi's house. Jostled by the crowds, she walked slowly, watching her step for fear of tripping over the unfamiliar sharara, and almost immediately collided with someone with his back to her.

'Sorry,' she said and found herself facing Sudhir Tyagi, the young man who belonged firmly in the five pm English tuition slot at her house and was not to be seen outside of it.

'What are you doing here?' she demanded of him, before she could stop herself.

'Ah, Master ji's granddaughter, the memsahib from London. I was hoping I'd see you here,' he laughed.

'Also, what's wrong with my being here?'

'Be quiet, I am not a memsahib. I just assumed that, you know, uh...'

'That I'm not good enough for the "genteel" crowd?' he teased, now laughing openly. Sukanya rolled her eyes.

'Something like that,' she said, and began walking again, a bit faster now, hoping to get away but Sudhir kept up easily, walking alongside her.

'Why are you following me?' she asked, exasperated.

'I am just looking out for you, memsahib.'

'I'll be fine,' she scowled at him.

'I know, I'll make sure of it.'

Distracted by his presence, Sukanya forgot to watch her step and nearly tripped before he caught her and straightened her, suddenly making her feel very flustered, her arms tingling where he had held her.

'This is the green sharara from that evening,' he observed, as she caught her breath and resumed walking, looking for the bride-to-be. 'Makes you look like a summer's day on this winter evening.'

'Oof, very poetic. A poet with guns. Where are they, your guns, I mean?'

'Ah, I see my reputation precedes me,' he laughed again. 'Not to worry, they are safely hidden.'

'Where is Gumbi?' Sukanya asked of a woman passing by.

'Upstairs, sulking,' said the woman without breaking her step and casting a curious glance at Sudhir.

'I'd be sulking too if grown people behaved like

savages with me, making me marry someone I don't want to,' grumbled Sukanya under her breath as she climbed up the stairs where more tiny rooms lined the floor. Sudhir continued to walk with her, his hands behind his back, his eyes not leaving her face. Sukanya finally located Gumbi's room and turned around to face him.

'Are you planning to accompany me inside as well?' she asked.

'Do you need me to?' he asked, leaning against the wall of the narrow corridor, completely at ease, smiling at her.

'I need you to vanish from here. Shoo, go away,' said Sukanya, and breathed a sigh of relief when he finally obeyed. What an insolent character. Trust Bade Papa to collect these specimens of humanity. A Shakespeare-loving goonda.

Shaking her head, she took a deep breath, knocked at the door, and entered it without much preamble. Gumbi was sitting on the bed, a couple of young girls keeping her company. They left when they saw Sukanya. Sukanya was struck by how different Gumbi looked, thinner, paler, withdrawn. It took her a moment to find her voice.

'How are you, Gumbi? Did you eat anything?' asked Sukanya, a note of kindness creeping into her voice. Gumbi shook her head and smiled faintly at Sukanya. Sukanya hesitated, unsure of how to approach her. She remembered what she had come for and held out the gift.

'I brought something for you,' she said. 'Congratulations, Gumbi.'

Gumbi's eyes lit up, and she took the packet eagerly.

'This is so nice! Thank you, jeeji,' she said, her voice warm, as she opened the packet and found the cosmetics inside. For a moment she brightened.

'Oh, you shouldn't be calling me that,' protested Sukanya. 'I am younger.'

Gumbi nodded, sadness wafting from her once again. Sukanya cleared her throat. Her flippant promise to Aman flashed through her mind – *my lips are sealed* – but at that moment, she needed to say something, anything to disconnect herself from them, the people who were pushing an unwilling Gumbi on a path that she did not want to tread. *I am not one of them, I am not one of them.*

'I...I'm sorry, Gumbi,' she finally blurted. 'They shouldn't be marrying you off without your permission. It's just...plain wrong.'

Gumbi didn't respond and gazed at her feet, looking drained and wretched. She didn't ask any questions of Sukanya.

One of the young girls came back into the room, carrying Gumbi's dinner in a thali, and placed it in front of her. Gumbi ignored her food, her head slung low. The noise from the courtyard grew louder, the shrill sounds of the professional singers drowning out the muffled sounds from the rest of the house. Sukanya did not have the heart to join in the festivities after having seen Gumbi's misery and sat there quietly till it was time to leave.

19.

Meerut, November 2006 – The Church at Sardhana

Each morning brought a little less of Badi Mummy to see. Sukanya would sit on the takht, the cup of tea forgotten, her chest tight with a ball of fear, chewing on her nails, and watching as her grandmother seemed to vanish into nothingness. At some point in those fear-filled days, she began to believe – entirely irrationally – that if only her father could come home, things would turn around, that Badi Mummy would get better, but Bade Papa seemed to have forgotten about her plea. He looked a little lost these days, his gaze often unfocused, and Sukanya didn't have the heart to reach into the place where he stored all his hurt.

'Sukanya,' Badi Mummy was calling her name in her frail voice, Sukanya realised with a jolt and smiled at her grandmother.

'What is it, Badi Mummy, what do you need?' she asked, straightening her blanket.

'I need you to cheer up,' said Badi Mummy. 'This is no way for a young girl to be. Go out, see things. Why do you sit here all day, next to an old woman?'

'I'll go later, Badi Mummy, once you feel better.' Sukanya laughed, trying to placate her but Badi Mummy was not to be distracted.

'I've been thinking, gudiya. There's a famous church at Sardhana; you should go and see that.'

'I live in Europe, Badi Mummy, I have seen enough churches to last me a lifetime.' Sukanya tried to brush off this new plan.

'This is not like those churches, bitiya, it is a mix of all sorts of styles.' Badi Mummy said, not to be defeated, 'It was built by Begam Samru. Have you heard of her? She was a nautch girl who went on to rule Sardhana. She owned a mercenary army, inherited from her dead husband. She built the church in his honour.'

'Sounds like a cool lady,' said Sukanya, absentmindedly reaching out to stroke the grumpy Tinku who allowed a little bit of affection, flicking his ears back.

'Go with Natwar. He knows the place well, and he will protect you from the guides that will swarm once you speak and the foreign accent slips out,' smiled Badi Mummy. Sukanya sighed, resigning herself to the idea of visiting this famous church.

It was settled that the following Saturday would be earmarked for the excursion. Sukanya braced herself for Natwar Chacha's protective ways, which always involved glaring at anyone who as much as glanced her way and making barely concealed threats of violence.

As it happened, Natwar came down with a severe case of food poisoning the night before the planned excursion and had to be taken to the hospital. Too much roadside chhole-bhature was the doctor's verdict. Sukanya and Bade Papa went to meet him, Sukanya feeling guiltily relieved that she wouldn't have to go for the day trip anymore.

'Hai, Bade Papa,' wailed Natwar Chacha, a saline drip still running into his arm. Spread out on his bed, his rough hair standing around his face, he looked like a disgruntled child, disappointed in his own body. 'I have let you down. I won't be able to take gudiya to the girijaghar.' He did not look too good, his dark, swarthy face still a peculiar shade of grey-green.

'Arrey nahi, beta,' soothed Bade Papa, resting a hand on Natwar's shoulder. 'Relax, try to get better. Sukanya can go next Saturday. No problem.'

'Nahin,' Natwar's voice was firm now, a surge of indignation running through it. 'Sukanya will go tomorrow, as planned. Puru will take her. Puru! PURU! Anni, call Puru!'

Puru came into the room, his usual sullen expression firmly in place.

'Kya hai?' he asked, crossing his arms. In response, his affectionate sibling muffled a string of expletives that would have made a sailor blush.

'Tell the seth of the video library of yours that you're taking the day off tomorrow. Borrow Balvinder's car and drive Sukanya to Sardhana.'

'But Saturday is the busiest day for the library. I can't just take leave on a whim,' protested Puru piteously.

'Nonsense, either tell them yourself or I'll handle it my way,' Natwar cut him off.

'Err, it's okay, really, Natwar Chacha,' said Sukanya, weakly supporting Puru who looked like he wanted to stamp his foot in rage. 'We can go some other time.'

'No, you will go tomorrow. Anyway, this idiot Puru doesn't do any real work in that library of his. All he does is hand out DVDs. You go with him, gudiya. I am sorry, I can't take you. I'd even picked out my merchanta shirt and pants out for the day.'

Sukanya shot a confused look at Bade Papa.

'Magenta,' he clarified tonelessly. Sukanya gulped, suddenly relieved at the thought of not having to spend the day with Natwar in all his magenta finery.

'Okay, Puru Chacha,' she turned to Puru and said, 'I will see you tomorrow morning.'

'Meet me at Bibi's chowk, gudiya,' said Puru with a sigh. 'That's the only place I can park the car.'

The next day was a crisp, clear one. Sukanya looked at herself in the old mirror, and the girl in blue stared back, long curly hair tied up with a red scarf, gold hoops in her ears, her eyes meeting their own bright gaze in the reflection. She touched the silver, engraved buttons from her father's old kurta, the one he wore in college, now sewn over the pocket of this dress by Api. The lucky buttons, he called them.

'Going to church, young lady?' she demanded of herself, and stepped out of her room.

She walked to Bibi's chowk, arriving well in time to sit on the steps outside her house, looking at all the comings and goings of the mohalla, Mithu and Mishri squawking from their cages. Nandi came out to throw the trash, wearing a gigantic nightie, and smiled at her.

'Arrey Sukanya lalli, why are you sitting out in the cold? Waiting for someone?' she asked.

'Yes, for Puru Chacha, he is taking me to Sardhana to see Begum Samru's church,' replied Sukanya, fiddling with the picnic basket that Sunita had insisted on packing for her.

'Arrey, take my Gumbi also with you,' exclaimed Nandi, suddenly excited. 'She just keeps moping all the time these days. And she loves that church. If she goes with you, I won't have to worry about her. Take her with you, rani bitiya, I'll go ask her to change.'

Before Sukanya could say anything, Nandi had taken off to look for Gumbi. Sukanya looked after her, unsure of what to do next. Take the sullen little Gumbi with her? How would Puru respond to that? Puru and Gumbi, while Sukanya played the unwanted third wheel? Should she bail out and make an excuse to not go?

While Sukanya was still dithering over her options, Bibi came out, a small bowl of seeds in her hand, looking to feed her parrots. She was very supportive of this new plan when Sukanya told her about it.

'Yes, you must take Gumbi with you. She needs a change. How pale that girl looks these days, not at all like a bride-to-be. A change of scene should do her good. And you'll have place in the car.'

Before Sukanya could decide, Gumbi stepped out of her house, dressed in a shiny, and clearly, new salwar-kameez, her long hair plaited and ribboned, looking shy and pleased at this unexpected outing.

'Sukanya jeeji, should I come along?' she asked, though of course it was a foregone conclusion at this point.

'Uh, yes, of course, Gumbi,' she said. Before she could say anything else, Puru had brought the car around. It was almost comical, his double-take at seeing his beloved Gumbi standing on the steps with Sukanya, all set to picnic. Suddenly the idea of taking his niece to see a church was not an unwelcome one. Gumbi flushed a deep pink and started to dig the floor with her toes.

'*All the world's a stage, And all the men and women merely players*,' one of the lines that Bade Papa had been explaining to his class came floating to Sukanya.

'Puru Chacha, Gumbi is coming with us,' she said, quite unnecessarily.

'Um,' said Puru, trying his hand at nonchalance and failing, his mouth curving into a grin.

'Do you want to sit in the front, Gumbi?' she asked, as they prepared to leave.

'No, no, jeeji,' said the panicked Gumbi, looking left and right and diving into the back seat. Sukanya sat in the front.

'Let's see, it's not too far, only about twenty minutes,' said Puru, ostensibly to Sukanya but looking at the blushing Gumbi in the rearview mirror. 'We can be back after lunch after you have seen the church, gudiya. Take your time, take your time.' Clearly, Puru would be happy if she spent a couple of months exploring the church.

The car made its way through the streets of Meerut. It was still early, so there was not too much traffic, but as they neared the university, they ran into a large crowd of students. Something was up; it was not an ordinary gathering. Bespectacled, idealistic-looking young men milled about, some of them carrying flags. Some amount of *naarebaazi* was in evidence, the chants rising in the morning air. 'Jogeshwar Singh, waapas jao! Chhatra Ekta, Zindabaad. Long Live Student Unity.' Some students sat on the ground in front of the university gate, sipping on cups of tea.

'Some sort of a student dharna,' said Puru, rolling the glass down to lean out and take a look. 'Oh look, there is Sudhir. Your cousin, Gumbi.' Gumbi did not bother to look out for her cousin, seeming to have eyes only for Puru, but Sukanya, intrigued, craned her neck out of the window and caught a glimpse of Sudhir Tyagi, very much a student leader at the moment, a white kurta over blue jeans, sunglasses in place. He seemed to have just finished a speech; there seemed to be a lot of energy and excitement in the rally, with students shouting slogans against the administration.

Even in the chaos, Sudhir spotted Sukanya almost immediately, and grinned at her, sliding his sunglasses down his nose to take a better look at this unlikely addition to his rally. Sukanya tried to ignore him and turned towards Gumbi to ask a question.

'I didn't know he was your cousin, Gumbi, though I did see him at your sagai,' she said, a little flustered to her annoyance, remembering how he had followed her up to Gumbi's room at her engagement.

'Sudhir? Yes, he's my brother of sorts. His father had helped rescue our land in Asauda – Mummy is from there – some goons had occupied it. Mummy had tied him a rakhi after that incident. That's how we are related to them,' replied Gumbi in her soft voice. 'And then, one of my aunts looked after him after his mother passed away. He has no one left in his family now. Reckless fellow, doesn't pay heed to anyone.'

'Reckless is right. He's protesting again the vice-chancellor this time,' said Puru as the car moved away from rally, and towards Sardhana. 'That's a bad idea, like all of Sudhir's ideas. Hazari Babu, the VC is a bada aadmi. Not advisable to take pangas with him, if you ask me. Ex-MLA, you know. Corrupt as hell, of course. There was the whole fraudulent degree scandal last year, in which he was involved in issuing degrees free for money. He got out of that scot-free. And now this. Sudhir should stay away from all this, but he doesn't listen.'

Sukanya looked at the rearview mirror as Sudhir and his fellow protestors slowly faded from view. The car moved away from the university rally towards the cantonment, very different in spirit from the Meerut of congested gullies and brick-paved roads. The roads were wider here, cleaner, the trees pruned. She could see canteens, dining and social clubs for commissioned officers, training centres for servicemen and residential enclaves named after army greats like Sam Manekshaw. The boundary walls marking the buildings looked freshly painted in red and white, and the blooming dahlias seemed to be saluting the passersby.

'This part of the city hits different, Puru Chacha,' she said, looking around. Puru nodded enthusiastically.

'Yes, because it belongs to the military; it was built to accommodate the Europeans when the East India Company took charge. That church you see there is St. Paul's Methodist Church, built sometime in the 1940s. It served the military garrison. British soldiers used to pray there.'

In the distance, she could see a small, red-bricked church built in the English style and set in a garden.

'Hmm, pretty structure,' she said, noticing its beautiful arches and warm timber roofing.

'And that's the M-48 Patton tank that we captured from Pakistan during the 1965 war,' Puru continued, pointing to an enclosure by the roadside with considerable pride. 'It was one of ninety-seven tanks, including Chaffees and Shermans, souvenirs of the war, now spread in cantonments all over India.' Gumbi looked very impressed at this impromptu history lesson delivered by Puru. Sukanya nodded along, she had heard a lot of these stories from Shiladitya already.

The road grew bumpier as they neared Sardhana, cycles and bikes weaving towards them from the opposite direction. But by now, Sukanya had grown somewhat accustomed to the chaos of the traffic of Meerut, ruled by a completely different set of gods than the ones presiding over London.

The car slowed as they approached the church. Outside the gates of the basilica, several ubiquitous candle and rosary sellers had set up shop. Sukanya stepped out to buy candles, while Puru went off to find a place to park, Gumbi still with him in the car.

A long, hedged driveway, lined with statues depicting the crucifixion of Jesus, led to the side of the church, which stood quietly in the midst of a large, silent mango grove. The church faced west, allowing the worshippers to face the rising sun during prayers. A statue of Jesus, arms outstretched in love and forgiveness, loomed above them, its peace and serenity quieting visitors almost instantly.

Sukanya looked up at the statue, then climbed up the bright steps and wandered around to the front of the church, hoping to give Puru and Gumbi some privacy. Badi Mummy had been right – there were so many different architectural styles here. Doric pillars, Roman detailing, and even hints of Muslim influence, with the onion-shaped domes. She explored further, her eyes drawn up to the lofty spires.

She entered the church and walked up to the marble altar, struck by its beauty, and looked up at the serene figure of Our Lady of Graces. She lit the candle that she had brought along, and closed her eyes. 'You know what I want.' She found herself sending up a prayer in unformed words, asking for all the things that people ask for. Health and happiness. Harmony and hope.

She felt someone step to the altar next to her, heard them shift softly as they lit a candle.

'Praying for something, memsahib?' she heard a familiar voice ask of her.

She opened her eyes, turned around and found herself face-to-face with Sudhir Tyagi, in the flesh, his expression amused, his eyes full of laughter.

20.

Meerut, November 2006 – The Church and Sudhir Tyagi

Sukanya's first thought upon seeing Sudhir wasn't about how or why he had appeared there so suddenly, but rather whether he had seen Puru and Gumbi together. He didn't seem concerned with his cousin's whereabouts, though. Instead, he was gazing around the church with a satisfied smile, his hands stuffed into the pockets of his jeans, looking entirely at ease and very pleased with himself.

'Begum Samru came a long way from a nautch girl, eh?' he remarked, his voice carrying a note of approval. 'I'd say things were better for women back then. A girl could rise from an absolute nobody to an empress who ruled and commissioned churches. These days, they can't even pick a husband without a hundred different questions – at least, not here in India. Things must be different for you in London.'

'What are you doing here?' asked Sukanya, stepping away from the altar, wondering where Gumbi and Puru might have gone. Likely out on the church grounds, whispering sweet nothings to each other. 'Don't you have student rallies to organize and people to lead?'

'I do, I do, but then I saw you, and then, I know not how, I got onto my bike and here I am,' he said, looking down at himself as if surprised at finding himself there.

'You shouldn't follow me around like this, Sudhir,' Sukanya began, sounding prim even to her own ears, but Sudhir was clutching his heart and pretending to swoon.

'This is the first time you've actually said my name,' he declared theatrically, still clasping his hands to his heart, making Sukanya smile despite herself.

'You are certainly very dramatic, but now I need to see this church,' she said. He followed her with a lazy, self-assured stride as she wandered through the church, glancing at the plastic flowers and at the paintings on the wall, all the while worrying about Gumbi and Puru.

'Tell me,' she asked. 'What were you protesting about so enthusiastically back at the university?'

Sudhir paused a moment, his usual easy smile slipping into something more serious.

'I don't know where to start,' he said, uncharacteristically hesitant.

'Try at the beginning,' said Sukanya, looking up the vaulted ceiling of the church and admiring its intricate design.

'Well, it's fairly simple. That Hazari Babu wants to invite Jogeshwar Singh as the chief guest for the university's Founder's Day. And I won't let that happen,' he said, his tone lowering.

Sukanya looked up, surprised by the intensity in his voice. He stared back defiantly at her.

'What's wrong with this Jogeshwar Singh?' she asked, her brow furrowing.

Sudhir burst into laughter, drawing curious glances from the other visitors to the church. Sukanya quickly pulled him away to a quiet corner, putting a finger to her lips, signalling at him to quieten down.

'Ab, where do I even start when you ask questions like that?' he said, his voice lowering again, more serious now. 'But sample this. Jogeshwar Singh ordered an entire colony to be burnt down last year, memsahib. There were riots for weeks after that. Forty-nine people died; seven of them were children. Two were infants.'

Sukanya felt light-headed, as though the cool, stone floor had shifted underneath her feet. The peaceful stillness of the church seemed to float away.

'Which colony?' she forced the words out. 'Who were these people? Why did he do this to them?' Sudhir led the way out of the church; they were now standing on the grounds.

'Wrong jaati, that's all,' said Sudhir, picking up a stick from the ground and twirling it around.

'Jaati...that means caste,' said Sukanya softly, the word unfamiliar in her mouth, too large to be swallowed. Sudhir nodded.

'I guess you would know about it,' he said, his eyes distant. Sukanya knew he was probably thinking of all the stories about her parents – the rumours that had swirled around for years. Each retelling, each gossip-laden whisper, dirtying it a little bit more.

'And you don't believe in this, this, jaativaad?' she asked of him, her voice quiet.

'The ethnographic system of social classification based on castes?' Sudhir laughed, as if reading an academic text while tossing the stick into the distance. 'I'd say not, though of course I must practice it without knowing of it. It comes easy to us, given to us at birth.'

'Sudhir, I didn't think you were an idealist,' said Sukanya, a thought forming in her mind. 'But you are. Very much so.'

'Maybe, but I didn't come here to discuss jaativaad with you, memsahib.'

'No? Then why did you come?' she asked, straining to see if Gumbi and Puru could be spotted loitering on the church grounds.

'I was thinking more along the lines of *My mistress' eyes are nothing like the sun.*'

'Ah yes, Bade Papa mentioned that you are quite the Shakespeare aficionado.'

'Can you blame me when he writes stuff like this?'

'Which sonnet is your favourite?' asked Sukanya, still scanning the grounds for the missing pair. Where could they be?

Sudhir studied her for a moment, as if trying to gauge whether she was being serious.

'Go on,' she insisted, noticing his hesitation. 'Let's see what you've got.'

Sudhir took a deep breath and, for a brief moment, looked almost uncertain, a strange sight for someone so self-assured.

'Well, I might be a cliché but it's Sonnet 29.'

'That doesn't tell me anything. Don't you have it memorized?' she asked and laughed when he stayed quiet. 'You do! I can see it in your face. Go ahead, give the crowds what they want.'

'Well, you asked for it,' he said and launched into it.

'When, in disgrace with fortune and men's eyes,
I all alone beweep my outcast state,
And trouble deaf heaven with my bootless cries,
And look upon myself and curse my fate,
Wishing me like to one more rich in hope,
Featured like him, like him with friends possessed,
Desiring this man's art and that man's scope,
With what I most enjoy contented least.'

He stopped here, his eyes briefly wandering, before returning to Sukanya.

'That's lovely, it truly is,' said Sukanya, distracted by the words. 'Is there more?'

'Maybe there is,' he said with a half-smile, looking down at his shoes.

'Well, well, so who do we have here?' teased Sukanya, hoping to lighten the mood. 'A Shakespeare-spouting politician in the making? Haven't they taught you? Art and politics don't mix.'

Sudhir laughed, shaking his head, but before he could respond, his gaze shifted, and he suddenly froze.

'Is that Gumbi?' he asked, his voice filled with disbelief. She followed his line of light and saw Gumbi, walking with Puru under the mango trees, his arm slung around her shoulder. One of her hands was intertwined with his, and in the other she was holding flowers that Puru must have brought her from one of the stalls. They looked so at ease, so happy, so very much in love. Sukanya groaned.

'With that Paresh, the DVD fellow,' muttered Sudhir, his voice full of shock. 'She is going to get married!' He turned to Sukanya, narrow-eyed. 'Did you know about this?'

'Of course I knew about this. Now, Sudhir, listen to me,' said Sukanya, suddenly making up her mind and pulling Sudhir away to a secluded pillar where they wouldn't be overheard. 'I have some Shakespeare for you too. Not sure if this is how it goes but something about not letting impediments get in the way of true hearts or something.'

'*Let me not to the marriage of true minds admit impediments*,' Sudhir said almost automatically.

'Yes, yes, same thing. Gumbi doesn't want to get married to that fellow the family has chosen for her. She wants to marry my Puru Chacha. And as you can see, he reciprocates. Don't ask me how I know this. It was by accident that I found out, but yes, there it is.'

Sudhir stood frozen for a moment, as if trying to make sense of it all. Then he shook his head as if to clear it. He stared at Sukanya, as if seeing her for the first time.

'What do you mean? Those people – the boy she is supposed to marry, is engaged to – they are the largest landowners in Baghpat. It's Durgesh ji, Sukanya! Gumbi has to be fucking nuts to even think about messing with him! Has she lost her mind?'

Sukanya felt her temper rising at this. His outrage, his hypocrisy – her disappointment in him felt bitter to the tongue.

'Weren't you going on about justice just a moment ago? Equality and all of that bullshit? Hypocrites, all of you!' she snapped. 'Go back to your stupid student rally and pretend to care about what's fair while things go to hell in your own backyard.'

'Listen to me, Sukanya,' said Sudhir, taken aback by her sudden outburst and clearly not used to being told off so summarily.

'No, you listen to me, Sudhir Tyagi,' she said, feeling the sharp edges of her own voice. 'I may not know anything about the twisted politics of this place and all that goes on in the name of the blasted sugarcane, but I do know that if I find out that you have betrayed Gumbi, you will...I will...well, you will have me to answer to.'

A smile tugged at Sudhir's lips, despite the heated exchange.

'A fate worse than death, to be sure,' he said. 'Fret not. I will not say a word. And now, memsahib, I'll take your leave. The twisted politics awaits.'

He turned and walked off, heading back to where his bike was parked. Sukanya, her heart still pounding, reached up instinctively for the lucky silver buttons on the pocket of her dress and found them missing.

21.

Meerut, November 2006 – An Encounter with Roshni

Sukanya and Aman sat in the verandah of his splendid ancestral haveli once again, the old portraits on the walls in their intricately carved Muradabadi frames looking down at them. A tanpura lay in one corner, though there was no sign of the one who must play it. Sukanya knew that there was a library on the first floor of the haveli, and that it had historical papers preserved in glass cabinets, but Aman had never offered to show it to her. In fact, she had never made it past the verandah at all.

And now he was sitting across, his eyes bloodshot and bags under them. He wasn't getting much sleep, that much was evident. The crushing workload of medical school was defeating him, it was there in the restless shaking of his legs and the light air of irritability he carried with him that day. Sukanya had just finished telling him about her recent meeting with Sudhir.

'You shouldn't have let him find out about Gumbi, Sukanya,' he said, with knitted brows. 'What do you know about the likes of Sudhir Tyagi? What do you know about any of this? Next thing you know, he has taken out his katta and shot six through Gumbi.'

'He will do no such thing, he might even help her,' said Sukanya but a note of doubt crept into her voice. Was this true? Had she landed the unsuspecting Gumbi into a lot of trouble? What else could she have done; the lovebirds had been canoodling in plain sight. And also, for some reason, she didn't want to lie to Sudhir.

Aman scoffed, giving her a shrewd look. 'Sukanya, please don't be one of those girls who get blindsided by a little bit of flattery and attention from the local boys. Keep your wits about you.'

Sukanya felt her temper rise, the tips of her ears burning. She rose in a huff. 'Good to know this is how you feel about me but if I need your advice, I'll ask for it,' she said, and walked to the gate to leave. But before she could do so, the rustle of a sari made her stop in her tracks.

A woman entered through the window-gate, straightened up and adjusted the pleats of her yellow chiffon sari. Her head was covered with her pallu, a custom that was now outdated in cities but it did frame her face in a most becoming way. She looked up and smiled at Sukanya with long-lashed eyes, who stared at her, unable to look away. She was certainly getting on in years but she was radiant in a way described in books. The kind of face artists would want to commit to a canvas. Sudhir could probably recite three or four sonnets befitting this woman.

'Aman, won't you introduce me to your lovely young guest,' asked the woman, looking at her with such affection that Sukanya wanted to reach out and touch her. Aman walked up and stood next to Sukanya.

'Sukanya, this is my aunt Roshni, she stays here,' he said shortly, put his hands in his pockets, and started to take undue interest in the pattern on the floor.

'Namaste, Aunty,' said Sukanya, still a little mesmerized, folding her hands. Who was this woman, intrigue coming off her like a haunting perfume?

'Namaste, beta, have you eaten? Should I make something for you?' she asked, much like every woman in that mohalla always did, except that Sukanya could not imagine her, not in a thousand years, slaving over a hot stove. She wasn't one of the women in the mohalla, not with her covered head, her staid sari and her polite offers to feed the visitor.

'No, no, Aunty, I was just about to leave,' Sukanya said but didn't move. Roshni kept her gaze on her, searching her face for something, until Aman coughed, indicating that it was time for Sukanya to leave.

'All right, Aunty, I'll be on my way now. Bibi must be waiting,' she said. Roshni nodded, her eyes unreadable.

'Ah yes, Bibi of the parrots, she is very kind,' she said, her voice trailing off in an absent whisper. Sukanya nodded and still simmering at Aman, left without a word of goodbye.

That evening Sukanya told Badi Mummy about Roshni. Badi Mummy, her frail form nearly blending with the faded flowers on the razai that was always draped over her these days, nodded quietly. She cherished these evening sessions with Sukanya, listening raptly to her granddaughter's retelling of this mohalla – a place which she had known all her life, had in fact never known anything outside of it. She didn't tell Sukanya that it was becoming harder to even gather enough air in her lungs to speak. Soon, too soon, it would be time for goodbyes, except for the one goodbye that really mattered. Shila... Shila.

'I haven't seen this Roshni, but I've heard there's some charismatic woman living in Nawabon Ki Haveli these days,' she said, her voice tinged with memories of the past. 'That haveli...what can I say about it? All sorts of people have stayed there over the years. There was a woman who kept about a dozen stray dogs, then someone who vanished after a chit fund scam in the eighties reappeared in the haveli till he was arrested, and yes even a small-time gang leader. I can't keep track of the ajeeb pagals it attracted.'

'I liked her,' Sukanya said, her face resting against her folded knees. 'I hope I get to see her again.' Outside, the familiar sounds of scooters and bikes screeching to a halt echoed through the gully. Bade Papa's nalaayaks had arrived, all set to absorb a bit of literature. To Sukanya's immense irritation, she found herself looking out the window, scanning the group to see if that troublemaker Sudhir was among them. He most certainly was – and clearly he was looking for her too, grinning broadly as he spotted her.

Sukanya quickly turned away, remembering Aman's dire warnings about that Tyagi boy, not wanting to do anything with him. A brute really – uncivilized, a junglee. Sure, he knew a bit of Shakespeare, but that didn't change a thing. Anybody could learn a sonnet or two. Well, not anybody, but still...he was bad news all the same. Better to stay away.

Badi Mummy drifted into sleep, and Sukanya slipped away to the terrace to speak with her mother, the Dugar girl who had never set foot in this house and yet somehow belonged here anyway, her presence woven in the whispered words spoken about her.

On the terrace, Natwar's pigeons cooed softly in the small room where he kept them. There had always been pigeons in that room, even when Shila was the one pacing the timeless terrace, worrying over things. Natwar had kept them since he was very young. Sukanya would often see him tending to his birds, filling their bowl with grains, and stroking their delicate feathers.

'Did you eat, Suku?' This was always the first question Api asked, always worried that Sukanya must be wasting away in the absence of her cooking. Sukanya laughed, thinking of the glorious flavours of the town's old alleys, food that she had been homesick for without even knowing of it.

'Yes, Mama, I ate. How is Daddy? Has he finally settled down about my visit to Meerut?' she asked, turning the conversation to her father. Aparajita sighed.

'He longs to be with you, Suku,' she said, her voice soft. 'There's nothing he wants more than to walk those roads with you. Did I tell you? He has been looking at flight options – for both of us, just on the off chance, you know...'

Sukanya's mind turned to Bade Papa, his jaw set, his endless pain at Shila's betrayal still a raw, festering wound. His cold words had made it clear – reconciliation was impossible, no matter how many visas Shila managed to organize.

After her mother hung up, Sukanya sat in her room, her thoughts drifting to Badi Mummy's face, growing paler with each passing day, her cat a constant companion, never leaving her side, as if sensing that she would soon disappear. Sukanya wiped her cheeks, taking a few deep, shuddering breaths. No. She couldn't let herself fall apart like this. She stood up and made her way downstairs to get some water. The sooty kitchen was dim and warm, and she poured herself a glass of water. She was about to go back when she saw a figure walking towards her.

'So, church is done. What will it be this time – mandir or masjid?' Sudhir said as he came to a halt in front of her. Now that he was closer, she realized he looked a little haggard, a bandage wrapped around his forehead. He was still smiling though – *like a wolf*, she thought. His teeth flashed through his beard; he was clearly delighted to have found her. He never made an effort to hide how pleased he was to see her.

Stay away, stay away, stay away.

'What do you want?' she snapped, her tone sharper than she intended. But Sudhir didn't seem to mind. His eyes lingered on her, noticing the faint traces of tears still wet on her face.

'Some water, please,' he said, and Sukanya noticed the steel tumbler in his hand. So, he really had come for water after all – not to stalk her, as she'd imagined.

'Fine, give it here,' she snatched the tumbler from his hand and poured him some water. She watched as he took a tablet from his pocket and swallowed it with the water.

'What's that for?' she asked, despite herself, trying not to sound interested.

'For the pain,' he sighed theatrically, then chuckled. 'Just a small scuffle. But you should see the other guys.'

'I don't want to see them. I've heard enough all about your fights. You're a strange bunch, all of you.'

'What can I say, memsahib? This is a land where you never know when a fight will break out. I mean, just look at the mutiny of 1857. That's who we are, mutineers.'

'What you are is an idiot,' said Sukanya.

'Jogeshwar's party sent out goondas to crush our protest; what were we supposed to do? Lay out the red carpet like one baraat of chutiyas?' he leaned in closer, searching her face for a flicker, a trace of understanding. Something, anything to show that she grasped his situation. But her steady gaze betrayed nothing.

'Sudhir, nalayak,' Bade Papa called from the baithak. 'I can wait forever but Othello won't, so you decide.'

'Coming, Master ji,' he called back, and then turned to Sukanya with a grin. 'Othello calls. So tell me, should I leave or stay and compare thee to a summer's day?' He waited for a long moment, then he stepped out of the warm, sooty kitchen, whistling a small tune, leaving behind Sukanya standing within her ancestral walls.

22.

Meerut, December 2006 – Fine Movie Lab

Several days passed by. Sukanya was still not talking to Aman and had no idea if he was in the haveli or staying back in the hostel. She took to reading *A Christmas Carol* and thought of just how different her London was at Christmas from the cold, dark, unfriendly one in the book. Yes, hers was bleak and beautiful and frosty and festive and exciting and exhausting, and she missed having Angie to share it with, feeling gloomier as the days went by. One evening as she was returning from Bibi's courtyard, she found Natwar deep in conversation with Bade Papa outside the house. Natwar glanced up, his face softening as he caught sight of her shadowed face.

'Are you getting bored, bitiya?' he asked, noting the downward tilt of her gaze.

'No, no, Natwar Chacha,' she protested, a little too quickly, fearing another excursion if she showed any sign of boredom. 'I am not at all bored. Everything's fine – just perfect.'

Bade Papa's smile wavered. 'Maybe it's time for you to return to London,' he said, his voice trembling a little.

'No, it isn't,' she said, linking her arm in his. His long, gnarly finger closed over hers. He was hers, those weathered hands seemed to say.

'I'll go back when it's time but not now,' she added.

'I know what you should do, bitiya,' Natwar exclaimed suddenly. 'Get some DVDs from Puru's shop. You can watch them on your laptop.'

'Okay, Chacha ji, I will,' said Sukanya but Natwar was a man of action. Before Sukanya could protest, he had untangled her arm from Bade Papa's and taken charge. Determined to banish even the shadow of boredom, he herded her briskly through the maze of narrow gullies, dodging the dirt mounds and mangy dogs, towards the small and cramped DVD library where Puru worked. Fine Movie Lab – known to the world only as FML.

'Go on inside,' said Natwar, as he stopped in front of the shop, its door painted a bright blue, paint peeling off in places. 'Get some movies. I've got some work to do – will you be all right getting back on your own?'

Sukanya nodded and sighed as she watched Natwar clomp off. She looked up at the signboard and couldn't help but snigger, but when she entered, she had to admit that FML was very charming, the walls lined with film posters and wooden shelves that stretched right up to the ceiling, crammed with DVDs and a few errant VHS tapes, relics of the eighties. A couple of exposed bulbs hung from the ceiling, bravely providing a bit of dim light to the space.

Once, this shop had been the baithak of an old house but had served as a shop for so many years that people had all but forgotten that a door at the back still led to the house's courtyard.

Behind the counter – a solid slab of wood that spanned the width of the shop – Puru would sit, the de facto proprietor of the shop. He ran the shop single-handedly, the elusive owner always absent for some reason. Several thick albums lay scattered on the counter, their plastic sleeves filled with miniature movie covers. Browsing them felt like flipping through India's cinematic history, from *Mughal-E-Azam* to *Sholay* to *Kaho Naa... Pyaar Hai*. In a few more years, DVDs would fade into obsolescence, but for now, people still came to FML to borrow movies.

Puru was stationed behind the counter, as usual, engrossed in a movie playing on the small, battered television set perched precariously on a wooden stool. He looked up as Sukanya stepped in and his face broke into a wide, unreserved smile. This, this smile – she would remember it years later. This was the best thing about her time at Bulandwada, this affection that flowed to her like an endless river. She didn't know if it was acceptance; there was much about her that these people didn't accept, but the love was given to her anyway.

'Aha, gudiya, what brings you here today?' Puru

called out, standing up to greet here. 'Looking for a movie?'

'Yes, Natwar Chacha insists I must,' she sighed, rolling her eyes. Puru laughed.

'What's good then, Puru Chacha?' she asked, leaning casually over the counter. Puru reached for an album and handed it to her with a flourish. 'English Moveez,' said the handwritten legend on the cover. Sukanya flipped it open, thumbing through the pages. *Jaws*, *Star Wars*, *Back to the Future*. A variety of James Bond films, the covers brimming with guns, explosions and very glamorous women. Everything seemed dated, though, as if the western world had frozen in the eighties and had never quite come out of it.

And then her finger stopped. *Love Story*.

Oliver and Jenny smiled at her from the cover. How many times had she heard her parents sing 'Where do I begin' on long car rides and at Christmas parties?

Her parents' story, her parents' song, her parents' love.

Suddenly the homesickness that had been building in small pieces hit her like a wave. London with its cobblestoned streets and medieval spires and the fog over Thames and its rain-soaked air, felt light-years away. She found herself aching for the two people who seemed to watch over her even in their sleep.

Maybe Bade Papa was right then, it was time to return.

But then, what about Badi Mummy, a few whiffs of air all that was left to her? And Bade Papa with his weathered hands and tired smile, who seemed so lonely already? How was she to leave this place, this life and never return?

'Sukanya, kya hua?' Puru's voice broke through her thoughts. 'Come here, sit down. It's a cold day.'

'And I need tea?' she smiled through her tears. Puru laughed at this.

'Yes, everyone always needs tea. Let me get some for you.' Puru opened the back door of the shop and disappeared into the depths of the house to fetch tea for his niece.

Sukanya sank down onto one of the stools scattered about, her head throbbing faintly. Puru's phone, lying on the counter, buzzed loudly just as he came back into the shop. Sukanya glanced at it and knew it was Gumbi. Puru looked sheepish; it was by now very obvious that Sukanya knew all about his clandestine relationship.

'Go ahead, Puru Chacha,' Sukanya said. 'I'll finish picking out a movie while you take the call.'

'No, no, it's fine. I'll call her back,' he mumbled, his hands fidgeting nervously with random things on the counter, looking distinctly uncomfortable. There was a pause, and then he spoke again.

'I'll always remember the ehsaan you did for me by agreeing to take Gumbi to Begam Samru's church that day. It may well be the first and last time that I got to see her like that,' he said. *Ehsaan*. A favour. Indebtedness. Perhaps because of the way he had phrased it, Sukanya's natural candour surfaced, cutting through the awkwardness.

'Why don't you do something about this situation, Puru Chacha?' she asked. 'You can't just let them go ahead with this wedding.'

Puru lowered his gaze, tearing apart an unfortunate fingernail. 'What can I say?' he muttered. 'People must have told you about me, Sukanya. I am nobody, just an unknown.'

'What rubbish!' Sukanya shot back, indignant. 'You're very much known to all of us. You are Rajni Mausi's son, Natwar Chacha's brother – and my uncle!'

To Sukanya's dismay, Puru lowered his head down onto the counter where he spent all his waking hours and began to cry. Great, heaving, shuddering sobs wracked his body, as Hindi film legends gazed down at him with sympathy from the walls of FML.

It was hard to tell who was more distressed – the grown man or the young girl. Sukanya glanced around uncertainly, wondering how to help him. She reached out and patted his shoulder tentatively.

Fortunately, at that moment, that panacea for all ills known as tea arrived. The young boy tasked with delivering it hesitated at the scene before him, his eyes darting between Puru and Sukanya, but he said nothing. He darted off after setting the cups on the counter.

Without saying a word, Puru took a deep, shuddering breath, wiping his tear-streaked face with the back of his sleeve. He picked up one cup and wordlessly handed it to Sukanya. He began blowing over his own teacup, cooling it before taking tentative sips.

They sat together in companionable silence, drinking their tea. Somewhere between the clarion call for the tea and its arrival, something intangible had shifted. He was no longer just Puru Chacha, one of her many uncles in this sprawling new-old world, about whom she knew nothing, in whose life she had no role to play. He had become someone real, a person with hidden depths, with worries and pain and a great, life-changing love.

'Have you been to see Munto yet?' Puru asked, his voice now steady.

'Who?' Sukanya replied before remembering that Munto Baba was the missing brother of the triumvirate. 'Oh, I didn't know he was in town. Isn't visiting family kind of...against the rules for these ascetics? You know, all that renunciation and detachment and so on?'

Puru scoffed, his voice filled with amusement.

'Ascetic, ha! He's a charlatan; that's what he is. He was too lazy to work, get a real job, get married, raise a family. So what does he do? Claims that he's had some divine revelation and runs off to the mountains. Spends his days smoking up and pretending to do sadhana. And when the loneliness gets too much, he shows up in Bibi's courtyard every now and then. Anyway, you should go and see him. If nothing else, he's good for some free entertainment.'

'I will,' said Sukanya, scanning Puru's face. She studied him, but he seemed to have pulled himself back together, his composure in place. The moment had passed.

23.

Meerut, December 2006 – Munto Baba's Prophecy

The next morning Sukanya walked into Bibi's courtyard to find it completely transformed. The air was thick with swirling incense smoke, and stray marigold strings hung haphazardly. Closer observation revealed that Munto Baba had indeed arrived from Banaras where he dabbled in part-time sadhuhood and full-time narcotics.

He was perched in a shaded corner of the chowk, apparently lost in a deep, meditative trance. Around him, the local bhajan mandli had gathered in a semicircle, belting out a disjointed medley of off-tune bhajans, indecisive as to which deity they were paying obeisance to. Many of them were clutching fruits and flowers, hoping to ask him about various things – missing jewellery, wayward husbands, children's exam results – improbable wish lists of hopeful people.

Nearby, the street dogs, Moti and Shera, lounged lazily, feigning indifference but acutely aware of the proceedings. Sukanya stepped closer to take a look at

Munto Baba. He must have been a handsome young fellow once, before he grew his unkempt beard to his belly and forbade his dark hair from meeting a comb in years. He wasn't wearing much despite the cold, a saffron dhoti and nothing else, his ribs starkly visible under the thin fabric. For a while, Sukanya stood watching this theatrical spectacle. Then she went inside in search of Bibi to discuss this at greater length.

'Bibi, did you see Munto Baba?' Sukanya asked, stepping into the tiny, gleaming kitchen where everything was polished to a gloss, every surface sparkled, and air was wet with the unmistakable aroma of fresh rice. Steam billowed from a pot, as Bibi lifted the lid to check on the contents.

'Baba-waba nothing,' dismissed Bibi in her characteristic style, as she picked out a single grain of rice and pressed it to check for softness. 'He is just high on hashish or whatever he smokes these days.'

'But there are so many women waiting outside to see him, Bibi,' Sukanya insisted.

Bibi snorted, putting the lid away with a clang. 'Munto cannot tell his ass from his elbow and if those women are foolish enough to believe that he can indeed divine their fortunes, they deserve to be taken for a ride.' She took out a couple of steel plates from the shelf and ladled steaming khichdi onto them. 'Anyway,' she continued, handing one plate to Sukanya. 'This khichdi looks ready. Here, take this plate to him, and one for yourself. Let's go and feed that dhongi before he passes out from too much sadhana.'

They made their way back to the courtyard, Sukanya balancing the plates in her hands. She hesitated for a moment, unsure how to rouse Munto Baba from his samadhi. As it turned out, this was not needed. The moment the familiar aroma of his grandmother's food reached his nose, Munto Baba's eyes fluttered open, his nostrils flaring. Without a word, he took the plate from Sukanya.

She settled down beside him, her own plate in hand, and bit into a luscious piece of mango pickle while watching him with great interest.

'Is she eating the same food as Baba ji?' exclaimed one of the women devotees, scandalized and clutching her pallu. 'What ghor paap! What kalyug! Eating the same food as what we serve to the sadhus, who would have thought it would come to this?'

'Sukanya will eat the same food,' said the ever-combative Bibi, placing her bony hands on her shrunken hips. 'If Munto has a problem with it, well, it's not too late – I can take it right back.'

'No, no,' Munto Baba protested hastily, clearly terrified that the food would be taken away. 'Let the child eat. Baba does not mind. We are all Shiv ji's children, after all.' He turned to the group of women. 'Mata ji, take all these women with you and leave. Come back for the aarti later.'

The women left, albeit reluctantly, darting disapproving glances at Sukanya, muttering something about Bibi allowing all sorts of blasphemy.

Bibi snorted, turned on her heel, and marched back into the house.

Left alone, Munto Baba and Sukanya, both Shiv ji's children, devoured the food in silence, their plates wiped clean. Once the meal was over, Baba announced the next step.

'Alakh niranjan,' Baba proclaimed, the words lolling off his tongue as he lit up a chillum. The smoke began to curl upwards and drifted into the corners and crevices of the chowk.

From inside the house rang out Bibi's sharp voice. 'Arrey, if I put salt instead of sugar in the tea today, don't blame me. It will all be Baba ji's doing,' she called out to Nandi as the thick, heady smoke snaked its way to her kitchen.

Sukanya sat there, feeling a slow drowsiness settle over her. The smoke seemed to have a peculiar effect, almost like it was drugging her too. She blinked, trying to clear the fog in her mind, deepening with every passing second.

'My child,' Munto Baba's voice drifted over her. 'We have shared food today. If there is anything you wish to ask, ask and it shall be answered.'

His eyes, now a peculiar shade of red, locked into hers with an unsettling intensity. Like Mama's scarlet geraniums, thought Sukanya to herself. She shook her head, trying to focus, but her head was swimming, and the world seemed to be coming at her in swirls. The air smelled strangely familiar – like the nightclubs in London, pungent and foreign, but it was far more potent. What was in that chillum? What should she ask of Munto Baba?

What would become of her family? Would Badi Mummy ever see her only son again before she passed away? Would her grandfather ever forgive her father? Would Shiladitya ever return to the home he had pined for most of his life? Would her mother ever step back into the house with the Nathdwara pichwai again? What would become of Puru, who had wept in front of her like a child? Who was Roshni, and why did she feel so inexplicably drawn to her? Why did she find herself so unsettled by the thought of that junglee Sudhir Tyagi?

'I don't want to ask anything,' she said abruptly, her words sharp.

'Why not?' Munto Baba's laugh rang out, his voice drifting to her from far, far away. 'You are young. You must have worries, some concerns, whether big or small we do not know, but enough to make you anxious, ha-ha-ha.'

'I am worried about my family,' Sukanya found herself saying, almost against her will. Was Munto Baba some kind of a hypnotist too? She felt a little drunk. The winter sun now hung high in the sky, beating down on the chowk and making everything shimmer. Any moment now there would be strains of Purple Haze ringing through the air, she thought.

'Everyone is worried, my child, everyone,' Munto Baba said. 'Everyone, except us sadhus, who have gone into the shelter of Shiv ji. Why are you worried? Have you done something to worry your family?'

Sukanya shook her head. 'Not me, I haven't done anything.' *Not if I stay away from Sudhir Tyagi. But will I?* The thought hung there, heavy and uncertain.

Munto Baba fixed her with a penetrating gaze, his eyes narrowing. Then without a warning, he burst into a loud guffaw.

'Ah, child,' he said, his voice low. 'Things will get worse before they get better. You must be brave. Death must come. To some, in time. To others, way before it's due. But you must have courage.' His eyes gleamed as he spoke. Then, abruptly, he snuffed out the chillum, lay down on his side and – without missing a beat – began to snore. He was asleep. Just like that.

Sukanya stared at him. The little hair on her arm stood on end, the chill of the evening settling into her spine. *Death must come.* What was she supposed to make of this? Was this a warning? Or the ramblings of a madman?

Later that evening, back at the house, she dialled Angie's number, desperate to share the strangeness of the experience. Angie answered, like Api did, on the first ring.

'Angie, it was weird, a psychedelic experience really,' Sukanya said, trying to articulate her feelings. 'Do you think Munto Baba has ESP?'

'STD is more like it,' scoffed Angie, 'Don't believe a word of what he said, would be my suggestion. You yourself said that everyone in your family, especially your feisty great-grandma, thinks he is a fraud. Stick with that.'

Sukanya nodded along, but she wasn't sure it would be all that easy to forget all that the sadhu in a dhoti, smoking a chillum under the winter sun beating down on a small-town courtyard, had told her.

24.

Meerut, December 2006 – The Hospital

Sukanya came down from her room, rubbing the sleep from her eyes, to find the plump Dr Goswami talking to Bade Papa, dressed in another one of her signature flowing floral salwar-kameez sets, her thick-framed glasses hanging from a gold chain around her neck, her ever-present stethoscope competing with it for space.

'What happened, Bade Papa?' Sukanya asked, her pulse quickening as she glanced anxiously towards at the baithak where Badi Mummy rested. 'Is everything okay? Did Badi Mummy feel unwell during the night?'

'She wouldn't wake up this morning,' Bade Papa said, his voice heavy as he rubbed his stubbled cheek, looking more fragile than she had seen him in all her time there. 'Natwar had to fetch the doctor.'

'Why didn't you wake me?' Sukanya asked, Munto's words still fresh in her mind. *Death must come.*

Before Bade Papa could reply, Dr Goswami spoke again. 'It's nothing unusual, beta,' she said in her booming, brusque way, not one for a gentle bedside manner at all. 'These things happen with her condition. Blood pressure tends to drop sharply in the mornings. Like I said, the best thing would be to shift her to the hospital for a few days so that we can monitor her more closely.'

The doctor and Bade Papa talked at length about the details of moving Badi Mummy to the hospital. Sukanya felt her head spin, her thoughts swirling. This was it, then. The beginning of the end. Badi Mummy would go to the hospital, and she would never return.

What did this impending grief feel like? A knot in her heart that would remain forever tangled. A weight in her chest that would never lift. Sukanya felt as if she were only just beginning to map the landscape of sorrow, of loss and it already felt like a losing game. I'm coming, death seemed to call out, and there's absolutely nothing you can do to stop me.

Natwar entered quietly, leaning in close to whisper something to Bade Papa. He nodded, his face briefly clouded with worry, before softening as he met Sukanya's eyes.

'It's just for a few days,' he tried to reassure her. 'She's determined to attend Gumbi's wedding. You'll see – she'll come back stronger.' Then after a pause he added, 'Why don't you call Sunita Chachi over now and help her pack a bag for the hospital?'

Sunita needed no help, of course. Sukanya spent the day lingering on the sidelines, watching silently as things unfolded. By evening, Badi Mummy was moved to the teaching hospital attached to the medical college. Sukanya insisted on accompanying her and stayed by her side in the stark, desolate room as Badi Mummy was connected to a tangle of tubes and wires, drifting in and out of consciousness. Meanwhile, Bade Papa and Natwar busied themselves with the seemingly endless admission formalities.

Cheerful, competent nurses with names like Elsie and Betsy drifted in and out of the room to take all manners of readings, their smiles like cool salves to Sukanya's frayed heart.

'Your grandmother, eh? Such a beautiful woman, ha-ha, just like you! Don't worry. Bahut jaldi theek ho jayega – she will get better in no time,' Betsy declared to Sukanya as she caught her worried gaze. Patting her arm, she added. 'I have given her a sedative; she will sleep for a while now. Go get yourself some coffee from the canteen. No sense in you fainting here too!'

Betsy didn't seem like someone one could argue with, so Sukanya reluctantly obeyed, stepping outside onto the hospital grounds. The sun warmed her face. Why did all hospitals smell the same? That sharp tang of antiseptic, the metallic sting of iodine and the heavy scent of thick, viscous anxiety?

The hospital was part of the sprawling medical college campus. It was crowded and dusty and seemed to stretch in all directions, leading to different blocks housing the various departments. Sukanya wandered aimlessly, feeling a little unmoored as she took in the sights and smells of the place, reading the signs – Medicine, Oncology, Pathology – thinking about how little she knew of the city. The past weeks had been confined to the old, dilapidated crevices and crumbling lanes of Bulandwada but here was the other side of this old town, where it was sending modern shoots out of its prehistoric core, growing haphazardly and chaotically.

Someone was waving and running towards her. She squinted her eyes against the sun. Ah, Aman, of course. She had almost forgotten that this was where he spent his days. Aman looked as he always did – bloodshot eyes, overworked, a little frazzled, and smelling of smoke and something else, and expensive cologne to hide it all.

'I ran into your Natwar Chacha outside at the paan-shop,' he said, panting slightly as he bent down to catch his breath. 'He told me you were here with your grandparents. I tried calling you – where's your phone? How is your Badi Mummy now? I'll come in to check on her.'

'The doctors are keeping an eye on her,' Sukanya replied, her voice flat, unsure of what to say. Aman, noticing her distant tone, cleared his throat awkwardly.

'Look here, Sukanya,' he began. 'I am sorry about the way I spoke to you the other day at the haveli.'

'It's fine, Aman. I suppose that's how you see me – as some attention-hungry gori,' she said briskly, her steps quickening, her temper rising afresh as she remembered his words. Aman sighed and hurried after her, shaking his head.

'Of course that's not how I see you,' he said, already a little breathless again as he tried to keep up with her pace. 'The thing is – for God's sake, Sukanya, slow down – my lungs are wrecked from all the smoking – I just don't want you to getting mixed up with the likes of Sudhir Tyagi.'

Sukanya came to an abrupt halt, turning to face him. Aman bent over again, holding on to his sides. She felt a little alarmed.

'Okay, okay, Aman, I've stopped,' she said, her voice softer this time. 'But seriously, why do you smoke so much? How will you ever lecture your patients about the evils of smoking?'

Aman straightened up and laughed weakly.

'If only all doctors followed their own advice,' he said. 'I know a surgeon who can't step inside the operation theatre without a bit of Dutch courage.'

Sukanya wasn't sure if he was joking but she didn't respond. She looked around. The search for coffee seemed pointless in this maze of a hospital.

'I'll go back to Badi Mummy's room, Aman,' she said and turned to go.

'Have you been to see Sudhir?' Aman called after her, knowing that this would stop her in her tracks. She froze, turning to face him, her heart sinking. 'Sudhir? What do you mean?'

'He's here,' said Aman, looking at her closely.

'Why is he here? I saw him the other day – he just had a bandage around his head. He said it was a minor injury.'

Aman looked at her incredulously. 'Don't you know? Where have you been?'

She stared back, confusion deepening in the lines of her face.

'That Jogeshwar Singh sent his goons to break up the protest on campus. There was a massive brawl that broke out. You know how these boys are, all brawn, no brain. Jisse dekho, he is a rebel without a cause. Anyway, some bright mind from the students' side decided to lob a beer bottle at the goons. That was it, all hell broke loose. Dhishoom dhishoom and all that. Many of the boys got seriously injured. Our friend obviously led from the front.'

Sukanya heard in silence as Aman continued.

'It could have been worse. Luckily, Sudhir has some solid backing in some wealthy sugarcane farmers from Asauda. They aren't short on goons either. It was a proper showdown, lasting for a couple of hours, I'm told, and then the police finally showed up and broke it all up. That is how it ended. And now, our hero is nursing his broken bones and flirting with the nurses while he's at it. You should go see him.'

Sukanya looked at Aman in stunned silence. Aman's face softened at her shocked expression. He understood.

'Listen to me, Sukanya, this is why I said what I did the other day. It's better not to get tangled up with these people,' he said gently. She didn't respond and turned to climb the steps leading back into the hospital.

He looked at her as she walked away.

'Although something tells me it's already too late for that,' she heard him say.

25.

Meerut, December 2006 – The Hospital (continued)

Sukanya knew nothing of the sugarcane belt and even less of its complex, Hydra-headed politics. Sugarcane, the ten-month crop, a hardy grass, no more, loaded in trucks every season and carried off far and wide. Sugarcane, which made its way to the kolhu and the sugar mills, the sweet, syrupy plant made into a thing of love and hate. Sugarcane, shaping the fortunes of millions of farmers and about a hundred electoral seats. No, she knew nothing of this.

What she did know was that Sudhir Tyagi looked terrible that day. He lay on his side in an old, white hospital bed, thin and weak, a sinuous drip snaking into his arm. He was floating in a sea of other patients and their attendants, the air thick with an overpowering medicinal scent, determined to suffocate everything that came in its wake.

Why was she even here? She had nothing to do with him. Sudhir Tyagi was her grandfather's student, a little more than an acquaintance – someone she saw in the common areas of her home, someone who had stories following him about like a trail. A person of violence, of pain, someone to be avoided at all costs. And yet, here she was, standing in the general ward of the hospital, her gaze fixed on Sudhir, drawing curious glances from the people in the nearby beds. She didn't belong here – not in this setting, not with her appearance.

Sudhir lay alone. Where was his family? Was there no one to ask after him from the village with the ancestral home, where were the aunts and uncles and cousins? And surely there must be comrades from the college, fellow protestors? Where was everyone? Who was to care for him? As if in response to her silent question, his eyes snapped open, locking onto the worried face at the foot of his bed.

'There you are, memsahib,' he grinned through his pain, his face twisting slightly as he strained to remember something. 'How does that line go – we are such stuff as dreams are made on...?'

'Hush now,' she interrupted. 'You can save the poetry for tomorrow.'

'Tomorrow, and tomorrow, and tomorrow,' he said.

'The mutineering seems to be progressing well, I must say,' she said, touching his blanket because suddenly her hands didn't know what to do. 'Every time I see you, you have new injuries, new wounds.'

'Ah yes, looks like I've broken something this time,'

he said, casually pointing to his leg. 'At this rate, I should be dead by the time Gumbi's wedding rolls around.'

Sukanya winced at his words, a shiver running down her spine.

'I am kidding, of course,' he said, with a grin, catching her look. He tugged at his shirt to reveal a small amulet around his neck, wrapped in black fabric. 'Look, I got a taweez made. I'm very well-protected indeed. Don't roll your eyes like that! Things just got ugly this time, that's all. That behenchod Jogeshwar Singh will need to think twice before messing with the students. We're not going down without a fight, that's for sure.'

Sukanya glanced around, suddenly feeling a bit ill herself, the colour draining from her face.

'You should go home,' she heard Sudhir say. 'You don't look too good.'

'Well, aren't you chivalrous?' she replied and heard him laugh, a low guttural sound that she had come to recognize all too well. 'Where is everybody? Aren't they supposed to be tending to their fearless warrior?'

'Naren was here, I think he's gone out to pick up some medicines they didn't have at the hospital. The others are at the police station.'

Sukanya's throat tightened at this. Police–Protest–Politics. *Death must come. To some, in time. To others, way before it's due.* Yes, she really should leave. She turned to go, but hesitated, then faced him again. It was not in her to not say what she had to.

'I have something to say,' she declared.

Sudhir watched her, waiting for her to speak, looking at her long curls specked with all sorts of colours, her eyes that always seemed to laugh at him, her beautiful skin glowing in the soft sunlight pouring through from the dirty hospital window. How out of place she looked in this town, forever fumbling, a being who had fallen from the skies in this mess, *his* mess.

'Irshaad,' he said, propping himself up on one elbow with some difficulty.

'I never thought I'd say this,' she began, listening to her own resolute voice. 'But I've come to realize that people are right. There really are different worlds we've been assigned to here. And people from one world don't cross into the other.'

'And I live in a different world than yours,' he finished, looking straight at her. There it was again – how quickly he understood her, how easily he followed her words, her thoughts. She looked at him, momentarily forgetting what she had meant to say, and then remembered it.

'You seem to have chosen, well, this,' she said, her hand sweeping towards the hospital, his wounds, his life, and everything in it. 'And this is not a wall I can scale, so this is where it must end. What I am saying is don't try to meet me again.'

He didn't say anything, only watched her walk away until she disappeared from sight. Then a faint smile played at the corner of his mouth. Of course he was a cynic, through and through, born in a world of feuds and conflict.

And yet.

And yet, Sudhir Tyagi didn't doubt for a moment he would see Sukanya Pandey again. It was inevitable, much like the first time he had laid eyes on her, the girl in a green sharara, standing in the dalaan of an old, crumbling house in the light of a flashlight. Whatever else happened, that moment, frozen in time, was one he would carry to his grave.

He reached under his pillow and pulled out the book he had been reading that week, trying to focus on the words despite the throbbing pain that seemed to pulse like blood through his veins.

Visiting hours at the hospital were between four and six in the evening, and Sukanya watched in disbelief as a constant stream of visitors poured in to see Badi Mummy. Entire families – some with newborns and small children, others guiding elderly parents, hard of hearing, weary of spirit –made their way to the tiny room. They came to express something – hope? Camaraderie? Neighbourly spirit? – she wasn't sure, but she could see Badi Mummy growing more and more worn out with each passing minute.

Finally, unable to bear it any longer, Sukanya stepped out into the corridor outside the room, pressing a hand to her aching forehead and leaning against the cool wall.

'How is your Dadi ji doing?' asked a soft voice,

breaking the silence. Sukanya looked up in surprise, only to find Aman's aunt Roshni standing there in the corridor.

Sukanya blinked. It seemed that everything about this day was strange. Yes, Roshni stood there, in her customary sari, head covered as always, composed, her small diamond nose pin catching the dim light in the grey of the hospital.

'She's better, I'll take you to see her.' Sukanya said, turning to open the door, but Roshni moved closer gently placed a hand on her arm. She smelt of something familiar, a perfume of some kind, but that was not it entirely.

'There is no need,' Roshni replied softly. 'There are too many people inside. I came by to see how you were doing, Sukanya.'

'I am all right, just a bit tired,' she answered, studying Roshni's beautiful face – familiar and distant at the same time, a little puzzled by her concern.

'You must not think badly of Aman,' Roshni said suddenly, her voice earnest. 'He doesn't mean badly. It is just that things are a little complicated. In his life and mine.'

Sukanya froze, unsure of how to respond. A sudden thought struck her. Was Roshni more than an aunt to Aman, a Mrs Robinson to his Benjamin Braddock? Had she stepped into some sort of amorous, forbidden cesspool underway in that otherworldly Nawabon Ki

Haveli? She looked at Roshni with renewed interest, her curiosity piqued. Roshni was possibly older than her mother but had that timeless allure some women seemed to be born with.

She realized suddenly that she had been staring when Roshni put a self-conscious hand to her own cheek.

'I cannot explain anymore, not right now, anyway,' Roshni said. 'But yes, you must not be angry with young Aman; he means well. I just wanted to say this. I need to leave. I have a meeting. Come by the haveli when things are better at home.'

The door opened and a sudden clamour of voices could be heard from inside, visitors prolonging their goodbye to Badi Mummy, giving some last-minute instructions to keep her faith in God and try some new totka that would be sure to cure her in a jiffy.

Before these visitors could emerge from the room, Roshni nodded at Sukanya, turned, and walked away, a faint perfume trailing in her wake, leaving Sukanya with more questions than answers.

26.

Meerut, January 2007 – Badi Mummy Returns from Hospital

Badi Mummy returned home, declaring with great enthusiasm that the oxygen that the hospital had given her had done wonders, that she could breathe again, that she would now live to be a hundred, no less.

Sukanya listened to her blustering claims, nodding along and pretending to believe every word, all the while noticing how Badi Mummy's hands had grown colder to the touch, how she seemed completely disinterested in the soft food that Sunita religiously brought for her; how her skin seemed to have taken on a faint bluish tinge. Even her breathing sounded different, thought Sukanya to herself, as she lay on the bed beside hers, staring at the ceiling in silence. The new year had slipped into their lives quietly, without any celebration or fanfare except for the new calendar gifted by the medical store that sold them Badi Mummy's medicines. It hung on the wall of the dalaan, the fresh paper marking the passage of time. And Sukanya had quietly turned a year older.

That afternoon, a knock at the door broke into her thoughts. Sukanya got up to answer it and found Bibi standing in the doorway, holding a basket of fruit. It was an unusual sight. Apparently Bibi had made an exception to her rule, deciding to step out of her house to visit her ailing daughter.

'You didn't need to, Bibi, she doesn't even eat fruit,' said Sukanya, taking the basket from Bibi's hands.

'Ah, doesn't matter,' Bibi replied with a shrug. 'I cannot go to my married daughter's house empty-handed, can I?'

Sukanya felt a flicker of irritation. Every day seemed to bring yet another archaic belief her way, delivered with such unwavering certainty and without the slightest room for debate. In these moments, she would feel a twinge of guilty relief that she didn't have to stay in Bulandwada forever.

'Come inside, Bibi, I'll wake Badi Mummy. Bade Papa has gone to the university for some work.' She listened to Bibi cluck in disapproval at the general state of the house, clean enough but not washed every morning like her own.

Bibi cried copiously as she sat next to Badi Mummy, asking after her health. Badi Mummy tried to assure her that she felt better, but Bibi wasn't convinced, offering her own remedies for the illness.

'You should apply Ricks on her chest,' she told Sukanya, who blinked in confusion.

'She means Vicks,' Badi Mummy said in a tired voice.

'Haan, haan, that is what I said, Ricks. It helps. I had put it on my hand the other night when I cut it while cutting mooli. First class by morning. Go, gudiya, go and get a jar of Ricks.'

Sukanya assured Bibi that she would apply the ointment at the earliest and wondered if one could get tetanus from a knife cut. Fortunately, before further paeans to Ricks could be sung, Sunita came in, bearing, as she almost always did, a tray of tea. Rajni Mausi followed soon after. Badi Mummy seemed visibly drained by Bibi's seemingly endless, copious tears.

'Stop crying, Bibi, I am not dead yet,' she said in exasperation, her patience wearing thin.

'Don't worry so much, Bibi, the doctors have all said that there is nothing to worry about.' Sunita said, offered the tea in an attempt to comfort Bibi but Bibi shrugged off the reassurances, continuing to lament her misfortunes.

'Arrey, what will doctors do? It's the curse on my head. I have to see all my children go before me,' said Bibi, wiping a tear from her cheek with the pallu of her white sari.

'I am sure there is no curse,' said Rajni Mausi hopefully, not wanting to die before her time.

Bibi stopped to sigh loudly, her voice filled with resignation.

'This Rajni is all right I guess,' she remarked to

Sukanya, as though Rajni Mausi wasn't sitting right there. 'But she barely gets anything to eat, works so hard, poor thing, what with her three hulks turning out the way they did, especially that Munto. You should have seen her at the age of sixteen. She was so beautiful. Now, of course, she looks like she may go before your Badi Mummy.'

Rajni Mausi had clearly had enough of Bibi. She got up and left in a huff, announcing that she would be at the sewing machine if anyone needed her. Bibi paid no attention to this display of sulking. Eventually, as Badi Mummy drifted off to sleep, Bibi finally decided it was time to leave. Sukanya decided to walk her home, determined to see her deposited back in her own house.

'You should ask Shiladitya to come back,' Bibi said suddenly, her tone firm as they walked through the gully. 'If she dies now, without seeing him, she will not have peace. Shila should come back, meet her once, and look after his father.'

Sukanya bristled, feeling the familiar protective instinct flare up.

'It's not like Daddy doesn't want to return, Bibi,' she said defensively. 'But Bade Papa won't allow it.'

Badi Mummy waved this off. 'I don't think they are upset about him marrying that Dugar girl, though of course it was out of line,' she said, with scant regard for Sukanya's feelings, stung at this insult flung at her mother. 'It's got more to do with the promise he broke.

They had set all their expectations on that boy, and he didn't even afford them the courtesy of letting them know that he would be marrying and moving to vilayat before he made that decision.'

'He was just scared, Bibi, surely you know that,' Sukanya said, her jaw tightening. 'And he tried to mend bridges later, but you people sure know how to carry a grudge far beyond its expiry date.'

'Don't get uppity,' Bibi replied calmly, unfazed. 'He was my grandson long before he became your father. I want only good things for him. Yes, and for you too.'

'Even though I am half-Dugar?' asked Sukanya with a sly half-smile.

'Yes, despite that,' Bibi smiled back, unperturbed. 'Arrey, tell me, I have never asked this before, but is your mother very beautiful? Shiladitya could have had his pick of girls. And everyone said he would become a collector. She had better be exceptional, I say.'

Sukanya paused, thinking of her mother, with her large, sad eyes and her long hair that cascaded down her back, and the small smile that always played at the corners of her mouth. Her mother, whose quiet presence lit up any room she walked into. She thought of the way her father looked at her – like she was the sun itself that shone on everything in his world.

'Yes, she is very beautiful,' she answered, simply.

'Speak to your Bade Papa, lalli,' said Bibi again, as they reached her courtyard. 'You are the only one who can make him see the reason why Shila should come back.'

'I can only try. Also I've decided, Bibi,' she said. 'I'll return home after Gumbi's wedding.'

Then Sukanya walked back home, lost in thought, kicking a stray pebble with the edge of her white sneakers.

27.

Meerut, January 2007 – Gumbi's Mehndi

Gumbi's wedding was fast approaching, now just a week away, but before that could happen, there were other, smaller celebrations to get through. Sukanya found herself standing in Bibi's courtyard, marvelling at the many lives this square piece of land had lived. A place of endless gossip and tales told, a refuge from the blazing midday sun, and the place where Munto Baba had briefly taken up residence, it was today alive with festive colours and genda phools once more.

The shamiana was up once again, its colourful canopy covering the entire chowk, reaching for the skies, allowing only soft beams of sun inside. Bright garlands of marigold and other assorted flowers were draped from every corner, their mild fragrance mixing with the air. It was oddly charming – the fresh greens adorning the weathered, mouldering walls. *Like Angkor Wat,* Sukanya thought to herself.

The temperamental genius, Balram Halwai, had claimed his post beside giant karahis, tins of desi ghee, and mounds of grain that could easily feed an army. The sharp, acrid scent of freshly ground spices spiralled into the winding gully, carried out by a light breeze. His team of skinny cooks looked harried as the thickset, short-tempered Balram barked orders and tasted this and that, invoking the illustrious lineage of seven generations of halwais that had served in the historic kitchens of Balli Maran of Purani Delhi, including, he claimed, for the Mughal Badshah himself.

Nearby, the mehndi-wali had arrived with her small entourage of girls. They had carefully laid out their albums filled with some fairly complex designs and cones brimming with smooth henna paste, from which tendrils would emerge onto palms, creating swirling, delicate, intricate patterns.

Mithu and Mishri screeched from their cages, startling Sukanya out of her reverie. Mithu ka bhi pata hai? – What about Mithu?

She felt a wet nose press into her hand and turned to see Shera's wise, deep-brown eyes gazing at her. She gave his head a quick scratch, and comforted by this, he returned to his spot in the sun beside Moti, always keeping a vigilant eye on the activity in the chowk, where much frenzied preparation was in evidence. Sukanya had a strange feeling of déjà vu, this-has-happened-before-this-will-happen-again, a brief glimpse of a time when, much older, she would have two dogs, one small and one large, and she would walk them on a beach, a house built with coral and limestone walls and a red-tiled roof behind her. A foreign land, a foreign life but the dogs would be called Moti and Shera.

Sukanya stepped across the courtyard, to make her way to Bibi's house, her slippers sinking into the carpet that now covered the uneven ground, unaccustomed to its softness.

'Today you look as desi as a kalai ka glass,' Bibi called out in delight, as Sukanya approached. Sukanya smiled ruefully, glancing down at her feet, trying to will the silken pleats of her sari into submission.

'I have no idea how this sari business works, Bibi,' Sukanya confessed, making her careful ascent up the steps. 'And I also don't understand how you manage to wear saris every day. I feel like I'm one step away from tripping and falling flat on my face.'

'No such thing will happen,' Bibi declared with her usual certainty. 'You'll get used to it soon enough. But what's the point of that anyway? You said you are going back to Ing-land. You won't wear these six-yard numbers there.'

'I have to return, Bibi,' said Sukanya, the familiar pang going around her heart. 'This gap year won't last forever.'

Bibi reached out, took Sukanya's hand, and sat there holding it awhile, lost in thought. Then with a sigh, she got to her feet, her knees protesting audibly.

Sukanya watched her, *her* Bibi, the charming bigot,

trying to commit everything about Bibi to her memory. Her silver hair that still gleamed in the sunlight. How busy she always was, her thin wrists always moving, her eyes still sharp behind the thick-framed spectacles, her wiry, spare frame forever in a whirlwind of activity. She would not see Bibi again, that much was certain. This part of her life was slipping away. Before too long it would be lost to her, swallowed by time, to resurface only in the unpredictable flashes of nostalgia.

'Sukanya,' Nandi's voice cut through the din, calling her from across the courtyard. She stood out in a violent shade of purple, the fabric clinging to the folds of flesh. 'Come on, it's your turn for mehndi. Gumbi's finished.'

Sukanya followed her inside.

Gumbi sat in her room, dressed in a garish yellow sari that seemed to dull her radiant complexion. The small room was warm and oppressive. A bunch of young girls sat around her, their palms stretched, marvelling at the intricate patterns of mehndi emerging from the cones. The air was thick with the sharp, earthy scent of mehndi and cheap perfume. Loud wedding songs blared from an old stereo nearby, the tinny sound adding to the chaos.

Gumbi's bridal mehndi was certainly very elaborate. Sukanya peered at her hands and arms, now stained a deep red-brown, a tangle of vines and paisleys, the swirls and curves leading into each other, twining around her fingers and ankles, wrapping around her wrists, leaving not a single patch of skin untouched. Somewhere within that maze of patterns, Sukanya knew, the mehndi-wali had hidden her husband's name, to be spotted by him in a gesture of playful, impending intimacy.

'It's stunning,' Sukanya whispered, leaning closer to admire the artwork but she faltered as she caught sight of Gumbi's face. Beneath the ornaments and adornments, she was pale and hollow, the perfect lines of her face dulled by sadness.

'Look at her,' Nandi grumbled loudly, leaning over Sukanya's shoulder. 'Is this how a dulhan is supposed to look? She's so lucky – marrying into that family, khandaani ameer – and yet she sits there looking washed-out like she hasn't eaten in a week. Then she'll wonder why her husband leaves her within a month of the wedding, bewaqoof.'

Sukanya turned quickly, cutting Nandi off before she could gain further momentum. 'You are right, Nandi Chachi,' she said, with forced cheer. 'She does need to eat. Can you ask that halwai outside to send two plates for us? I'll make her eat, I promise. And let's empty out this room, Chachi – she needs to rest for a bit.'

Nandi grumbled but obeyed. 'Accha, ladkiyon, out to the shamiana for tea,' she announced to the gathered girls and the mehndi-walis. The room emptied gradually amidst the khus-khus of silk lehengas and tasselled dupattas. Nandi thundered off to arrange the food, an excess of purple, her heavy footsteps echoing across the courtyard.

Sukanya turned the music down; the room became bearable.

'Sukanya jeeji,' Gumbi whispered from her corner. 'Did you see Puru today? Mummy has taken my phone.'

'No, Gumbi, I haven't seen him.' Sukanya felt her throat tighten at Gumbi's forlorn voice. Gumbi nodded faintly but didn't say anything more, fatigued and defeated.

Nandi returned in a short while, carrying two heaped plates of food. Sukanya took the plates from her and asked her to return to the hundreds of tasks that called to her while she took care of Gumbi.

Sukanya sat beside Gumbi and coaxed her to eat. Gumbi complied with visible effort, though she looked nauseous.

'Rest for a while, Gumbi,' Sukanya said once they had eaten. 'I'll put this away and come back to check on you later.'

'See if you can find Puru, jeeji, see how he is doing,' said Gumbi again, as she lay down on her bed, holding out both arms by her sides, trying not to smudge her mehndi.

Sukanya stepped into the shamiana, the din of laughter, music, and clattering utensils immediately engulfing her. So many people, so much noise, so much movement. She jostled through the throngs of guests, her slippers catching on the edge of the carpet as she finally stepped out. The cool winter breeze brushed her face, soothing her flushed cheeks. She checked on her sari. It was holding up so far, but just about.

She went to put away the empty plates outside the shamiana and saw Sudhir slouched against a wall, his cigarette dangling between his fingers. His appearance made her uneasy – this was the first time they had crossed paths since that day at the hospital when she had vowed never to see him again. The recent scuffle with Jogeshwar's goons hadn't done him any favours though the fracture had clearly been a false alarm. He was thinner, drawn, the strain of pain visible on his face. He was looking straight at her. There was no place to hide.

'Have you seen my Puru Chacha around?' she asked abruptly, glancing past him to scan the gully.

'No,' he said, exhaling a plume of smoke. 'But then, why would he be here? I mean, this would be the last place you could expect to find him, right?'

'Maybe. I don't know what to think anymore,' said Sukanya, feeling uneasy. Something about Puru's absence felt wrong. 'I thought maybe he had come to check on Gumbi. I'll go to FML and check if he is there.'

'Should I drop you?' asked Sudhir suddenly. 'You don't look like you can walk too well in that sari.'

This was true. She wouldn't get very far in her sari and brand-new heels, a gift from the doting Badi Mummy. But also, Sudhir had to be avoided at all costs, except that she didn't want to. As she hesitated, Sudhir, sensing an opportunity, stabbed his cigarette out with his shoe and went off to get his motorcycle. He brought it around and gestured for Sukanya to get on. Sukanya eyed it warily, as if expecting it to go up in flames at any moment.

'It's clean,' said Sudhir, uncertainly, looking nervously at the seat behind him.

Sukanya examined the bike, her gaze lingering on the fuel tank.

'That Tyagi Boy,' she read aloud, the legend scrawled in cursive lettering, no less, on the fuel tank, and rolled her eyes so dramatically that Sudhir thought they might exit via her head. 'Jesus really needs to take the wheel on this one.'

'I know, I know,' he tried to explain, embarrassed, as she laughed aloud. 'It's a joke. Everyone does it in this part of the world you know. If it's not Gujjar King, it's Jaat Pride or Yadav Prince. I just thought I'd get in on the fun, you know? Well, I'll put on my helmet if that'll make you more comfortable?'

'It would,' Sukanya said, still laughing. 'I don't want to be seen with you.'

'You really know how to spare my feelings, don't you? Well, here we go.'

Sukanya would remember the ride through the old gullies, perched behind Sudhir, struggling to keep her billowing sari in place as he manoeuvred the motorcycle through narrow, winding lanes. The familiar sights of dilapidated houses and bustling neighbours whizzed by in a kaleidoscopic blur.

'That was quick,' she remarked as the motorcycle pulled up outside FML. She gingerly dismounted, the sari threatening to give way.

'Too quick, memsahib, too quick,' he grinned. 'I'll wait here in case you need to be ferried back.'

'No need,' she said, annoyed at how pleased she was with his attention. *That Tyagi Boy. Well, see if I care.* In her mind, where she had silent conversations with Angie, she found herself defensive. *No, of course there is nothing there. How can there be, when he is a junglee, a boor, a ganwar really? The question doesn't arise.*

Sukanya tried the door to the shop only to find it locked from the inside, a knot of dread beginning to form in her stomach. She turned to leave but then remembered the backdoor of the library, which opened directly onto the courtyard of the house.

She walked around her way to the main entrance of the house, like any other in the neighbourhood – a small tulsi plant sat in the middle of the aangan, and all the rooms were arranged to look out over it. The house was quiet, save for a child – the same one who had brought her tea the other day – playing on the floor, drawing patterns with coloured chalk.

'Hello, baby,' called Sukanya, her voice wavering. 'Can you take me to the DVD library from here?'

The child nodded silently, taking her hand and leading her to the one of the rooms overlooking the space. He pointed to a green door that was presumably the library. Sukanya approached it, her unease mounting. She tried the door, and it opened with a creak, revealing the dim, shadowy interiors of the DVD library.

She squinted into the murky light, her eyes struggling to make sense of the blurred shapes. Almost immediately, her gaze fell upon Puru, slumped over the counter. For a moment, she thought he was simply napping, worn out by the day and everything that had happened in it. Then the truth dawned on her. The overturned bottle of pills. The half-empty bottle of Old Monk rum. Her hand flew to her mouth, muffling a cry of horror, garbled words escaping her lips that she couldn't quite comprehend.

Heart pounding, Sukanya turned and bolted for the main door, unlocking it with shaking hands that just wouldn't cooperate, stumbling out into the open air. Her eyes darted left and right, frantically searching for Sudhir. Mercifully, he was still there, waiting for her by his motorcycle, his helmet glinting faintly in the early evening.

'Sudhir!' she cried. 'Come inside quickly...I mean, go, get help, get someone!'

He stood frozen for a moment as her words tumbled out in a frantic torrent. Her body shook violently, and the precarious pleats from the sari finally gave way, collapsing in a silken puddle around her feet.

'Puru Chacha has...has...I think he has killed himself.'

28.

Meerut, January 2007 – The Aftermath of Puru's Shenanigans

The next several hours passed in an underwater world, where voices and words swam up to her but made no sense and could not be heard. Sukanya only remembered flashes of these moments later. There was Natwar, clutching his *tehmet* with one hand as he ran, looking haggard, rivulets of sweat running down his stubbled face in the winter evening, dark with worry. There was Sudhir, but also Aman, shouting brisk orders, no trace of his usual sardonic self. Others from the mohalla were there, panicked and frightened. And all this while, the same merciless thought played on a tireless loop in her mind – *he's dead, he's dead, he's dead*. With a bottle of Old Monk and some pills for company, he's dead.

How many seconds, minutes, or hours passed before the battered, dented ambulance arrived? How long before the two paramedics, calm and efficient, emerged from the ambulance, unfolding a stretcher, their practiced movements so alien amidst the chaos? For how long did they disappear into the annals of the shop, where Puru must have lain slumped over the counter before they carried out his pale, listless form on a stretcher? How long after the heavy, metal ambulance doors slammed shut was Sukanya still sitting outside, frozen, on the steps of the DVD library?

And then Sudhir was crouching in front of her, his face shadowed beneath the pale light of the streetlamp, whispering to her, holding her hands. It was his hands – bruised, scraped, scabbed, warm, firm – that brought her back to that moment. She looked down at them and then around at the dark walls of the gully, light spilling from the open windows of some of the houses. She realized she was very cold, and had been so for a long time.

'Sukanya,' Sudhir was saying. 'Listen to me, he isn't dead. The paramedics got there in time; his pulse was weak, but he's alive. They have pumped his stomach. You saved him.'

The knot lodged deep in her heart began to loosen. She was mumbling thanks to Hanuman-Jesus-God-Creator-Shiva-Mother, someone who had answered her unformed, wordless prayer to save the defeated Puru.

'Are you sure he isn't dead?' she now asked of Sudhir, still crouching in front of her, still holding her hands.

'I just heard from Aman, the pills were not strong

enough; he'd gone unconscious,' said Sudhir. 'But he'll be okay.'

There it was, the relief, flooding through her veins. He smiled at her, and almost of her own accord, she leaned forward and kissed him. She kissed him, and all of this, this mohalla, its gnarled, ruined brick walls, all the childhood ghosts of her time-weathered past, this fucked-up missing piece of her life. He didn't pull away, he didn't lean in, he allowed it to happen, and he waited till she let go of his hands, and folded her own in her lap.

He rose to his feet, then sat beside her on the cold stone steps and lit a cigarette. He offered it to her, and she took a drag, the smoke filling the moment and making it familiar and lived-in. This had happened before; this would happen again.

'He could have died,' said Sudhir, rubbing his stubbled cheek. 'Easily. This is more serious than I thought. For that silly little Gumbi. Who can tell the ways of the heart, which is, all things told, a complete kameena?'

What could Sukanya say to that, her own rogue heart playing tricks on her as she stood by?

'I must go and meet Gumbi,' she said. 'I must tell her what happened, that he's okay. What time is it? It's late. Would the mehndi be over? I really thought Puru Chacha was...you know...' A couple of helpless tears escaped, catching her by surprise. Sudhir looked away as she hastily wiped them off.

'Would you like me to drop you back to the chowk, my objectionable bike notwithstanding?' he asked.

Sukanya smiled tentatively at the feeble joke and shook her head. *That Tyagi Boy.*

'I'll walk. You've already done enough,' she said, rising to her feet and checking the mussed pleats of her sari. She couldn't believe that she had draped it only a few hours ago, with Badi Mummy taking her through the steps, urging her to try, try, try.

'Nowhere near,' said Sudhir, still perched on the steps, the lit cigarette sending out wiry plumes into the last rays of the weak evening sun. A light fog descended upon the mohalla, obscuring the houses. In the stillness, they could hear the distant azaan, calling the faithful to *maghrib*. The gully was dark and silent, no trace of the commotion of a few hours ago. Two young boys came out with a cricket ball and bat and headed off, looking for others to play with.

'This is a strange place,' Sukanya gave a small, bitter laugh, shaking her head. 'Everybody's in everybody's business, and yet, someone like Puru Chacha is completely invisible. He doesn't count. Gumbi doesn't count. They are in love, right here, under the collective nose of this mohalla, but nobody knows, nobody cares. They are not enough to disturb matters, to create ripples.'

She paused, meeting Sudhir's look. He opened his mouth as if to speak, but she was preparing to walk away, carefully gathering the pleats of her sari. Never again, she told herself. *Never again what?*

'I better hurry home. Bade Papa must be wondering where I've disappeared to,' she said, lifting her hand in farewell.

Sudhir watched as she made her way home with unsteady steps, the troublesome sari clutched in her hands, the pallu trailing in her wake. Her heels wobbled with each step, and she stumbled every now and then.

'What is your substance, whereof are you made, that millions of strange shadows on you tend?' he muttered to himself, wincing as a fresh surge of pain shot through his injured leg. He watched her vanish from view, then flinched as the dying cigarette burned the tip of his finger. With a start, he stood up and walked away to his motorcycle, the faint glow of the solitary streetlamp casting a weak light on the spot where Puru had once tried to end it all.

By the time Sukanya got to Bibi's chowk, the festivities had wrapped up and Gumbi had already gone to bed. There was no point in sticking around. Her grandparents were already asleep when Sukanya got back, oblivious to everything that had happened with Puru. Sukanya let herself in through the heavy, weathered wooden door and stood in the dalaan, watching the two of them lying there, covered in thick black blankets. In their sleep, they looked older, their faces softened, the sharp edges of the day smoothed away. Was this one of the last few times she would see them like this? She fought a sudden urge to cry and quietly went upstairs to her room – her father's room once – and sat on the bed, trying to make sense of the day and its chaos late into the night.

As expected, by the time Sukanya woke up the next morning, Bade Papa had already been informed of the previous evening's events by at least twenty different people. The errant Puru had been given a few bottles of glucose and after a stern word from the attending doctor, had been discharged from the hospital. He had gone with Natwar to the police station, where Puru's statement had to be recorded. Then there was the medico-legal report and the psychiatric evaluation – Puru's troubles were far from over.

When Sukanya came downstairs, Rajni Mausi was sitting with Badi Mummy, weeping inconsolably. Sukanya had always been struck by how freely people cried in this place, without a shred of shame or embarrassment. Badi Mummy continued with her usual, quotidian questions directed at Sukanya – had she eaten? How was Gumbi's mehndi? What was her plan for the day? – even as Rajni Mausi's tears soaked the edge of her pallu. Grief and the tears it birthed were everyday things, not to be hidden.

After a while, it became clear that the source of Rajni Mausi's despair was not just the shock of Puru's attempt but his silence afterward. He had been tight-lipped about the recent events, and no one had been able to coax out the reason for his act of such abject desperation.

'Everyone will say that I mistreated him because he's adopted,' Rajni Mausi wailed, her voice thick with guilt. 'That is why he swallowed all those neend ki goli.'

'Be quiet, Rajni,' snapped Badi Mummy, her patience clearly wearing thin with her sister's endless self-flagellation. 'Nobody has said that about you. And they won't start now.'

Rajni Mausi honked in her pallu, damp and crumpled, dabbing at her eyes.

'But we need to know what's bothering him,' she said. 'I think someone has done kala-jaadu on him.'

Badi Mummy scoffed audibly at this, rolling her eyes.

'Of all the people in the world, why would they choose your Puru for kala-jaadu, Rajni? He doesn't have enough going for him to merit that much effort. Kala-jaadu takes work, you know. No, it must be something else – a girl, or some other trouble. Let it go. He will tell you when he's ready.'

Sukanya had grown used to the bluntness and lack of charity in the mohalla, the unapologetic way people spoke their minds, with not even a cursory attempt at political correctness. Yet, hearing Badi Mummy speak this way was still jarring.

She would soon find that Badi Mummy's view was hardly unique. In fact, it was the prevailing sentiment. If Sukanya had harboured any hope that Puru's desperate act might stir sympathy or concern, she was mistaken.

In the eyes of most, it was merely dismissed as an impulsive, youthful antic – a childish attempt at attention, nothing more. And even if it had been a cry for visibility, it hadn't worked. Puru remained as invisible as ever. Nothing stopped. No hearts softened. Time marched on, and with it, Gumbi's wedding preparations continued unabated without interruption, unaffected by the shadow of despair that had briefly loomed.

Days passed and Bibi's courtyard remained a place of festivity and celebration, vibrant with marigold garlands strung across every corner, their stray golden petals drifting down to the time-worn brick floor.

Yet, Gumbi herself was seldom seen, a solitary figure, thin and withdrawn, uncomfortable in her new clothes, too big for her, as though she were wearing someone else's decisions, which didn't quite fit.

Sukanya herself wandered through the days in a daze, feeling as though the mohalla was a timeless river, its rhythms and rhymes unaltered by the small dramas and fleeting acts of rebellion attempted by its people. She drifted through the motions, trying on dresses for the wedding functions, coaxing the frail Badi Mummy to eat a little more, and watching Bade Papa's face grow ever more drawn with the passing days. And through all of this, she waited for this short tryst with her past to come to an end.

There was no denying it. She had fallen in love with Bulandwada, but even as she surrendered to this love, she could feel the pull of London, the constant tugs of the life she had left behind, her mother often appearing in her dreams, urging her to return, and her father, waiting for her by the fog-covered Thames.

29.

Meerut, January 2007 – Gumbi's Haldi

The day of Gumbi's haldi fell on a freezing Sunday, when the sun couldn't quite break through the cold mist in the gullies. As Sukanya dressed in the baithak under the keen eyes of Badi Mummy, she kept blowing into her hands, trying to warm them. An electric heater glowed in a corner, trying valiantly to stave off the chill, but the room was too open to the outside world, letting in a draught. Bade Papa was lounging in his customary armchair in the dalaan outside, one leg draped over the arm, wrapped in a thick blanket over his kurta-pajama, wearing a makhmal topi even indoors. He sipped from a cup of sweet, black tea, fragrant with cardamom and cloves, and hummed an old ghazal under his breath as he read Hindi and Urdu newspapers, informing Badi Mummy of the day's goings-on every now and then.

There had been some debate among the women of Bulandwada about the order of Gumbi's mehndi and haldi ceremonies, but finally, much to Nandi's relief, an uncomfortable consensus had been reached – mehndi could precede haldi by a few days. On this day, everyone was expected to wear yellow, to mirror the deep, earthy, sun-soaked gold of the turmeric paste that would be applied to the bride and groom. Sukanya now held up a yellow churidar pajama and kurta against herself, lovingly made by Rajni Mausi from a delicate piece of Lucknow chikankari, and presented herself to her grandmother.

Another day, another dress to be worn and paraded before Badi Mummy in the baithak. Carry on as if nothing had happened, as if the young man next door hadn't tried to kill himself.

'It's too cold to be putting cold haldi paste on anyone, honestly,' Sukanya announced. 'And just how many more functions will Gumbi have before she's married, Badi Mummy? One would think we're just about done. Clearly *Hum Aapke Hain Koun..!* was a case of art following real life.' Her father loved that movie and watched it repeatedly, but of course she couldn't say that to Badi Mummy.

'I don't know about art and all that, but this much you have to do for a wedding. Khair, it's not like I ever got the opportunity,' said Badi Mummy with a sigh. Sukanya felt Badi Mummy's mood shift and immediately changed the topic to that of clothes and jewels, sure to bring cheer to the old lady. Even with her limited means, even in poor health and hardship, Badi Mummy had paid meticulous attention to herself. She had carefully guarded her silks and organzas, each piece painstakingly wrapped in mulmul and stored in a wooden peti. Till she could do it on her own, she'd bathed with the finest soaps that she could afford, concocted face packs with strands of saffron and warm milk in the confines of her small, dim kitchen, and had religiously oiled and plaited her long, once-glossy hair with her trusty Parachute Coconut Oil. All this in the service of vanity, until the cruel hands of illness had reached out and said, 'No more.' No more, that is, till Sukanya – beautiful girl – had emerged from the mists of London, stepping into her house. It was all Badi Mummy could do to wrap her in the fabric of her incomplete dreams and all the finery that was no longer hers.

'I don't think yellow does anything for my skin tone, Badi Mummy,' Sukanya pretended to grumble, knowing exactly how it would affect Badi Mummy. Sure enough, Badi Mummy bristled, just as she had intended.

'Of course it does, yellow makes you look so fair,' Badi Mummy declared, leaving no room for disagreement. In Badi Mummy's world, to be called fair was the highest praise, the symbolic pinnacle of beauty. Sukanya scowled but didn't argue. She had long since learned that Bulandwada's obsession with fairness probably predated colonialism. Rang saaf hai, they would say with bobbing heads and approving smiles, the complexion is clean. To be fair was to be clean.

'Badi Mummy, I must say, you look good today,'

Sukanya said, giving her two thumbs up, and it was true. There seemed to be a flush of colour on the old woman's face, a hint of life running beneath the delicate, papery shell of her skin.

'I feel good today,' said Badi Mummy, smiling broadly, trying to hide how pleased this made her as she adjusted her shawl. Sukanya felt a familiar pang, a rush of love towards these old people – *hers, hers, hers.*

'It's because you are here, bitiya,' Bade Papa called out from the dalaan. 'I couldn't manage it on my own. How has Ghalib put it? Mat pooch ke kya haal hai mera tere peeche, tu dekh ke kya rang hai mera tere aage.'

Sukanya burst out laughing at this, causing Badi Mummy to blush – a rare, endearing sight.

'Go now,' Badi Mummy said, eyeing Sukanya's appearance. 'You look lovely, and at least you won't trip all over the place in this one. And don't forget to take the matching cardigan and Kashmiri shawl from my cupboard.'

Sukanya smiled at the pleasure in Badi Mummy's words and took the warm things, faintly smelling of neem leaves. Matching things was Badi Mummy's big style statement, and if she had had her way, Sukanya would be draped in yellow from head to toe.

How do I look, Sudhir? The thought came unbidden, and Sukanya pushed it away just as sharply as she stepped out of the house to make her way to Bibi's chowk, a journey she had made nearly every day in her time at

Bulandwada. *Just a silly kiss, really; it didn't mean a thing. Not to me.*

As expected, Gumbi was once again at the centre of attention on that day. She sat on a short, squat wooden stool, encircled by a group of women in swishing silks and bindis and gajras. Dressed in a simple yellow sari, Gumbi had no trace of any lotion or potion on her. Her long hair cascaded down her shoulders, framing her perfect, oval face.

No longer despondent, Gumbi had become a glowing picture of a textbook bride, aglow and radiant, serenely smiling, and seemed almost completely detached from the chaos swirling all around her, lost in a daydream only she could see.

Dozens of relatives had descended upon Nandi's home, a buzzing hive of corpulent mamis, irritable cousins, and petulant buas. They bustled about, decked out in bright colours, casting appraising glances at each other's gold jewellery with petty precision. A distant phoopha ji sulked in a corner over some imagined slight, his pout aimed at garnering attention.

Balram Halwai, ever the perfectionist, was in his element, loudly lamenting the lack of ghee needed to prepare the vast thaals of laddus. Meanwhile, the dholak-walis were in full swing, singing playful, borderline vulgar songs, leading to sudden eruptions of laughter from the women.

Sukanya felt unexpectedly moved by the scene

unfolding before her. This was happening more and more these days, this sudden surge of emotion for the smallest of things, the tiniest of moments. It would give way to sudden despair, a deep plunge into unexplainable sadness.

The haldi ceremony was to begin once the groom's family arrived. In the meanwhile, Nandi darted around the courtyard like a wind-up toy, her energy seemingly endless, except for the occasional pause when she'd come to a sudden stop, panting like a dog, before picking up speed again. The air buzzed with activity; everyone had a job to do, everyone was busy.

Sukanya slipped away from the centre of this frenzied activity to Bibi's house. The normally serene house had been utterly transformed by the influx of wedding guests. Children tore through the rooms, their shrieks of laughter ringing through the air. The floor was cluttered with a mess of bags, stray footwear, and half-eaten plates of food. Sukanya was amazed that the usually fastidious Bibi had allowed this chaos to unfold in her pristine house. Just then, Bibi emerged from her kitchen, looking very flustered.

'Look at these jaahils,' she said, gesturing to the mess around her. 'That Nandi begged me to lend her my house so I gave in. You know me, bitto – generous to a fault. Soft heart, like a motichoor laddu.'

Sukanya rolled her eyes at this blatantly inaccurate self-description, but Bibi, needing no encouragement, steamrolled ahead with her usual gusto.

'People should have some sense. Is this any way to behave in someone else's house?' Bibi grumbled loudly. 'It is only because it's Gumbi's wedding that I've allowed all this. Anyway, this is no place for you today, bitiya. Should I ask someone to open Gumbi's room for you? You might find some peace and quiet there.'

'No need, Bibi, I'll be all right,' replied Sukanya with a small smile. 'You should feed your parrots, though – they're screaming their heads off.'

'They are not the only ones,' Bibi said, looking pointedly at the clamorous children. She stormed off, loudly cursing Nandi, her eight siblings and their many children, now ensconced in her house, but secretly enjoying the mess and chaos. Sukanya, suddenly feeling out of place in the bedlam and commotion, felt an urge to escape.

No, not just to escape. To see someone. Aman, whom she hadn't seen since the day he had helped ferry Puru to the hospital, taking charge with his quiet, focused intensity. Maybe today he would be in the haveli, smoking in his room, the familiar burnt scent of his cigarettes mingling with his musky cologne, loud rock music filling the air. Without quite meaning to, her feet carried her out of the house and down the street, towards Nawabon Ki Haveli.

But the haveli was silent. Basheeran answered the door and informed her that Aman was not yet home, but that he was expected soon. Disappointed, Sukanya turned to return to the raucous haldi celebrations when a familiar, sweet voice called from inside the haveli. 'Sukanya, is that you?'

Roshni emerged from her room, a pair of gold-framed spectacles on her forehead, a thick book in her hand, dressed in a simple ikat sari, but looking for all the world like Mallika-e-Hindustan – regal and upright, composed and elegant.

'Ji, hello, I just came by to thank Aman for his help in, uh...' Here, Sukanya stumbled, unsure whether Puru's shame had crossed the threshold of this stately haveli, but Roshni understood almost immediately.

'How is your uncle doing now?' Roshni asked. What was it about her that made Sukanya feel so unsettled?

'He's better, uh, stable,' she replied – embarrassed that she hadn't visited Puru Chacha at home, hadn't found the courage to face him after all that he had been through. Ashamed that she, like everyone else, continued to participate in Gumbi's wedding festivities as if nothing of consequence had happened. Guilty for pretending that she hadn't heard his heart break.

'He's better,' she repeated, almost to herself.

'Would you like to come inside?' Roshni asked her. Sukanya came out of her reverie and immediately began to make excuses. No, she must leave right away; the haldi ceremony must have started; Bibi might need her help. But then something in Roshni's expression made her pause, made her want to stay – if only for a moment.

'Yes, sure, just for a few minutes,' she finally said, stepping inside the haveli.

'Basheeran, please get chai,' Roshni asked of the old caretaker, who flung her broom into a corner, and flounced off to do Roshni's bidding with impressive ill-humour.

'Thyroid,' Roshni explained with a straight face. Sukanya stifled the snigger that rose in her at this.

Cruel but funny – this was the recurring motif in most conversations in Bulandwada, where no topic was too sacred or too sensitive. Racism, sexism, bigotry – everything was fair game in the pursuit of a good laugh.

'She makes excellent tea though,' said Roshni, settling into one of the armchairs in the verandah, the hunting trophies and gilt-framed mirrors looking down at them. From the kitchen, Basheeran clanged dishes and thumped around in protest.

'Yes, Aman always speaks of Basheeran with great fondness ,' said Sukanya, lowering herself into the chair opposite Roshni's. She shifted uneasily, wondering what it was that she actually wanted to talk to her about. Roshni carefully marked her place in Auden's poems with a bookmark and laid the tome aside.

'How have you been?' Roshni asked, looking at her from beneath those dark, thick lashes. It couldn't be denied; the woman was striking beyond measure. The kind of face you could catch a glimpse of in a moving train and never quite get out of your mind.

'Ji, all is well,' Sukanya said, already beginning to regret her decision. Why did Roshni look at her this way, with such deep affection and something like compassion?

'And you are dressed for that young girl's haldi, yes?' she asked, gesturing to the yellow churidar, a playful glint in her eyes.

'Oh, yes, yes, of course, I normally don't wear yellow,' Sukanya replied, glancing down at her clothes.

'You should; it makes you look...'

'Fair?' Sukanya completed the sentence for her.

'No,' Roshni looked surprised. 'I was about to go for a ray of sunshine at dawn.' She broke off with a chuckle as Basheeran entered, the clatter of dishes announcing her arrival. 'But here comes Basheeran with our chai.'

'And Irani biskoot,' Basheeran added, looking very pleased with herself, her mood noticeably mellower after having smoked a beedi in the kitchen. 'Do you want one, bitiya?'

Sukanya helped herself to a biscuit to placate Basheeran, and she left, wrapping her dupatta around her head to ward off the cold.

'Um, have you lived here long?' Sukanya asked Roshni, trying her best to make conversation, but also aware that she had promised Aman that she wouldn't dig deep into the exact nature of his relationship with Roshni. Something was definitely not quite right there.

'Long enough,' said Roshni, looking around the

haveli, as if seeing its pillars and carved beams for the first time. Sukanya took a hasty sip of the hot tea in an attempt to finish quickly and scalded her lips. *Listen, Angie, maybe Roshni is not quite all right in the head? She certainly seemed like she could be hiding a body or two under her bed.*

'But let's not talk about me, Sukanya,' Roshni continued. 'What about you? Aman tells me you are visiting your grandparents? Your father's parents?'

Sukanya nodded, reluctant to share any details about her family situation – the estrangement, the anger, the fractures that defined her strange, broken family. *Yes, I'm visiting my happy, idyllic grandparental home, where my mother's name must not be uttered and where my father has been a stranger for twenty years and more.*

'Ji, that's correct,' she said briefly, hoping to steer the conversation away.

'And your mother?' Roshni prodded.

'She's in London,' Sukanya replied, and placed her empty cup on the ornate coffee table. She rose to her feet and folded her hands in a namaste. 'I should leave now, Aunty, Gumbi's haldi will be starting soon. I'd better hurry.'

'Is your mother also Indian? Where does she come from?' Roshni asked. She remained seated, not quite granting Sukanya the unspoken permission to leave.

'Somewhere in North Delhi, I am told – a road called Shankar Marg,' she could hear the clipped British inflection in her voice, excessively polite because she was annoyed. 'Thank you for the tea, Aunty, I will take your leave now.'

She turned and walked out, leaving the older woman sitting there in the decaying old haveli, still holding the fine porcelain cup in her lap, her tea untasted, weak plumes of steam rising from it, her gaze following the young girl until Sukanya disappeared from view, the yellow of her churidar a fleeting flash in the fading light of the haveli.

30.

Meerut, January 2007 – Gumbi's Haldi (continued)

Sukanya returned from the haveli to find the haldi ceremony in full swing, the chowk humming with laughter and music. Gumbi was covered in turmeric, shivering a little in the cold. Her dulha sat next to her, looking pleased, stealing nervous glances at Gumbi every now and then, unable to believe his luck. Sukanya tried to smile as she applied handfuls of the wet, squelching paste to their faces and then stepped back. She assessed the groom-to-be, a plump boy-man, clearly well-fed through the years on deep-fried goodness, a pearl necklace glinting over his yellow sherwani that stretched over his small potbelly.

This is to be the pretty Gumbi's husband, this human laddu, she thought uncharitably to herself.

'Not a patch on your Puru Chacha, is he, memsahib?' Sudhir whispered in her ear, appearing out of nowhere, as he always did.

She turned around to look at him, determined to ignore her body with all its restless flutters and light-headedness and that bloody euphoric delight in seeing him. *Just a silly kiss, really, Angie, nothing more.* Sudhir didn't look dressed for the function, wearing a black kurta of all things in that sea of yellow, looking wan and overdrawn behind his stubbled, smiling face.

'Sorry, did I surprise you? But I could see you thinking unkind thoughts about my delectable little jija-to-be, and I couldn't let that pass, could I?'

'What rubbish! I was thinking no such thing,' Sukanya replied, flushing. 'When did you get here? I didn't see you around earlier.'

'I just got here, couldn't get away from college. Mahaul theek nahin hai,' he said, looking down at his shoes and shaking his head. A woman next to Sudhir gave him a once-over before turning to whisper to her friend. Sukanya gestured for him to follow her and stepped away from the crowd.

'What do you mean, mahaul and all that? Is it safe?' she asked when they were away from the crowds, in a quiet corner of the chowk, only the walls listening to them.

'Everything boils down to ego in this place,' he said, frowning. 'It's not like that haraami Jogeshwar cares about speaking at the freaking Founder's Day, but what good is he if he gets sent back by a bunch of laundas?'

'But your side, I've heard you have a lot of support

also, from the sugarcane farmers of Asauda. Henchmen standing by to protect you. Is that true?'

Sudhir looked at her, and for a moment she felt a sense of unease creeping up her spine. *Nothing at all, Angie, just a little holiday thing. Meaningless.* Then he grinned and looked away.

'Of course I do. I will be fine. Plus, don't forget my taweez,' he said, pointing to the amulet around his neck.

Then why don't I believe you? she wanted to ask him but didn't.

'I think they've opened the buffet,' she said. 'I'm starving. Have you eaten?'

'Go ahead, I'll go meet Gumbi's in-laws and come back in a bit.' She watched him walk up to the groom's family to shake hands and say his namastes. They seemed to greet him with great enthusiasm, specially the patriarch, the groom's father. She turned away and went to the buffet, a typical UP-style array with dishes like kaddu ki sabzi, boondi ka raita, and fat pooris stuffed with urad dal.

Sukanya would remember the food that she ate in her time in Bulandwada, the flavours that she had been homesick for, even without ever having tasted them. Years later, an Indian lab assistant would return from home with a round steel container filled with sweets, offering them to everyone. Sukanya would take one bite of the mithai, and before she knew it, tears would spring to her eyes. The syrupy, fragrant mouthful would transport her back to Bibi's chowk, smiling women looking down at her from their balconies, calling her in for a cup of tea, asking after this and that. The breeze fragrant upon her brown skin, so much like theirs, the sounds of home all around.

The guests, tired and spent from the day's festivities, gathered around the food, clamouring like hungry children. Sukanya knew Badi Mummy would want to know exactly what had been served and would be delighted by her granddaughter's long-drawn descriptions of the food. She served herself a plate and sat down on one of the many chairs scattered around, grateful that she didn't have to struggle with a sari that day. Sudhir returned, his eyes scanning the crowds to look for her.

'How's the khana?' he asked, sounding a bit distracted, his gaze flicking over his shoulder at the groom's family.

'I'll miss this food, that's all I know, trying to eat as much as possible before I go,' she said, trying to sound flippant about her impending departure. *No big deal, really.*

'When do you leave?' he asked, and she could hear the quiver in his voice. Not so nonchalant after all.

'Soon after the wedding,' she replied, and felt the silence creep over him. Then he shook his head and laughed.

'But you haven't seen anything of the city! I'm sure there's another church or two that you need to explore.'

'I've seen enough,' she said. 'I have just enough left in me to see this wedding through and then return. There's the whole university thing to tackle back home. My grandparents won't allow my parents back, my Badi Mummy...' She fell silent, searching for words to describe this impending loss, clearly written on the wall. 'Sudhir, she doesn't have much time left. And then, what will become of my Bade Papa? How will he stay here all alone?'

'Stay,' he said simply. 'Don't go back, not just yet. You don't know what might happen. Things have a way of resolving themselves.'

'Look at you, being so philosophical.'

He shrugged. 'I'll leave now. God knows what's happening at the morcha.'

'I'm finished here too. And this is criminal, but I can't finish this rasmalai. All right, I guess I'll see you at the wedding,' she said, turning to put away her plate. In a gesture that took her by surprise, he took the remaining piece of sweet from her bowl and ate it. And then he was gone.

Something made Sukanya turn around, feeling someone's gaze upon her. Aman stood in the distance, watching her, his brows knitted, his face flushed with rage. Sukanya was used to seeing Aman look tired, but did he always have those sunken, bloodshot eyes? He didn't say anything – just turned on his feet and left. She would have followed him, but one of Gumbi's aunts came by and took her by the arm.

'Ah, Sukanya lalli,' she said. 'How's everything going? How are you liking the taam-jhaam of this Indian wedding?'

'Yes, Bua ji,' said Sukanya, watching the retreating figure of Aman and wondering if he was going to the haveli where the mysterious Roshni read thick books and smoked slim cigarettes. 'This is all very nice.'

'Arrey bhai, what nice? Now everyone knows Gumbi is manglik,' said Bua Ji, helping herself to some more food. 'But Nandi bribed the pundit and got the kundali changed. She thinks she is very smart, but tell me, bitiya, can anyone change the girl's destiny? And what of that poor gabdu, he doesn't know he is being married to Gumbi under false pretences, does he?'

'Yes, Bua ji, I'm sure the planet Mars will manage Gumbi's destiny just fine,' said Sukanya automatically, wondering how soon she could leave without appearing to be downright rude. Bibi had told her that this particular aunt was given to extreme jealousy, and it was better to steer clear of her.

'Anyway, what is it to us?' said Bua ji piously, ploughing into the food.

'What indeed, Bua ji?'

31.

Meerut, January 2007 – A Brief Conversation with Puru

Sukanya glanced at her passport, lying next to her bag, a reminder that this sojourn was coming to an end. She sighed and sat down on the stool in front of the mirror, looking at herself, delaying getting dressed for as long as she could. All this time had passed, and what did she have to show for it? What could she have done better? Not falling for the local goonda–chhatra neta hybrid would certainly have been a good start. The face in the mirror looked back at her, her father's eyes flashing from it. *Come back now, Sukanya, enough of this.*

There was something that she had to do before leaving. She brushed her hair and put on her jeans and boots. There would be more than enough Indian finery at Gumbi's wedding the next day (finally!) but for now, she needed to feel like herself, not a pretend Indian princess. Then, without waiting for her inner voice to start protesting, she went downstairs and walked into the house next door. It was too early and too cold for

Rajni Mausi to be sitting outside at her sewing machine. Sukanya stepped inside, calling for Natwar.

Natwar was there, dressed in his usual checked tehmet and a dirty, holey vest, tending to some undefined broken appliance. A large blender? A small cement mixer? The house looked as unkempt as ever, piles of unattended laundry lying in a corner, splashes of water in the courtyard that nobody had bothered to wipe down, broken bits and bobs of a hundred different machines, and peeling walls that hadn't seen a coat of fresh paint in decades. Natwar brightened when he saw her and rose to his feet.

'Aha, look who's here first thing in the morning! Come inside, though you're already inside, ha-ha-ha! Should I get you milk or chai, gudiya?'

Gudiya, bitiya, lalli, rani.

'Chai is fine, Natwar Chacha,' she said, swallowing the lump that had appeared in her throat at the warmth in his voice. 'Is Puru Chacha in his room? May I see him?'

'Of course he is in his room. Where else would the nalayak be? You should drill some sense into that thick head of his. In fact, I was saying the same thing to Sudhir when he came to see him. Maybe you young people understand all this. But finally, it is Puru's kismet,' he said, walking to the closed door of Puru's room and banging on it with his fist.

'Puru! Abbey uth, darwaza khol! Sukanya is here to

see you,' he bellowed. A moment's silence. Then the door opened. Natwar walked off, calling his wife to make tea.

Puru's room was dark and dank, the kind of place that seemed to invite illness and despair. Sukanya squinted as she stepped in from the sunlight, struggling to make out the shapes, trying not to think of that other dark room where she had last seen Puru. He was standing next to his bed, dressed in a faded white vest and pajama bottoms. He reached for a shirt as Sukanya walked in, smiling at her.

'Come in, Sukanya,' he said. 'It's going to be a good day, seeing you first thing in the morning.'

This was the first time she'd seen him since he'd taken the pills. He had always been one of those tall, spare men who seem underfed, but now his ribs were sticking out. His cheekbones jutted out, his hair was longer and hung loose. *The body keeps the score*, they say, and his seemed to bear the marks of a recent tragedy, drooping down and hollowing out.

'Puru Chacha,' she said, not knowing what to say to this man who had been lonely enough to wish to sleep forever. This was the moment that had kept her away for days. He sat down on his bed, a sorry wooden affair covered with a tattered bedsheet. Sukanya went up to him and took his hands in hers. Puru was surprised, but he held on to her hand. He didn't trust himself to say anything, but he nodded to the spot next to him. They sat in silence for a while.

'Gudiya,' he said. 'If you hadn't come into the shop

that day...'

'Then someone else would have come,' Sukanya finished his sentence. 'I shouldn't be saying all this, Puru Chacha, given that I am younger than you, but things will get better. You will feel better. Don't despair.'

'It felt like bahaduri for a moment,' he suddenly said. 'Bravery, you know? As if I'd taken charge of my life for a single moment. Fearless, finally. Not looking over my shoulder, not wondering, not feeling worthless – just... in control. But afterwards, after they'd pumped my stomach, after I woke up, after I saw the nurses calmly going about their business...I feared it; I feared death. What is it I might have missed out on if I'd gone away?'

Sukanya had no words. He sat there, still clasping her hand, finally letting it go when Natwar's wife knocked at the door and entered with two cups of tea, her head covered with a long ghunghat as always, smiling at Sukanya.

'Did Puru Bhaiyya tell you why he took all the pills?' she demanded of Sukanya. Embarrassed, Sukanya shook her head and began to sip the tea aggressively, too milky, too sweet.

'I was telling *him*,' she said, referring to her husband, whom she was not allowed to address by name, 'that we should call Munto Baba. He'll help us get the bhoot-pret off Puru.'

Puru looked sickened by this. Sukanya coughed into her tea.

'There is no need for all that, Bhabhi. I will be fine.' Puru's spine straightened as he said this. His sister-in-law shrugged and left; she had to get her four squalling children dressed for the day.

'Sukanya, Bade Papa is looking for you,' Natwar called from outside.

'Coming!' Sukanya replied, rising to her feet. She turned around to take one last look at Puru. He wasn't her family by blood, but they were connected in a deeper way, this young man that she had brought back from the brink of death. There was nothing else left to say, except goodbye.

32.

Meerut, January 2007 – Gumbi's Wedding

On that winter morning, Sukanya stepped out onto the balcony outside her room, still in her dressing gown – a very English habit, as Badi Mummy liked to remind her – and craned her neck to look up at the sky, her hair up in rollers.

'Ah, Sukanya, all set for Gumbi's wedding today?' Sunita came out on her balcony to hang some washing to dry.

'Getting started, Chachi. But doesn't look like a clear day,' she said, pointing to the grey clouds gathering into woolly blankets across the sky.

'Yes, sometimes we get these storms in the winter; I'm sure it will clear up,' said Sunita, cheerful as always. 'Let me know if you need any help dressing up.'

That evening would be the saptapadi, the seven pheras that would bind Gumbi to her new husband. It was time to get dressed for the wedding. It was the weekend, and nearly everyone from the mohalla would gather in Bibi's courtyard from the afternoon and stay well into the night, to attend the pheras, and then bid goodbye to Gumbi in a tear-filled vidai.

Sukanya walked back to her room. She opened her suitcase, and as always, a bit of London perfumed the air. She took out the only sari she had carried with her, her mother's wedding sari, the one she had worn to the temple where she married Shila, the one she had repeated for the civil ceremony in the courtroom. The silken length of the gold muga sari, gifted to Api by Charu's mother after a trip to Assam, unfurled almost of its own accord on the bed. Sukanya touched its delicate, golden folds, and for a brief moment, the slightest bit of her mother entered the room. Her mother, who waited endlessly for the time she would come back home.

Mama, if only they could see you once.

She draped the sari, not struggling this time. Maybe she had finally learnt the art and science of it after all. A gift to carry back with her when she left. She made her way down the steps and then blinked in surprise, not quite believing her eyes.

'Badi Mummy, you're not in bed!' she exclaimed as she saw her grandmother, sitting in her wheelchair for the first time since Sukanya had arrived in Bulandwada, resplendent in a Banarasi brocade, flowers in her hair. Her grandparents laughed like children at her delight, exulting in the success of their effort. The secretive moments spent plotting and planning this moment had been worth it.

'I told you I'll get well enough to go for Gumbi's wedding,' said Badi Mummy. 'But here is the thing – now your Bade Papa will have to wheel me all over the place. But he can do it, for at least some time.'

'I'll do it, Badi Mummy,' said Sukanya, taking the handles of the wheelchair from Bade Papa, dressed today in a bandgala and his makhmal topi, a poet from another era, someone who played shatranj by the banks of the Yamuna. 'This is going to be a fantastic day.'

They made their way through the gullies of Bulandwada towards Bibi's courtyard, Badi Mummy taking in everything eagerly, as if seeing it for the first time. This had been her home forever; she had known no life outside of it. She knew everyone's stories, and they knew hers, and now they came forward to greet her, to ask after her health, and to express their delight at her appearance. Sukanya lost count of the number of times they stopped to meet and greet people.

'Sukanya, go now, take a look around; I'll stay with your Badi Mummy. Meet everyone, beta; you'll be gone soon,' said Bade Papa, as they reached the chowk. Sukanya, suddenly dispirited by the thought, smiled bravely at him and went off to find Bibi. When she glanced back, she saw him bending attentively to listen to what his wife had to say.

Brought up on a steady diet of Hindi films by Shiladitya, Sukanya had seen more than enough Indian weddings on screen, but still, nothing could have prepared her for this, an overwhelming demand on the senses. Strains of shehnai filled the air. Bright green mango leaves filled the space, the yellow of the marigold vivid against them, though of course mango season was still many months and a lifetime of loo-winds away, and Sukanya would be gone before then. Children darted about, no game tiring enough after their breakfast of milk and jalebis. Men in pagdis discussed the finer nuances of the dowry that Gumbi was taking with her. Women were dressed in their heaviest zaridaar Banarasi saris, saved for this day. Where would Gumbi be? Would she be covered in all of her finery already, silk veils and gold all over her body? Sukanya made her way through the throngs of people and bumped into Bibi.

Bibi always wore white, but today she, too, was wearing a new sari with zari on the border.

'Wow, Bibi, look at you!' Sukanya teased her great-grandmother. 'Be careful, you might give the oldies a collective heart attack!'

'Uff, nothing like that. Nandi gifted me this for Gumbi's wedding, that's why I am wearing this. Otherwise, you know me – always simply dressed,' said Bibi, trying to brush off Sukanya's comment. Sukanya, who could never quite decode the politics of sari exchanges in the community, let it go.

Someone came up to her holding a tray of glasses of sherbet. Just a few months ago, she would've refused it, finding it too syrupy, too cloying. But now, holding a glass of rose-flavoured, sweetened water, she could walk around, mingling with the guests. She was no longer a stranger here; she was one of them, everyone knew her, had spent time with her over the past weeks. There was Sunita, with her portly husband, looking wistfully at the clamorous children. And there was Natwar, discreetly drunk already, with his ghunghat-covered wife and their four brats in tow. Bade Papa and Badi Mummy sat in a corner, eating from the same plate. Rajni Mausi was there, not looking quite so miserable today, talking animatedly to Bibi who seemed to pay her no attention. Hari Mama was there, tending to someone's infant that had been deposited in his lap. Nandi and Atma Ram and their sons were there, busy tending to the million pieces of preparation that went into an Indian wedding.

This was the last of Sukanya's days here, and she was determined to see it through to the bitter end, the heartbreak and the hypocrisy, all of it.

33.

Meerut, January 2007 – An Unexpected Twist

Sukanya wanted to see Gumbi one last time before she went away. She searched for Nandi, tireless in her relentless pursuit of tasks for the day, to ask for permission. Nandi had been coiffed and dressed by professionals that day, draped in a bright crimson sari with a border golden enough to challenge the sun itself, her hair piled high in an overhead bun in an attempt to add height, and her feet in golden heels. Sukanya, momentarily blinded by all the shine and gleam, finally managed to corner Nandi for a moment as she paused for a breath.

'Aha, Sukanya,' Nandi paused to appraise Sukanya. 'Why are you wearing such a dull colour, hain? It's your sister's wedding! Hai, I wish your parents were also here on this day. Shila never even got to see my Gumbi. He was gone before she was even born.'

'Nandi Chachi,' Sukanya managed to squeeze a word in, amidst all the complaints and reminiscences. 'Do you think I could meet Gumbi for a minute?'

'Arrey, she has no time for anything today,' Nandi said proudly. 'She is going to the biggest beauty parlour in town for her make-up and hair. Her in-laws said that nothing but the best will do for our Gumbi. Don't tell anyone but they thought she looked a little dull on the day of the haldi.'

A rage began to build up in Sukanya's belly at this. Gumbi on the day of her haldi. That radiant, shimmering bride in yellow? Dull? How dare they? But before she could protest, Nandi was already moving on to have a tussle with Balram Halwai about just how much cardamom needed to be allotted to the kheer. Sukanya decided to go and seek out Gumbi, despite Nandi's protestations. She made her way up the staircase which was draped in marigold garlands, as was everything else in the house. Right outside Gumbi's door was a familiar figure, leaning against the wall and, as always, smoking. One more gift, one more lasting memory of Bulandwada. Presenting, Mr Sudhir Tyagi himself.

'How dare you smoke here?' she said, her voice gruff. He started, already beginning to extinguish the offending cigarette, before turning around and seeing her laughing face.

'Memsahib,' he said, shaking his head as he took a long look at her. 'I nearly burnt my finger, but all for a good cause, I say. Look at you, a vision in gold.'

'Nandi Chachi thinks I look jaundiced. Anyway, what are you doing here? Guarding the bride? No more morchas and dharnas?' she asked.

'I've been asked to ferry Gumbi to the beauty parlour and back,' he said, pointing to the door. 'She'll be leaving in a minute.'

'I don't think she needs to go anywhere. She's perfect the way she is. Listen, Sudhir, can I see her for just a moment? I just want to say goodbye.'

'No, I'm sorry but you can't,' said Sudhir, his voice firm. 'She must go to the beauty parlour. That is what her in-laws want.' This wasn't the response Sukanya had hoped for. She looked up at him questioningly, but he turned away, stubbing out the cigarette.

'Can I at least come along with both of you to the parlour?' asked Sukanya. He hesitated.

'Maybe not,' he finally said. 'You might be needed here. Stay here; enjoy the wedding.'

'Oh, okay,' said Sukanya, hurt by his refusal. She had imagined he would be delighted at the thought of her company, and here he was, brushing her off like an errant fly. 'No problem then; I guess I'll go back. Give my love to Gumbi.'

He called her name, but she was already walking down the stairs. Stupid, arrogant Sudhir Tyagi, the sentinel outside Gumbi's door. Well, she did not intend to beg him to let her see Gumbi. Sukanya flounced off and found Badi Mummy, who was looking tired now but determined to stay through to the bitter end. Sukanya sat next to her and looked around.

There was always so much happening in an Indian

wedding, she thought, never any shortage of drama. Visiting relatives found something to squabble over; someone always had some peculiar dietary requirements that drove the hosting family nuts, others demanded the most outlandish things, and yet, somehow, the whole juggernaut moved forward.

Outside the shamiana, the winter sun had already set. The music went from melodious shehnai to raucous Bollywood, getting louder and louder with every passing minute. Appetizers and mocktails were being served to the guests while less innocent beverages were organized outside the venue, out of the boot of a car. Judging by the throngs of young men, happily dancing, whatever it was, it was adequately potent. Frenzied children ran around like little whirlwinds. Sukanya marvelled at the sheer number of people who seemed to be around and wheeled Badi Mummy around when she wanted to see something or meet someone, which was every second minute.

Things hit a crescendo when word spread through the crowd like wildfire. *The baraat is here, the baraat is here!*

'Sukanya, you can go see the baraat with the other girls from the terrace,' said Badi Mummy. 'I will be okay. Bade Papa is here.'

Sukanya made her way up to the terrace with all the other excited girls in their lehengas and shararas, competing to find a good spot from where they could see the incoming crowd of the baraat. Everyone had something to say about the groom, mostly highly critical. He was proclaimed too short, too fat, too retiring, and by and large, no match for the beauteous Gumbi.

Then why didn't someone say something when all of this was being fixed! Sukanya wanted to ask, but the juggernaut was moving forward still. The girls from the terrace dashed downstairs once again, jostling each other, the silks rustling, the anklets clinking, the flowers in their hair slowly wilting. Now the baraat was being welcomed inside with a sprinkling of rosewater and garlands. Nandi was holding the large plate for the aarti, placing a tika on the groom's forehead. Gumbi's father-in-law, an unsmiling, domineering man by all accounts, led everyone into the enclosure. There was a sudden deafening roar of thunder, and dark clouds rolled together, melding into dark, giant shapes in the sky.

'Ha-ha, looks like it's going to rain.' Atma Ram, his head covered by a pagdi, apologized on behalf of the weather gods. The baraatis tumbled inside, eager to escape the rain which seemed like it could come any moment now. There was much hospitality extended their way, a steady supply of food and drink being brought forth immediately. Sukanya and her grandparents watched from afar. Bade Papa shook his head and sighed heavily.

'That's Durgesh ji,' he said, moving his face in an aside to Sukanya, referring to the groom's father. 'Very influential in these parts. So much land in Baghpat. Pity the boy is so unimpressive.'

For a while, the focus of the gathering was on feeding the newly arrived guests – most of them quite boisterously drunk – and making them feel like royalty. There seemed to be some commotion happening inside the house as well but it was par for the course for a chaotic Indian wedding. Sukanya first felt uneasy when she saw Nandi rush past, her face pale beneath the multiple layers of make-up applied carefully by professionals, her hair coming loose from the elaborate hair-do. What was the crisis? Perhaps Gumbi's appearance had not met the standards set by her exacting in-laws? If only Sudhir had agreed to let her come along, she could have helped. She turned back to Badi Mummy, who was now sipping on a garish-looking drink and enjoying herself immensely.

A few moments later, Sukanya saw Atma Ram abandon the groom and his guests and rushing towards the house, the increasingly more dishevelled Nandi in tow. Something was wrong. Had a fire broken out? Why was everyone rushing around? What had happened? Sukanya left Badi Mummy with her grandfather and walked towards the house to investigate.

Ripples of shock and confusion seemed to flow between the house and the mandap. Women stood around in groups, holding their hands to their mouths. Someone shrieked. And then suddenly, the chaos began to build into something sinister. Sukanya looked around, bewildered, feeling the panic thick in the air. She tried asking Gumbi's aunt, but the woman wouldn't say anything. Who would tell her what had happened?

Then she felt a soft, wrinkled hand slide into hers, and turned around to see Bibi standing there, pale-faced but erect. Bibi knew everything, as she always did.

'Take your Badi Mummy and go home before it gets really chaotic, Sukanya. There will be no wedding. Gumbi, that silly child, has run away.'

Sukanya gasped.

'Run away? When? Now?'

'Yes,' Bibi nodded. 'Nandi went into her room to accompany her to the mandap and turned out, the girl has left a note and gone off. Apparently, she didn't want to get married to that idiot, and who can blame her? Leave now, Sukanya.'

Sukanya made her way back to where the wedding guests sat waiting, buzzing with thoughts, her hands shaking. Gumbi had finally run away. How? When? Fragments of the last few days started floating back to her as she tried to make sense of Bibi's words. The memory of Gumbi's glowing face on the day of her haldi. She remembered Puru's voice of conviction the day before. Everything will be all right, Sukanya. How certain he'd sounded.

She found Badi Mummy and mumbled some excuse to her to leave immediately, ignoring her surprised questions. The news was travelling through the pandaal. She could see groups forming, a collective rage building against the errant bride, who had flung dishonour in their faces, surely, and must be caught and punished. Bulandwada was not the safe haven that had welcomed young Sukanya with open arms, now it was a convulsing pit of misogyny that was itching to put its hands around the disgraced Gumbi and strangle her, much like it did to anyone who tried to break its rules. She turned around and caught the look on Durgesh ji's face, a look of such rage that she shivered.

She pushed Badi Mummy's wheelchair through the crowds, trying to get out of the wedding venue. A torrent of thoughts surged through her. This had been planned. Both Gumbi and Puru had known it all along. This was not some impulsive, spur-of-the-moment decision on Gumbi's part. But they couldn't have done this alone, not the piteous Puru and that faint-hearted Gumbi. Somebody must have helped them plan this escape. But the only people who knew about their affair were Aman and she, Sukanya. Then, who had helped Puru and Gumbi escape?

Something made Sukanya glance up at the terrace, and Sudhir was standing there, a dark figure silhouetted against the dark, rolling clouds. The fairy lights adorning the terrace flickered on and off, casting brief, erratic glimmers. He was staring directly at Sukanya, a smile playing on his lips. Then, with a silent toast, he raised his glass, turned on his heels and vanished from sight.

The clouds finally broke, and rain started falling in thick drops, filling the air with a wet, earthy scent.

34.

Meerut, January 2007 – The Past Becomes the Present

Badi Mummy looked ashen. Sukanya watched her with growing anxiety as she lay there in bed, utterly exhausted after the events of the day. They had been caught in the rain on their way back from Bibi's chowk, and she'd just helped Badi Mummy change into dry clothes.

'Poor Nandi,' Badi Mummy kept murmuring. 'What will become of her? Why did Gumbi leave? Why didn't she say anything? Will she come back? We have known this heartbreak for so many years. Now they have to face it.'

Sukanya flinched, her throat tightening as she turned away. The full weight of the parallels between her parents escape and Gumbi's hadn't hit her till then. Now she thought of the shame to be heaped on Gumbi and Puru, perhaps forever estranged from these people and their homes. Why couldn't the parents of this place just understand their children a little better, be a little more forgiving, and bend a bit? Hot words bubbled to her lips, but she looked at her grandmother, defenceless and old, a shadow of the vibrant woman who had left for the wedding just a few hours ago, and bit them back.

'Bade Papa,' she turned to her grandfather, her voice soft. 'I'll go back and check on Bibi once. I don't want her to be alone.' Bade Papa nodded silently, his gaze fixed on his wife's face. Was he thinking back to when his own son had disappeared like this, never to return? Sukanya felt she was carrying the burden of her parents' shame once again as she hurried back down the gully, the ground still wet beneath her feet. It had stopped raining, but the swirling grey clouds above told her the storm wasn't over yet.

The whole neighbourhood was abuzz with the news of Gumbi's disappearance. People couldn't talk of anything else; wherever she looked, she saw small groups of wedding guests, whispering and exchanging gossip. About midway to Bibi's chowk, she saw Sunita, rushing home from the looks of it, still dressed in her wedding guest finery, her sari pallu tucked into her waist with a measure of purpose. She stopped to provide Sukanya with the latest bulletin.

'What a day! What a mess! I don't know much, but I'm told that Sudhir took Gumbi to the beauty parlour. He couldn't go inside, obviously – it being a ladies' beauty parlour, so he dropped her outside and our beautiful Gumbi just vanished from there. After two hours he went back to pick her up, and the girls at the parlour told him that she'd never even shown up. That is when he came back and broke the news to Nandi. Look, it must have been some boy. Why else would she run off like this?'

Sukanya kept silent. No one had yet figured out that the boy was, in fact, Puru. In this space of shared walls, and balconies that looked into the neighbour's windows and no space that could really be called private, Gumbi and Puru's love had been an utter, closed secret. Nobody but the three unwitting people, who had come to know of it by accident, knew of it. That moment on the terrace when Aman and she had spied on the two lovers meeting in silence felt like it belonged to another time, another life, an eternity away.

'What, uh, what is happening with Gumbi's family?' she asked of Sunita, dreading to think of it.

Sunita looked at her, her expression softening as she made the connection. She reached out, her hand landing lightly on Sukanya's arm.

'It will settle down, gudiya. Right now, there is utter chaos. I would've stayed back at Bibi's chowk to help, but my husband wasn't feeling too well, probably ate too much at the wedding,' said Sunita, already beginning to leave. Sukanya continued to Bibi's chowk, part of her resisting, her feet dragging, but she knew she had to.

At the chowk, everything was still glittering, still shimmering, but something had altered. It had gone from being a place of celebration, of festivity, of joy to something else. A storm had blown through the chowk, and nothing looked the same. The family, relatives near and far, stood around in tight clusters, whispering opinions and judgements. It was through these whispers that Sukanya pieced together the news that Gumbi's note had been found in her room.

I cannot convince myself to go through with this wedding, she had said, *and so I must leave.*

Nandi was sitting in the same spot where, just a couple of days ago, her daughter had applied her bridal mehndi. She was wailing loudly, surrounded by some women. Sukanya winced at Nandi's confused, painful cries. Nandi had not once stopped to think whether Gumbi wanted this wedding at all, or perhaps she had and chosen to disregard it.

The men were conspicuous by their absence. Gumbi's brothers and cousins had taken it upon themselves to find the errant girl and had taken off on their motorcycles. The baraat had returned, led by the icy Durgesh ji. The groom had started crying when he found out that Gumbi would not be marrying him after all, and his efforts had been met with a resounding slap by his father before being marched away. Bibi stood in a corner, her face stern as she watched the proceedings. Apparently, a police report would be filed. There was not much else that could be done; the girl was not a minor.

Sukanya sent a silent prayer up for the runaways. Oh, there would be hell to pay if they were caught. Where could they be right now? In some train compartment, hiding their faces? On the road, in some bus lurching along a potholed road towards some unknown destination? Where would they go? Would they try to get married? What would become of a pair like them? Would they return after a few days, when tempers had cooled, hoping for a reconciliation, much like Shila and Api had done all these years? Or were they be lost forever, paying a lifelong price for making this choice?

Suddenly, loud sounds of a scuffle broke out in the gully outside. Sukanya hurried out. What now? It became clear almost immediately what had happened. Puru's involvement in the Gumbi fiasco had been discovered. His note had been found by his simple-minded, ghunghat-covered sister-in-law, who had announced to anyone who would care to listen that Puru was the one responsible for the elopement.

Now, Natwar and his group were up in arms with Gumbi's brothers and cousins. Both sides had been drinking in celebration just an hour ago, and now it was a full-blown, free-for-all, with everyone eager to assign blame as quickly as possible.

Natwar, his face flushed with fury, was defensive and aggressive all at once, charging like a bull at anyone who came his way, going after the boys like his life depended on it. He was older than most of the other ruffians in the fight, but he had thrived on this kind of thing his whole life, and he was terrifying to watch in action.

Here he was, dragging a boy by the hair; there he was, pummelling another, and a moment later, he was landing a punch on yet another. Impromptu weapons were being fashioned out of bricks, sticks, and even entire bicycles, which the boys hurled at each other with all their might. Sukanya watched in perverse horror as some of the boys began to bleed.

Finally, some men from unrelated parties stepped in to separate the two sides.

'Bas, bas, that's enough,' they said to the two groups, guiding them away in two different directions. Even at this stage, someone or the other would throw a parting gaali, and a boy or two from the opposite side would try to break free to respond in kind until they were shepherded back into their group by the border collie-like peacemakers.

'Sukanya,' she turned to hear Bibi's call. 'Come inside; it's going to rain again soon. I don't think the storm is over yet.'

'I just came by to check if you're all right,' Sukanya said.

'I will be all right, gudiya,' said Bibi, with a sigh. 'That's the problem. Nothing ever happens to me. Well, come inside.'

'No, Bibi, I won't come inside. I'll go home for now and come back again in the morning.'

Bibi watched her walk back, her expression unreadable, her back straight.

When Sukanya returned home, she entered quietly through the heavy wooden door, intricately carved, that had come to mean home for her, Bade Papa was sitting in the dark in his usual spot in the dalaan, a drink resting beside him. The harmonium he had been playing was silent now.

'Has Badi Mummy slept?' she whispered to him.

'Yes,' he whispered back. 'Sit down with me, bitiya.'

Sukanya sat down, the events of the day running through her mind on a loop.

'Sukanya,' Bade Papa said in the dark, his voice coming from a distance. 'You were right.'

'Right about what, Bade Papa?'

'About calling your parents home.'

Sukanya sat there, a frozen part of the stillness of that moment. Had she heard it right? Would this really happen? Would Shiladitya walk through this doorway again, a much older man now, back to claim this missing piece of his life? Would her mother, a presence only felt but never seen in this house for the last two decades, truly be welcomed here, into this old dalaan, this comforting baithak, this smoke-blackened kitchen?

'What do you mean, Bade Papa?'

'Call them home, Sukanya. Tell them I said so. No more runaways, child.'

Bade Papa rose slowly to his feet, all of his years visible in that one moment. He patted Sukanya's shoulder and walked to the baithak where Badi Mummy slept. Sukanya sat in silence for a long while, unable to comprehend this day with all of its vastness. It was true, it was true! The thing she had wanted with all her heart was finally being given to her. Her parents would return. She wouldn't have to exist in two worlds at the same time. She could have two homes.

The old woman, known only as Badi Mummy ever since she gave birth to Shila, dreamed a dream. In this dream, she had floated to a distant land. Here, the regrets, the complaints, the resentment had all disappeared. Here she was insignificant, everything was insignificant, but also bound in the same fabric, all floating in the same fluid. Here she was finally rid of the pain that had faithfully followed her through the years. Here the body was no longer a troublesome appendage. But this wasn't a dream, the dream was what she had lived in for a fleeting moment. This was home.

When her husband went to wake her up in the morning, he found that sometime in the early hours of the morning, she had passed away in her sleep.

Her name was Shakuntala.

35.

Meerut, February 2007 – The Funeral

Grief is a many-headed monster, and Sukanya was to find out that she couldn't keep up with all of them. How relentless the pain was, not a moment without it. Bereavement and loss, what do we know of these things until we are brought face to face with them? The woman she had known for such a short while, and had loved from afar for so long, was nowhere to be found. The fire had claimed her, and then water, until finally she became the air that Sukanya was breathing.

Her parents were here now, something she had wanted all along, and yet there was nothing to celebrate.

'Sukanya,' Aparajita called as she came into her room. 'Come outside, the pooja will start soon.' Sukanya looked at her mother, unsure when or how this house had received her. But Api seemed to have been here all along, never once stumbling. She walked up and down the ageing house as if she had grown old with it. She opened old armoires, knowing exactly how they creaked. She made tea in the soot-blackened kitchen without needing to ask anyone where the sugar canister stood. She went over to Rajni Mausi's house, without faltering on the loose stone on the second step. Her bones had absorbed all of Shila's stories about Bulandwada and it could not be a stranger to her. She would not allow it.

Perhaps she had to, there was no choice. Everyone was looking at her to tell them where to step next. Shila seemed to be disoriented those days, parts of him scattered all over time, some flung back to his childhood where his mother called him inside after the day was done, some had travelled to the time he had met the beautiful girl he was to give up so much for, and others were back here in this house, where his father still sat in the dalaan, an old, spent man.

Shila had spent so long trying to push his past away that he had succeeded. None of this made sense anymore. He did not want to be back. Too late, Shila realized that it was his mother that he had longed for, now no more. And now, the axis of Shila's being, around which he had spun forever, had been taken off by a cruel god, and he had been flung off into space, no longer knowing which way to go, floating, floating, untethered. Only Api knew; only she could tell.

Bade Papa was lost too, staring for hours together at the vacant bed where his wife had lain, the life he had spent with her flashing through like a slideshow playing in the dark theatre of his mind. Click, she was sixteen, hiring a rickshaw to go to the bazaar, and turning around to give him that look. Click, the shehnai was playing 'Shubh Abhinandan' in Raga Kajari, they were getting married. Click, a boy, a boy, the midwife was telling him as Shila was brought to him. Click, click, click, it would go, till he felt a warm hand on his shoulder and looked up to find an almond-eyed woman standing there, a cup of tea in her hand, a glass of water; a hot meal. If only Shakuntala could have seen her once, he would think, and then the tears would come.

The endless rituals of a Hindu death. Sukanya sat in one pooja after another, the timeless sounds washing over here, the fragrance of incense, flowers, and fruit in the air. Even in this mourning, there was food and feasts. People had to be fed, people who could ensure her grandmother's soul a place in heaven. Api took care of all of it. Neighbours and family were always in and out of the house. Sukanya didn't need to pay heed. She would be told by Api to come outside and greet someone and stay a while until it was safe once again to retreat into her room, to lie down on her bed, wait for the day to pass. Bibi and Rajni Mausi and Natwar – they all came, and Sukanya witnessed their tears, but wrapped up in her own grief, she couldn't quite reach them. Aman came too, but she was sleeping at the time, and he left after meeting her parents.

On one day, all of Bade Papa's tuition boys came, looking uncomfortable, huddling together in an awkward group. Bade Papa met them and asked them vague questions about their coursework and exams. Sukanya looked for Sudhir among the motley crew, but he wasn't there. Something made her step out of the house to look for him, and sure enough, there he was, sitting on the chabutra, the sitting platform outside the house. She didn't say anything to that desolate figure; there were no words left. He looked up at her and remained silent. He had known loss, many times over, he seemed to say, and there was no easy way around it. She would have to cross the seven seas and climb the seven mountains of fairytales, only to meet the monsters, over and over again.

One day when she came downstairs, Shila was talking to Bade Papa while Api stood nearby.

'You have to move with us, Bade Papa, you have to. What is left here now? The house is falling apart, and I don't even know where to begin the repairs...It will be uninhabitable in another ten years.'

'It doesn't have to last too long, only till I do,' Sukanya could hear the sad smile in Bade Papa's voice.

'Bade Papa, please,' Shila was pleading. 'Don't do this. I cannot leave you here. I've organized your passport and visa. You just need to agree to come. This town is not worth it, Bade Papa.'

'Maybe, Shila, maybe. Kaun jaye Zauq par dilli ki galiyan chhorh kar? This is the only home I have known, this is where your mother lived and died. How can I leave this place? You people should return after the terahvi. I will be all right,' Bade Papa replied.

'Badi Mummy would have wanted this too,' Shila was saying, but he was already defeated. His bull-headed father would not change his mind.

The same conversation replayed endlessly in the old house, as Badi Mummy's death became a less recent event. Sukanya drifted in and out of these moments, dreading the day she would have to leave, leaving her grandfather behind.

Thirteen days passed. Soon, too soon, it would be time to return to London. And then one morning, Sukanya woke up in the morning without the pressing weight that used to greet her in the morning, the night before filled with dreams and visions of Badi Mummy, chasing her, calling her back. On that day, she sat in bed and realized that she felt lighter. She got out of bed, washed her hair, and then stepped out onto the balcony to dry it, the way women did in the gully, no hair dryer needed. She looked up and down the gully, as if waking up from a long sleep. Winter was departing; the sharp chill of the past days already gone.

She walked downstairs, feeling hungry for the first time in weeks. Api was inside one of the rooms, rummaging through some old trunks and trying to sort out things collected over decades. She would empty and lock some of the rooms, she said, to make the house easier to manage. It was a mammoth task, things hoarded over generations tumbling out of each corner, piles of possessions that must have meant something to the people who collected them, but the meanings had been lost to time. Bade Papa was downstairs; the remnants of his breakfast lay nearby – a far cry from the tea and rusks that Sunita used to bring. He was reading the local newspaper, a thinning, wan man. Sukanya tried to ignore the pang in her heart, trying not to think of him as he would be after they left. As she walked in, he pointed to something in the paper, his eyes lighting up briefly at her presence.

'Look at this, this Sudhir has now made it to the papers. It is an impasse,' he said, his voice tight with anger. 'How many times have I told this boy not to get into all this? He should back off now. This has gone on long enough.'

'What about that Jogeshwar Singh?' said Sukanya, taking the paper from him and reading the text slowly, trying to make sense of the complex Hindi words. There was a blurred picture of Sudhir too, his fist raised, his face contorted, amidst a crowd of protestors. 'He won't back off either.'

'Kal ke chhokrey,' spat out Bade Papa. 'They have no idea who they are up against. He'll wipe them all out. Why fight someone like that? It takes real idiots to not recognize the danger in something like this.'

Sukanya put the paper away, her thoughts drifting back to the day she had seen Sudhir after Gumbi's wedding. What had he done? Did he have anything to do with her disappearance?

'Bade Papa, any news of Gumbi and Puru?' she asked, dreading the answer.

'None at all; they seem to have vanished off the face of the earth. Natwar has left no stone unturned in looking for them, but to no avail. Poor man, someone told him they were seen in some relative's house in Saharanpur, so he ran there to look for them. It is all a wild goose chase, and listen to me, he's not doing it because he is afraid of what people will say about Puru being adopted. Nandi and Atma Ram have given up hope. Wahan, that Durgesh is losing his mind; a baraat returning with no bride, well, people have killed for much less. People are very vengeful in these parts, bitiya. Feuds continue for generations. People kill each other for revenge long after the reasons are half-forgotten. Khair, you should not think about all this now. You will be gone soon enough. Shila says you will join university this autumn.'

'I don't want to return, Bade Papa,' Sukanya said. 'Not without you.'

'I'll be fine,' said Bade Papa. 'How to uproot myself at this age? It would kill the tree!'

36.

Meerut, March 2007 – Back at Bibi's Chowk

When Sukanya went back to Bibi's chowk the next morning, it was as if Gumbi's wedding had been a fever dream, no more. There was no trace left behind; there were no forgotten marigold garlands dried out in the sun, no haldi or mehndi stains left on the ground; no mithai boxes lying forgotten in a corner. It was as if the wedding had not happened at all, erased neatly and thoroughly. There was sorrow in the air.

Sukanya walked around, feeling the Chaitra sun on her face. The parrots screeched from their cages. The dogs came to meet her, sniffing at her hands, welcoming her like an old friend. The earth was still spinning. Her worries and pain too would fade with time.

Bibi was uncharacteristically in bed. She had become thinner, and Hari Mama had told Sukanya she had been having trouble getting up in the mornings these days. 'What, Bibi, no more washing the house at four in the morning then?' Sukanya asked, as she took Bibi's hand in her, caressing the sole gold bangle that seemed to slide all the way up her shrunken arm.

'I only stopped doing that because I was running a fever,' declared Bibi with bravado, tears running down her face but some of her old spirit returning at the sight of Sukanya. 'Come, help me get up; I will make something for you.' Sukanya pretended to be hungry so that Bibi would cook and eat with her. Later the two of them sat on the stone steps outside Bibi's house, looking out at the chowk, each lost in her own thoughts.

'Is your Bade Papa going with you, then?' Bibi asked finally, she never took her son-in-law's name. Sukanya shook her head.

'You know how he is,' she said. Before she could say anymore, a couple of young men came running across the chowk towards Nandi's house. Sukanya recognized them – they were Gumbi's cousins, who'd been embroiled in the fight with Natwar on the day of Gumbi's wedding. They seemed agitated, their faces flushed with anger, shouting at Gumbi's brothers to come out. The young men came out to meet them and conferred in low voices. There would be trouble; it was clear in the set lines of their jaws and in the defiant gestures.

'Arrey lalla, what happened, where are you going off in such a huff?' called out Bibi, but the boys didn't answer, grabbing their cricket bats and hockey sticks and storming off. Nandi came out, looking stricken, her sari mussed, her hair uncombed.

'What happened, Nandi? Have they found Gumbi?' asked Bibi, now beside herself with curiosity. Nandi sat down heavily next to Bibi and put her head in her hands. Bibi stroked her head, and Nandi burst into loud sobs.

'They are saying it was Sudhir who helped Gumbi and Puru run away. He told us that she ran away from the beauty parlour, but it was all planned by him. He helped that lafanga Puru get a car and take Gumbi away somewhere. It was Sudhir who planned all this; even his dead father will not forgive him for this. I tied him a rakhi!' Nandi couldn't manage any more words, her body wracked by sobs.

Bibi's sounds of confusion and shock as she consoled the weeping Nandi washed over Sukanya, she felt herself shiver. *They had found out; they had found out. It was Sudhir, and they had found out.*

'Honestly, all this sounds like nonsense to me, Nandi,' Bibi now said. 'Why would Sudhir do that? Who is spreading all these rumours?'

'They say Aman told them,' Nandi honked into her pallu.

'Aman? That half-baked doctor from the haveli? What does he know? This is all just a big lie.'

Aman knew. Of course he knew. Sukanya felt her heart sink when she thought back to that evening on the terrace, Aman and her hiding in the dark while Gumbi and Puru spoke of their future.

'Why didn't you say anything, Gumbi?'

'What could I say? What could I do?'

'I could have asked your mother. She would have agreed.'

'Never. You know that. It is not just the difference in caste, Puru. My father has borrowed money from them. We are indebted to them. I could not refuse.'

It was their secret to keep. Hers and Sudhir's and Aman's. And yet, Aman had given it away. Sukanya felt a ball of fury building in her belly. Why did Aman do that? What would happen to Sudhir now? Who could protect him now? What could she do? She couldn't bear to sit there, waiting for something to happen.

'Bibi, I'll go home now,' she said. 'Bade Papa might be waiting for me.'

Leaving Bibi with the red-eyed Nandi, she hurried back home. News had travelled fast. Outside the house, Bade Papa and Shiladitya were already trying to talk sense into Natwar and physically restraining him. Natwar was unwilling to listen to reason, but he couldn't brush off Shila. *Oh Sudhir, Sudhir, what have you done?*

'Bade Papa, he is your student; I understand that, but I cannot let this pass. Sudhir instigated Puru to run away with Gumbi. Even if Gumbi's brothers spare him, I won't.' Natwar was in tears of rage, his too-long hair standing around his dark, stubbled face like a dark halo, giving him the appearance of a dramatic player in a Ramleela.

'This is not some medieval war, Natwar,' said Shila, his voice like cold water. 'They ran away because they felt trapped. The boy had nothing to do with it. Go back inside. I am still your older brother, Natwar. If that is true, you will listen.'

This kind of emotional manipulation was normally effective in such situations in the mohalla. Natwar finally acquiesced, and Sunita's husband, Sandeep, who'd been watching wide-eyed from a safe distance, took him inside. Shila and Bade Papa continued to stand outside, still worried for Sudhir.

'Bade Papa,' Shiladitya told his father. 'I don't like the look of this. Let's go and see how Sudhir is doing. I'll borrow Sandeep's motorcycle and take you to the university. They will listen to you, these avenging angels.'

Sukanya wondered if she too could go with them, but it was futile to even ask. It was too dangerous. After the two men took off for the university, the hours ticked by painfully. Api was still bustling around busily in one of the rooms. Once or twice she came outside to ask Sukanya to eat, but Sukanya had no appetite, a strange disquiet gnawing at her insides. Finally, when she was ready to scream with the strain of all the imagined scenarios flashing through her mind, Bade Papa and Shila returned, looking exhausted beyond measure.

'What happened, what happened?' Sukanya was beside herself with worry.

Shila parked the motorcycle and took the keys off the ignition. 'That Sudhir is a strange one. He didn't even deny his involvement in the elopement. He kept saying that someone had to do something, given how unhappy the girl was. The pair was hiding in his ancestral house in Asauda for a while after they got married. They are in Mumbai now. Apparently, Puru has even found a job in some studio.'

'But is Sudhir okay?' asked Sukanya. Shila gave her a long look.

'The boys from Gumbi's family have all backed off for now, and Natwar is under my watch, so things should calm down for now. We will see how it all comes along. Go, return these bike keys to Sandeep and come inside to eat. This town, the more it changes, the more it stays the same.' Saying this and shaking his head, Shila went inside.

It didn't last, the tentative peace that Bade Papa had brokered. Even before the moon had risen over the spires and terraces of the mohalla that night, news came that Sudhir had been stabbed.

37.

Meerut, March 2007 – The Stabbing Incident

It was all over the papers. Sukanya stared at the news articles, unable to quite believe that they were written about Sudhir, the words swimming before her eyes.

Student Leader Stabbed Amid Violent Protests: Tensions Escalate

Student Leader's Stabbing Sparks Outrage and Calls for Justice Amid Ongoing Protests

Sudhir Tyagi in Critical Condition After Tensions Boil Over

Bade Papa was getting dressed to go to the hospital, his hands shaking slightly as he tried to strap his watch on. He hadn't slept at all since the news came late the previous night. Shila had somehow convinced him to stay back until morning. Sukanya listened to them with half an ear, as she read and reread the papers.

'Aur karo yeh sab,' Bade Papa was in tears. 'This is what we get old for, to see our young ones die. That Jogeshwar Singh is a snake, he was waiting for something like this.'

'What happened to all the henchmen who were supposed to protect Sudhir?' asked Api, handing Bade Papa his walking stick. He had been using it more and more these past few days, and Sukanya ached to see how he seemed to struggle to keep his balance.

'Obviously, Durgesh ji pulled them back after Sudhir's involvement in Gumbi's elopement became clear. He won't support Sudhir anymore. I don't understand what that boy was thinking,' said Bade Papa, adjusting his topi.

Sukanya looked up at this.

'Durgesh ji? You mean Gumbi's father-in-law?' she asked, sounding clueless even to her own ears. 'What did he have to do with Sudhir?'

'He had everything to do with it, bitiya,' said Bade Papa. 'He was Sudhir's protector. The zamindars support these young leaders so that they have a strong relationship by the time they reach a serious level in state politics. And Sudhir, well, he is very gifted, isn't he? Everyone expected him to rise in the system.' The steam suddenly went out of Bade Papa, and he sat down on the chabutra, tears welling up. This had been too much for him. Sukanya stared at him in silence.

Durgesh ji, the sugarcane baron, had been Sudhir's protector, and yet, Sudhir had chosen to betray him. Why had he done that? He must have known all along that helping Gumbi escape would be the end of him.

She had to see Sudhir; she just had to.

'Bade Papa, maybe you shouldn't go,' said Api in a voice that brooked no argument and looked over at Shila for support. 'I really don't think you're in any shape for this. Let Shila go and see Sudhir.'

'Yes, I'll go,' said Shila, wondering why he hadn't thought of this himself. 'I'll find out everything, Bade Papa. Don't worry so much. He is a young man; he'll pull through.' Bade Papa went inside with Api, muttering something about Sudhir's father and how he had died the same way, caught in a violent struggle.

'I'll come with you, Daddy,' said Sukanya, as Shila turned to go. It was unclear why Shila did not protest. He only looked at Sukanya once, nodded, and went off to get Sandeep's motorcycle once again.

The narrow street outside the colonial-era, red-bricked hospital was completely clogged with vehicles. Of course small towns like Meerut treat bullock carts the same as large trucks on any given day and everything coexists on the same road. But on that afternoon, there was complete chaos. How any ambulance was supposed to get past the crowds was anybody's guess. The hospital itself had transformed into a veritable fortress. There were police vans and barricades everywhere, trying to hold off the hundreds of students who had descended upon the hospital, up in arms, shouting slogans. Local activist groups had also joined the protests. The air was thick with tension. Sudhir's stabbing had ignited something even in the most peaceful of students.

'If he makes it, Sudhir's career will take off. Just look at the number of students who've turned up for him,' said Shila, as he looked through the crowd for someone who could help them get through. In this city, which he hadn't visited for decades, he was still armed with the certainty that he would be recognized and helped. Sure enough, two of Bade Papa's tuition boys saw them, detached themselves from the sloganeering crowd, and came over.

'It's not safe here, Shila Bhaiyya,' said one of them, looking pointedly at Sukanya. 'You should go back.'

'It's okay, don't worry,' said Shiladitya, but the polish of London was clear in his voice. This was no longer home for him; he didn't know how things worked here. 'I need to see Sudhir. Who's the cop in charge?'

'That woman there. Be careful though; her brains are fried after all of this,' said the boy, and Shila nodded and walked off to talk to the police officer. Sukanya started to follow him when the boy called her back. Surprised, she turned around to face him.

'Sukanya, we've never met, but I'm Naren. I've something of Sudhir's to give you,' he said and took something out of his pocket, pressing it into her hand. She held out her palm to look at it. It was the taweez, the charm that Sudhir had taken to wearing around his neck these past few weeks.

'It had fallen off during the protest,' the boy said with a wry smile. 'He would probably say that he got stabbed because it fell off. He had real faith in it.' And then wiping away the sudden tears that sprang from his eyes, he turned around and swiftly ran back to disappear into the crowd of boys, stamping their feet and raising a storm of dust, the police struggling to force them behind the perimeter.

Wait, Sukanya called for Naren, but he was nowhere to be seen. Why are you giving this to me, she wanted to ask him. Take it back to that Tyagi boy who lies somewhere in this hospital, a few breaths away from death, no family to speak of. He needs it now more than ever before.

Shila came back, looking harassed and fatigued. Apparently, the officer had been cordial, but had told him in no uncertain terms, that nobody could meet Sudhir. Not without her losing her job, anyway.

'It's just too risky,' he said. 'They are not letting anyone go past. He is in the ICU, it looks really bad. And you can see what a political wildfire this had become. When you strike at a king, you must kill him, right?'

'Can't we see him for just a minute?' she asked.

'No, the police are afraid they will try to finish the boy off. But somehow I think Sudhir will be all right. How does that line go, *Why should I be afraid now? Strange men have come to kill me ever since I twelve years old.*'

Shila made sense of things through books whenever he was nervous. Both Api and Sukanya knew this about him. Sukanya suddenly realized that in all the time that he had been away, her father had become a bigger stranger to this town than she was. It now frightened him in some ways, with its unpredictable restlessness and its underpinnings of chaos.

Sukanya took his hand in hers, the din around them growing louder and louder.

'Let's go back, Daddy,' she said.

'Are you sure?' he hesitated. 'Yes, you're right. Your mother must be waiting. Let's go.'

'No, Daddy,' she said. 'I meant let's go back to London.'

38.

Meerut, April 2007 – It's Goodbye Once Again

Api was packing; it was time to leave. In her last few days in Meerut, Sukanya took to roaming the gullies of Bulandwada, trying to impress each detail upon her soul so that it would last her a lifetime. She climbed the stone steps outside the houses, touching the heavy, wooden, panelled doors with their elaborate, intricately carved borders. She looked up at the chajjas, the overhanging eaves, supported beneath by heavy brackets, and at the decorated, arched gateways.

She sat on one of the two identical chabutras outside these houses, one on either side of the door, and watched the monkeys in the higher reaches, up to their usual antics. She placed her sunglasses in one of the two niches built into the wall above the platform and listened to the sounds of the mohalla – the temple bells, the hum of televisions, the sizzles and clinks of people's kitchens, the barks of street dogs, the cries of the sabzi-wala, the knife-sharpener, the balloon-seller – all of this to carry back.

This mohalla would disappear too, like many others had. Already cement had covered the original sandstone used to build the houses. In some homes, the open pavilion around the courtyards had been enclosed to create rooms, and the jharokhas were giving way to balconies with wrought-iron railings. Yes, all of this would disappear, and she would almost certainly never return. These were her last few glimpses into her past.

She would think back to all that had happened during her stint in Bulandwada and unable to make sense of its floating, dream-like contours, give up before too long.

Sudhir was still critical. Bade Papa had taken to going to the hospital every day, just to get news of the boy, nobody was allowed to see him just yet. Would Sudhir recover in time for her to see him before she left? Or were the wounds too much, and would he...no, she would not think about it.

Bade Papa wanted the house transferred to his son, and Shila was perpetually at the Town Hall or at the lawyers, trying to make sense of the timeless laws that governed a house such as theirs, difficult to define, difficult to name, difficult to bequeath. Api seemed more and more exhausted each evening. Sukanya would come home and find her sitting in a chair, looking completely drained after the day's labours, trying to find meaning of the past decades in the objects that populated the house, each one marked with invisible memories. If only she could make sense of the house, perhaps she could make sense of the lost years too.

'Mama, all you have done since you got back is stay in the house and sort through stuff,' Sukanya finally told Api one evening. 'Tomorrow, you're coming for a walk with me; we will explore the mohalla, and we will go and eat chaat for lunch.'

Api was loathe to go; the house was comforting, and she didn't really want to face the neighbours, but when Sukanya prodded her again the next day, she changed into a sari and agreed to step out. Sukanya guided her through this gully and that, and Api marvelled at how adept her London-born daughter seemed to be at navigating the maze of that neighbourhood – how she knew everyone, and everyone knew her. Api would have liked to walk through these pathways with Shila, to be introduced to the inmates as the mysterious Dugar girl that Shiladitya had forsaken everything for, but her husband seemed so disconnected these days. All he could talk of was his impending return, the endless red tape that he needed to unravel after Badi Mummy's death, and how everything would be better if they were all in London. Bulandwada had become Sukanya's inheritance, Shila wanted nothing to do with it anymore.

It was a strange day. Sukanya and Api spent it shopping at the local bazaars, small gifts and trinkets to take back to London, and eating at the roadside stalls and stepped into the various temples that lined the neighbourhood, some of them dating back to Vedic times. All the while, Api tried to see everything through Shila's eyes. And thought of the house with the Nathdwara pichwai, from which she had been banished forever. What would happen if she were to return today? Who would she meet? What would they say? How does one end an estrangement? How did one claim their legacy?

'Come on, Mama, let's go to Bibi's chowk,' she was pulled out of her reverie by Sukanya's voice. She looked at her daughter, tall and proud, her hands full of prasad and flowers given to her by the priest at the Hanuman temple. 'We will give some of this to her.'

Api was hesitant, she didn't like the chowk with all its surrounding houses and endless windows, windows through which people seemed to peer down at her with great disapproval. But Sukanya seemed happy at the thought of seeing her great-grandmother again. Api had found the stern, old woman quite forbidding but it was clear how besotted she was with the curly-haired girl with the same flashing eyes as her own. She would be heartbroken when Sukanya left for London, that much was certain.

'All right, let's go, but not for too long. There is some stuff I need to sort out at home,' she said.

Bibi was looking a bit better that evening and was sitting on a charpai, eating a guava. She hadn't lost a single tooth to age, she often told Sukanya, who insisted that she was lying and wore dentures. Nandi saw them sitting with Bibi and brought them tea and a plate of sweets.

'Why the mithai, Nandi Chachi?' asked Sukanya, taking a barfi, remembering how Badi Mummy liked this soft, milky sweet.

'Arrey, that Gumbi is coming back, na,' said Nandi, smiling broadly behind her pallu, feeling shy in the presence of the polished Api.

'What?' Sukanya couldn't believe her ears, the mithai frozen in her hand. 'What do you mean? Gumbi is coming back? Here? When did this happen? What about Puru Chacha?'

'Damaad ji is also coming,' said Nandi.

Sukanya gawped at Nandi in complete silence. Damaad ji, aka Puru Chacha? How did one even begin to make sense of this?

'Don't be surprised, lalli, this always happens,' interjected Bibi, seeing Sukanya's stricken face. 'After all that drama, these morons have accepted the girl's decision. Now the newlyweds are coming back to meet everyone. Puru has found a job; suddenly everyone has become very progressive and agrees that he is a very good match for Gumbi.'

'Um, that's great,' stammered Sukanya, not knowing what to say.

'What's so great about it? If they had listened to the girl before becoming moral police, none of these theatrics would've had to take place. Wahan, that Sudhir is ready to kick the bucket because of everything that happened, and over here these idiots are getting the pooja thaali ready to welcome the prodigals.' Bibi shook her head in disgust, and continued to eat her guava.

'Arrey, Bibi, the times are changing,' said Nandi piously, as if she were the one who had advocated for this reconciliation. 'We should also keep up with them. There's no harm in such marriages. I saw the mother in *Kkahani Rishton Ki* say the same thing.' *Kkahani Rishton Ki* was Nandi's favourite soap opera, and she took all of her life's advice from its myriad characters, constantly embroiled in some domestic crisis or the other.

'She could have said it in last month's episode,' said the indefatigable Bibi. 'Could have saved us a lot of heartache, and Sudhir a stab wound.'

'Here, bahu, eat barfi,' said Nandi, ignoring Bibi completely and addressing Aparajita. 'You've been through the same thing, running away from home and all that. You ought to understand. Tell me, am I right or wrong?'

Api looked like a deer caught in the headlights. Sukanya jumped to her rescue.

'Mama, we should leave now, don't you think?' she suggested, and Api rose with impressive alacrity. They left Bibi's chowk still hearing the old woman giving Nandi an earful about her hypocrisy. Bibi didn't take any prisoners. Api wiped her brow, glad to have escaped, and they slowly walked back home.

'What is this place?' she asked as they crossed Nawabon Ki Haveli, noticing its unusual symmetry and deisgn. 'It must have been beautiful once. It still is.'

'The people inside, not so much,' said Sukanya, thinking of Aman's betrayal. She suddenly wondered if he would be home. There was a lot she wanted to say to him, and not much time left. 'Want to go visiting, Mama? I know the folks here.'

'You seem to know everyone,' said Api. 'All right, let's visit, but just for a few minutes, okay? I don't think I've much left in me for people's antics in this place.'

Sukanya led the way to the small window-gate and bent down to enter the courtyard. Dusk was falling now, and she knew that Basheeran would have long since left after completing the day's tasks. She stood in the courtyard and called out.

'Aman, are you home?'

'He's not,' she heard Roshni's voice from inside. Then Roshni herself appeared, as always, holding a book she must have been reading. 'I haven't seen you in ages, Sukanya. I just got back. I was in Banaras for a...'

Exactly why Roshni had travelled to Banaras, Sukanya would never know, because Roshni stood frozen, the book slipping from her hand with a thud. Beside her, Sukanya felt her mother stiffen and then heard a strangled cry escape her.

'Gulshan,' said Api in a near whisper. 'Oh Gulshan, it's you.'

39.

Meerut, April 2007 – Gulshan, Again

Api, pale as if she had seen a ghost, looked as though she might faint at any moment. Sukanya and Gulshan helped her into a chair on the verandah, next to the courtyard. Gulshan switched on the rusty ceiling fan, and it laboriously whirred to life. The air began to cool. Api's eyes were fixed on Gulshan, unable to look away.

Gulshan seemed to have aged in a straight line, Api thought. She was the same she'd always been, only a little wrinkled, scrawnier, whereas she, Api, had been shattered into pieces and put together again, never quite the same again, a patchy, fractured imitation of her old self.

'How are you here, Gulshan? Why are you here?' Api kept asking her cousin, piteous in her bewilderment.

'Hush, now, Api, sometimes Basheeran comes back if she's forgotten something. Hold on a minute,' said Gulshan, and went off to lock the gate, which creaked in protest at this unusual demand on its old hinges. 'Yes, now it's safe. We can talk.'

But Api couldn't quite frame her questions. Sukanya had no such hesitation. She had plenty to ask and did not wish to hold back for a moment longer.

'You are *that* Gulshan, my aunt? I've heard so much about you,' she said, peering at her. 'When did you change your name? And why? What about Aman? Why does he call you his aunt? He can't be your nephew.'

Gulshan sighed and held up her hands, looking at Api worriedly. She poured her some water, then disappeared into the kitchen to make her the panacea for all ills – a cup of chai. She brought it out in an old porcelain cup, faint cracks visible on its surface. Api took a sip, and something about the familiar taste of cloves and cinnamon finally unlocked her tears. She cried silently while Sukanya and Gulshan watched. Finally, when Api seemed a little better, Gulshan took her hand in her own and spoke.

'Listen to me, Api, I had no choice. Let me start from the beginning. Once I got married, I thought it was all over for me, I was to be a shopkeeper's wife, no more. But all was not lost, Api, the man I married turned out to be my biggest blessing. Once he found out what had happened to me, the whole fiasco, he said he would support me, but I had to study in secret. We moved to a different town, supposedly to set up a business, and I continued my studies.'

'That's good,' said Sukanya, looking at her mother to prod her into saying something, but Api kept silent. Gulshan continued with her story.

'We decided not to have children till I finished my master's, and then my post-doc. He lied to his family, told them that he was medically unfit to have children, Api. Can you imagine that? It bought us a few years. Sometimes, I feel that he came into my life just for those years – to watch over me while I studied. A man who had himself never studied past grade eight.'

'Where is he now?' Api finally asked. Gulshan went quiet at this, removing her glasses and rubbing her temples.

'Just as things were starting to look better, we found out that all the years of khaini and cigarettes had finally caught up with him. He had aggressive throat cancer, very advanced by the time he went to the doctors. They said it had spread everywhere, and there was nothing they could do.'

Both Sukanya and Api listened, spellbound. Gulshan, the brightest star that family had ever seen, forced to study in secret.

Gulshan spoke again, looking at Api. 'Remember how Chacha ji used to get so enthusiastic about astrology every once in a while? He would draw our kundalis and spend hours poring over the planetary configurations guiding our lives and futures. Antardasha, Mahadasha, Shani this, Brihaspati that! Sometimes I want to ask him, did the planets ever tell him that my life would be spent in secret, that I would always be hiding, as if I'd done something terrible?'

Gulshan went quiet once again. Shadows were lengthening in the verandah. Sukanya felt compelled to ask what happened next, but before she could do so, Gulshan picked up the narrative that had fallen by the wayside.

'Once my husband passed away, I was faced with a choice again. Go back to his hometown and take up the role of his widow in a sprawling joint family. Or disappear once more and begin my life anew. This was what he wanted me to do. Soon after his funeral – the house was full of relatives who had come for the last rites – I left in the dark of the night, never to return. I moved to an obscure town, you wouldn't have heard of it, changed my name, and started teaching in a school, continuing my own coursework alongside. I got my doctorate, and when I found out they needed a professor in this town, I moved here, thinking that nobody knew me here, and I knew nobody.'

Gulshan smiled wryly, looking at Sukanya.

'How did you meet Aman?' asked Sukanya, listening to this fantastic account and trying to gather as many bits as she could, to put together this puzzle of a thousand pieces.

'It was serendipity, more than anything else. I was admitted to the medical college after a particularly bad bout of malaria, and he was just a student there. We started talking, and he found out I was looking to rent a quiet place. He needed the money, and he told me I could just tell everyone I was his aunt, that all sorts of people from his family stayed in Nawabon Ki Haveli, and that I'd be safe.'

'Aman needed the money?' echoed Sukanya, surprised. Didn't Aman come from a family of wealthy merchants? Why would he need to rent out his ancestral mansion?

'No amount is enough when you're funding an addiction,' said Gulshan with a sigh and a wave of her hand. 'He has a real problem, that boy. At first it was just alcohol, and once in a while, he'd go off to the local shops to buy bhaang. Then he started smoking weed, and now, of course, it's steadily getting worse. I think he is on dhatura and diazepam, or something worse. Who knows? He doesn't tell me.'

'Gulshan, you shouldn't be staying here.' Api seemed to come back to life, her eyes wide as looked around wildly at Nawabon Ki Haveli, no longer the beautiful residence of some long-gone royalty, but a sinister place, home to the most wretched dregs of society. 'Come, live with us in London. Shila would love to have you. And Sukanya too.'

Gulshan laughed softly at this. How innocent Api had remained, even after all these years.

'I can't move to London, can I?' she said with a rueful smile. 'No, Api, I've built my life here. And this haveli, it's fine, for now. I don't owe Aman anything, but I do feel concerned for him. I mean, he goes up in flames every time I bring up his troubles, but how can I just abandon him and walk away? And anyway, it's still not safe for me to go back to being Gulshan, and I don't think it ever will be.'

'You could just disown your biological family, couldn't you? Legally I mean? Have nothing to do with them,' Sukanya said, wondering at the power their families still held over these ageing women. Gulshan and Api exchanged a look.

'We could disown them,' Gulshan replied. 'And we have, haven't we? But if we try to be too brazen about it, they come at you with all the force of nature. I don't think I want that.'

'Did you know who I was?' Sukanya shifted the topic, still trying to piece together this tangled narrative. Gulshan smiled, as if she'd known Sukanya had always suspected she was not who she appeared to be.

'Well, I had heard bits and pieces about one Shila Pandey, the brightest boy from Bulandwada who crushed their collective heart when he ran off with a beautiful girl. I always knew that it could be the same Shila that Api had eloped with, but I didn't want to enquire too much, in case someone linked it back to me. Of all the mohallas in all the towns in all the world et cetera. When you arrived here, Sukanya, it was more or less confirmed. Everyone says you look like your father, and you do, but Api does lurk there somewhere. Then, when you said that your mother had once lived on

Shankar Marg, I knew for certain. I just didn't expect to see Api here, knowing that she was persona non grata with the Bulandwada regime.'

Api smiled faintly at Gulshan's turn of phrase, sharp as ever.

'She was asked to come back when Badi Mummy passed away,' Sukanya said automatically, her eyes focussed on something distant. 'They all come around in the end, after wasting years and years. Maybe it's a good thing that Gumbi's family didn't wait that long before coming to their senses.'

'What happens next?' Api looked at Gulshan, her voice filled with the same curiosity as when they were children, playing under the maulsari tree in the garden, Gulshan spinning intricate stories out of thin air, and Api always asking, *what happens next*?

'Nothing happens,' said Gulshan, patting Api's arm gently. 'You'll go back to London soon and get on with your life. And I'll do the same out here.'

'Pretending to be this...this...Roshni something?' Api's voice cracked. 'Living here in this strange haveli, in this dying mohalla, pretending to be some drug addict's family?'

'It's not so bad,' laughed Gulshan. 'I mean, I could have come up with a better name, but Roshni is non-committal, don't you think? And what outrageous fortune did being Gulshan bring me anyway that I should want to resurrect her?'

'And so we are just supposed to get up and walk away?' Api's voice was sharp now.

'I see no other way for you to get home, Api. Unless you take a rickshaw.'

At that, Api did get up, her nose turning up in that unmistakable gesture of annoyance, the one that Sukanya and Gulshan both knew too well. Sukanya watched helplessly as her mother stormed out, struggling with the creaking gate for a moment before finally managing to wrench it open. Sukanya made to follow her, but Gulshan placed a hand on her arm.

'You understand, don't you, Sukanya? I couldn't unravel this web, even if I tried,' she said, her tone no longer light. 'Take care of your mother. Be good to her. Move forward. There's really no point in looking back at all the would-haves and could-have-beens and if-onlys. Just take the next step, whatever it is.'

Sukanya squeezed her aunt's hand, then turned and walked out into the gully. Her mother stood there, her back turned to the haveli, sulking like a child. Yes, it had really been a strange day.

40.

Meerut, May 2007 – The Return of Gumbi (and Puru)

Gumbi returned to Bulandwada, this time a much-married woman, all of her old diffidence gone. She spoke comfortably of her new life in Mumbai, where she lived in a crowded chawl with hundreds of others, the roads always abuzz with traffic, and the ocean calling at all hours of the day.

Puru followed her around, ever the devoted husband, fetching her new shiny purse when she asked for it, taking her to the tailor to get new salwar-kameez stitched, and visiting her old friends. Sukanya couldn't quite believe it was the same girl who had once lacked the courage to stand up against a forced marriage. The elopement had clearly given her a great deal of strength. Now she ordered her new husband around and wore bold shades of lipstick. Puru had apparently found a job in a film studio, archiving and cataloguing their film library, a job he had prepared for his whole life. It was a well-paid position, and Gumbi was making the most of the newfound respect that came with it.

As expected, Bibi had a lot to say about it.

'Le bata,' she started when she saw Sukanya a couple of days before her flight was due, there to collect some of her things that she had left at Bibi's house. 'Who would have thought that Nandi and I could ever be related? Not really by blood, given that Puru is adopted, but still. Bhagwan knows I've always considered him my grandson. And now this Gumbi caterpillar has grown wings. She is lording over all and sundry, won't get up to even fetch herself water, won't put her dishes away after eating. Why isn't she going to her in-laws' house? You tell me. Rajni is useless, of course, I have no idea how she is my daughter, but that Natwar will put Gumbi in her place in no time, if she tries to show him any airs and graces.'

'Maybe that's why she is not going there, Bibi. Have you considered that? It's all good, Bibi, let it go,' said Sukanya, putting her clothes in a plastic bag to carry them back to Api, who was almost done packing. 'It's better than never opening her mouth and expressing herself.'

'Yes, but it cost that poor, motherless boy his life, didn't it?' said the ever-sharp Bibi.

'Sudhir is not dead yet, Bibi,' snapped Sukanya, before realizing that Bibi was giving her a shrewd look.

'Will you go and see him before you leave, lalli?' Bibi

asked, her tone softening slightly. Sukanya shook her head.

'It's unlikely. They are not allowing anyone except the closest family members to see him, Bibi,' she said.

'Well, something tells me he would have liked to see you, close family member or not,' Bibi said, sighing as she pulled herself up to her feet. Her knees creaked but only a little. 'Once you leave Bulandwada, I don't think you will ever return. At least go and see the boy. Ask what's-his-name, that doctor from Nawabon Ki Haveli to help you. He is not good for much else. I ran into him in the gully the other day while I was feeding the dogs, and he smelt like some of the Naga babas I've seen in Rishikesh and Banaras, the ones who smoke chillum. Khair, what's it to me. But if these are the doctors we'll be getting, I am better off relying only on Ricks.'

Bibi wouldn't let Sukanya go back that evening, so she stayed. Sukanya hadn't seen Aman since Gumbi's wedding. She was certain it was by design, but she knew she had to say her goodbyes – to him, to Sudhir, to everyone. That night, after dinner, she messaged Aman, asking him to meet her. To her surprise, he replied almost immediately.

In Bulandwada for tonight. See you on the terrace in ten minutes.

Bibi had gone over to Nandi's house for yet another pooja being held in Gumbi's honour. Sukanya knew she would be invited too if anyone saw her, so she tried to sneak up the stairs quietly, making her way to the terrace. But just as she was doing so, she bumped into someone.

'Puru Chacha, where are you coming from?' she asked, smiling as she caught the sharp scent of cigarette smoke clinging to him. He'd clearly tried to mask it with cardamom and fennel, but the faint trace was unmistakable.

'Bas, nothing, gudiya, just went up for some fresh air,' Puru said, relieved to see that it was just Sukanya. 'Come, sit with me for a minute. I heard you'll be gone soon.'

'I'm glad everything worked out with you and Gumbi, and I got to witness it,' Sukanya said. But Puru looked away, his face momentarily clouded with a fleeting expression of unhappiness that left Sukanya feeling disconcerted.

'What happened, Puru Chacha?' she asked, leaning in to whisper. 'Is everything okay in Mumbai? Do you like it?'

'It's a dump,' said Puru, flatly, with surprising intensity. 'I've never worked this hard in my life. We live in a tiny room in a chawl, with four other people. The local trains... uff. The stench, the crowds, the heat. It's unbearable. The people have all turned into zombies, Sukanya, like in the movies. Everyone is part-dead.' He shuddered at the memory. Sukanya looked at him in silence.

'But you get to be with Gumbi, and you wanted that all along,' she said, trying to offer some encouragement.

'I have realized one thing, Sukanya,' Puru replied, his voice low. 'That city comes with its own frequency. People like Gumbi, they're tuned into it, but people like me? We never will be. Not there, not ever.'

'Give it time, Puru Chacha. It will get better.' Sukanya offered, not knowing what else to say.

'No, gudiya, I don't want to wait. I want to come back. I want to return to FML, to our ramshackle house with Mummy and Natwar Bhaiyya and Bhabhi and the children. They aren't even talking to me, and I feel lost without them. I want to be next door to Bade Papa. I want to have naankhatai and kulhad ki chai. Sometimes I get so homesick I start crying. I don't want anything more than this mohalla.'

'Well then, you could come back to Meerut. Now there is no problem, everyone accepts your decision,' Sukanya said.

'Gumbi says she will leave me if I do that,' Puru said, his head slung low. 'She says she's waited a lifetime to be able to leave Bulandwada. She doesn't need me to stay in Mumbai. There are plenty of single women there, living on their own. Someone in the chawl even offered to get her a job as a junior artist. You know, dancing in films. She is beautiful, and she can dance. I am sure she'll find work before long. Mumbai recognizes her own, and Gumbi is one such.'

Sukanya nodded, the truth of his words sinking in. Gumbi looked like she had finally found her place. She was thriving in the way people do when they are planted in the right soil.

She couldn't help but think back to that moment in the DVD shop, when the desperate Puru was willing to give up his life for Gumbi. And now here he was, already regretting his decision.

And all the while, the one who had orchestrated it all – he was hanging by a thread, teetering between life and death. The sudden reminder of Sudhir brought her back to the present. Aman, she remembered, I've to meet him.

'I'll speak with you again, Puru Chacha, I need to finish some work,' she said. After saying goodbye to the despondent Puru, still sitting there on the stairs, she made her way up. Aman was already standing there. He was thinner than he had ever been, a little paler. Sukanya took in his face, the dimples caving on either side of his face, the eyes half-closed in mirth, and his hair speckled with a bit of red-gold. How beautiful and how cruel he looked, like a Greek god about to pull a prank on a mere mortal. He coughed as he saw her enter and took out a joint from his pocket, his hands trembling slightly. He lit it, took a deep drag, and offered it to Sukanya. She shook her head.

'You'd better be careful with that stuff,' she said. 'You are getting quite a reputation as a nashedi with the local populace.'

'Well, thanks, narc,' he scoffed, making her bristle

at once. Gone were the honourable intentions to keep it civil.

'Smoke up all you like, Aman. I just want to say – I hope you're wracked with guilt. And I hope you're not sleeping at night.'

'I sleep like a baby, thank you, ma'am,' Aman replied. 'And I don't know what you are so upset about.'

'You know exactly what I am talking about. Why did you tell everyone about Sudhir's involvement in Gumbi's elopement? It's because of that that Durgesh ji pulled his men back, and Jogeshwar's men had full access to him. They fucking stabbed him!'

'Hmmm, quite like the heroic Abhimanyu in that sense but I don't know if you get the reference. Broadly speaking, do not get into a mess that you don't know how to get out of.'

'What's come over you, Aman? What did Sudhir ever do to you? He might die, for God's sake.' Sukanya felt the angry tears welling up and brushed them away.

'I should ask you the same question, Sukanya,' Aman snarled suddenly, his eyes bloodshot. 'What's come over you? He's a ganwaar nobody, a two-bit goonda, born and raised in this violent, sickening hellhole, and you're carrying on with him?'

'Oh, so that's what's bothering you? That I should like him over a ganja-smoking doctor-to-be? That's all there is to it – that you are jealous?' she heard her own voice rise in rage.

'Yes, that's all there is to it. So tell me, how does it feel to go slumming with the nobodies?'

'Tell me, how are you going to be a surgeon with those trembling hands?'

'Fuck off.'

'No, Aman, you fuck off. And while you are at it, jump off the nearest terrace too.'

They stared at each other in silence, furious, fangs-bared furious, but already their fury was slowly subsiding. Aman sat down on one of the platforms on the terrace and put his head in his hands and passed the joint to her. Sukanya took a drag, sat next to him, and stared out at the twinkling lights of the mohalla in the distance, its sounds travelling up and wrapping around them. Minutes passed.

'How are you doing?' he asked, once again sounding like the old Aman, the friend who would jump over terraces just to see her for a moment, invite her into his home, and laugh at her badly told jokes.

'Pretty shit,' she said with a strange laugh-sob. 'I miss Badi Mummy terribly. I feel like I failed her in some way. My father is like a lost toddler ever since he got back, almost like he's coming here for the first time. Mama's doing some sort of intense self-therapy by sorting through truckloads of pointless things in the house. And Bade Papa...every time I think of leaving him here, all alone, I feel like my heart is being yanked out of its cavity. So yes, pretty shit.'

He reached out and took her hand.

'Such a brown girl. I like you, Sukanya. So much,' he said, his voice muffled. 'I always have.'

'I know,' she said. 'But that's a hell of a way to let someone know this. And honestly, it's a very Meerut move for someone who claims to despise the place.'

'I've stopped thinking straight,' he nodded, wiping his face with his sleeve.

'It's all the drugs,' she said, and he smiled.

'I'm not taking that bait. You're leaving soon, yes?' he asked. 'Will you meet me someplace, somewhere, later?'

'That's pretty specific, I'll try,' she laughed. She hesitated for a moment and then spoke again. 'Now listen, Aman. It's a bit cruel but I have nobody else to ask this of. Can you help me see Sudhir one last time? Without cutting off his oxygen supply or giving him a lethal injection or something, okay? I just want to say goodbye.'

He nodded. And they sat in silence, thinking about the time they had sat on the same terrace, eavesdropping on a private conversation. It felt like it had happened in another lifetime.

41.

Meerut, May 2007 – Gumbi and Puru Return to Mumbai

Gumbi and Puru returned to Mumbai. Sukanya stood with Badi Mummy and a large group of neighbours gathered to bid them farewell. She glanced at Puru in his shiny grey shirt, a shimmering gold chain around his neck, gifted to him by his adoring mother-in-law, as he helped load Gumbi's various bags and suitcases into the car. Gumbi was channelling her inner film star and had sourced a star-speckled velvet lounge set in deep maroon and stood at no risk of getting lost in a crowd. She hung her head out of the car window, and waved a cheery goodbye to her wailing mother, brothers, and numerous cousins as the car rolled down the gully. Puru seemed a lot more restrained. Natwar and Rajni Mausi stood there too, looking determinedly stony-faced, as if to say, *you can force us to be here but you can't make us be happy about it*. After much cajoling and scolding by both Bade Papa and Shiladitya, they had finally acquiesced to bless the newlyweds, but it was clear that things were far from peachy in that branch of the family.

'Tell me, Bibi, do you think Natwar Chacha will let it all go, maybe a few years from now?' asked Sukanya of her great-grandmother as the car disappeared from sight and everyone turned around to return. Bibi harrumphed.

'Listen to me, bitiya, if you hold your breath waiting for all branches of a family to be normal and balanced, you'll go blue in the face and eventually meet your maker,' Bibi informed her, starting to walk back towards her kitchen – the tiny place where she exerted complete control, where nothing was allowed to be out of line or unpredictable, and where there was no place for messiness.

'And honestly, I have no time for this. I'm making namakparas and mathris for you. Eat them in Ing land and think of your Bibi.'

Later that afternoon, Sukanya made her way to the city hospital, its boundary walls covered with public service messages about polio vaccinations, the numerous benefits of family planning, and the hazards of not washing one's hands. Inside, the compound was filled with entire families who seemed to have descended upon the hospital for no reason at all – sitting on chatais spread on the sun-burnt grass, eating copious amount of food brought from home, and freely littering the ground with peanut shells and orange peels. Industrious-looking paramedical staff walked around, accomplishing some mysterious tasks. It was very crowded and Sukanya was relieved to see Aman hurrying towards her, wearing a lab coat, checking his watch, still smelling of the cornucopia of uppers and downers that made up his life. He gestured for her to follow him.

'Things certainly look very different from the other day,' she told Aman as he swiftly guided her inside one of the buildings in the sprawling hospital complex. 'Where are all the passionate protestors from that day? The police, the media? Nobody is marching anymore.'

'They all got tired of it and went home,' he said. 'A movement like this needs a leader. Beyond a point, it loses steam.'

'So Jogeshwar Singh will address the university at Founder's Day after all?'

'I never doubted it for a moment,' said Aman. 'Sudhir was playing this game well; this whole thing could have catapulted him into city politics, but these things take a bit of luck.'

Luck that you wouldn't allow him, Sukanya bit back the words.

Their sneakers made squelching sounds on the disinfected floors of the hospital corridor, as if the rubber soles were melting into the concrete with every step. Bright tube lights shone overhead. It was quiet here; none of the madness and chaos from outside was permitted inside.

Specialized Trauma Centre, she read on the sign

outside one of the ward doors as they made their way inside. Aman came to a halt outside a room marked General Surgical Ward. He looked in both directions down the deserted corridor, then opened the door for her.

'Five minutes, Sukanya. That's all you get; the nurse is on her break, and this is the only window where he's unsupervised. I'll wait outside and keep a watch. Don't touch anything. Go on.'

Thank you, she mouthed and stepped inside. Sudhir was the only patient in the ward. He was conscious, awake, and reading a book – *The Meditations of Marcus Aurelius*. He put the book down and turned his head slightly when he heard her enter, seemingly unsurprised. He was connected to tubes and monitors, various liquids being pumped into him, trying to keep him alive. She thought back to the night the news had come that he'd been stabbed, when it had seemed that he wouldn't make it, and felt a surge of goodwill towards Aman and his tribe.

'Making your way into a unit like this...it hasn't taken you long to figure out the ways of this place, memsahib,' said Sudhir, his voice so much more feeble, as though it hurt him to talk.

'Well, thank goodness you recognize me. I thought maybe you had Hindi film–style amnesia,' she said, trying to keep her voice light as she walked up to stand at the foot of the medical bed. He smiled.

'I really fucked up, didn't I?' he asked, seeking reassurance that wasn't hers to give.

'We all did. You just ended up being the fall guy,' she said. The room was so brightly lit, it seemed there was nowhere to hide. 'I've been given only five minutes, of which two have already been spent. I came to see you, to say goodbye. I'm leaving tomorrow.'

He nodded. She cast a long look at his face – thinner, more drawn, in pain.

'Will you be okay, Sudhir Tyagi?'

'I think so, unless they have a go at me again. Baaki, you know I am meant *to take arms against a sea of trouble.*'

'A Shakespearean hero in the narrow gullies of Bulandwada – who would have thought?'

'Who indeed? And now you go back to London, the land of my hero. And my heroine.'

'I'm really sorry, Sudhir. I had no idea this is how it would turn out. It all feels so futile now.'

'I wasn't doing it for anyone else, but for myself. I had no choice in the matter. We're all guided by our instincts.'

'And yours is to get stabbed in the stomach?'

He laughed – a low, throaty sound that couldn't quite form fully.

'Not if I can help it.'

There was a soft knock from outside the door. There was no time to speak out the treatises they both wanted to speak.

'I'd better go before they arrest me or something, Sudhir. Here, I've got something of yours.' She took the taweez from her pocket and held it out to him. 'You dropped it that day, when...you know...before the incident. A friend of yours gave it to me.'

He stared at the locket in silence, then smiled a conspiratorial smile. 'It's come back,' he whispered almost to himself. Then, as if deciding something, he spoke again.

'The plan was to tell you about this in a happier setting, memsahib, but there is a tide in the affairs of men, I am told. Open it, won't you? It's not really a taweez, I mean, not in the traditional sense.'

Sukanya stared quizzically at him, and he nodded encouragingly at her hands. She struggled with the black cloth but finally managed to wrest it free of the two silver buttons linked by a chain that had once been sown on her dress. She looked at it, unable to comprehend, then glanced at him, perplexed.

'They'd fallen down at Begam Samru's church that day,' he said, smiling. 'I'd picked them up. I would have returned them, but I needed all the luck I could get, so I figured I'd borrow them for a while. They worked very well, I must say, till they didn't.'

Aman knocked more urgently this time. Sukanya took one last look at Sudhir, and leaving the buttons on the bed, stepped out of the room.

He needed all the luck he could get. That Tyagi Boy.

42.

Meerut, May 2007 – The Long Way Home

And now, the plane was flying over endless, dense swirls of white clouds. Sukanya couldn't tire of looking at the vast, uninterrupted expanse stretching below, a sea of white. Sunlight filtered through, lighting the clouds with an ethereal glow, artworks in a heavenly gallery. The earth below couldn't be seen. The blue sky couldn't be seen either. All there was were the clouds, shifting and sorting themselves into all sorts of shapes before tiring of them and dissolving them like an impatient artist. A ship sailing on a sea of cotton. Towering mountains, the unseen tops of which are hidden somewhere in the skies. A woolly-coated sheep. A trumpeting elephant. A giant dragon spitting fire across the firmament.

Look at that shape. Doesn't that look like Badi Mummy sitting on her bed, her indoor–outdoor cat at her feet? It would be many years before Sukanya could think of her grandmother without her eyes misting, her body always recognizing the grief before her mind did. What if she had known Badi Mummy all her life?

What might they have done together? Would she have gone on pilgrimages with her as a little girl – Rishikesh, Banaras, Haridwar? What would Badi Mummy have taught her, crocheting, cross-stitch, or macramé? Which family secrets would have spilled over cups of tea and loud, raucous laughter? Which writers would they have read sitting in the baithak of their home – Dinkar, Nirala, Mahadevi Verma? The deepest sadness lay in not knowing the answers to all of these, to be banished with only a shared, imagined past for company.

And right there was a parrot in the clouds. Mithu and Mishri, screeching from their cages, holding green chillies in their claws, snapping them with their scarlet beaks. So much of Bibi's chowk would stay with her forever, but she was only eighteen, and as the years went by, she would forget much – the ornate chajjas, the sunlit chowk, the *aala*s in the walls, the steps with the stone balustrades on either side. All this she may forget, but the industrious woman in white, the single gold bangle on her scrawny wrist too loose for her, waking up at four in the morning to wash the house, telling people off for their bigotry and hypocrisy in no uncertain terms, cooking for her great-granddaughter with all the enthusiasm of a much younger person – this she would never forget; this she would carry in her veins like blood. This she would become.

The clouds were parting, making way for sunlight, revealing faces to her. Gumbi, Puru, Nandi, Atma Ram

– they were all looking at her. How quickly she had become embroiled in their lives. How unwittingly she had participated in the drama unfolding around her. A drama that had concealed and revealed, teaching her the impermanence of people. And there was Natwar, a son to Bade Papa in the absence of Shila, fighting valiantly in the streets for the honour of his adopted brother, resigned to a life of poverty and squalor, yet hoping for better things for his four children. Rajni Mausi was there, and Munto Baba, whose path crossed hers so briefly. Sunita was there too, a neighbour, no more, she had said when Sukanya had first asked her, but so much more. A beloved aunt, who had sobbed inconsolably when Sukanya had touched her feet and sought permission to leave.

The shape-shifting clouds were showing her the stately Nawabon Ki Haveli, its large gate holding within it countless secrets. Gulshan was there in the haveli, elegant to the end, her head covered, reading a thick book, forever an enigma to everyone around her, sentenced to a life of secrecy, still dreading the family that she had left behind a long time back. And Aman was there, seemingly blessed with good fortune, the one who had done so much damage and gotten away with it, struggling with addiction now, a life full of promise in jeopardy. Basheeran was there, an old-timer, a symbol of times gone by, times that would never return.

The clouds were parting, and her parents were there,

as much younger people. They didn't know they would be torn from their homes like this. They had held on to each other, maybe they did love each other that much, or maybe the fates had left them with no choice in the matter. Shila, endlessly curious, unbound by the fetters of the neighbourhood he grew up in, lost when confronted with his own past, now muddled about who he was, who he had become. A motherless man. And his wife, who had not been given even that luxury, who was never asked to return, the doors of the house with the Nathdwara pichwai forever closed to her. A *missing piece*, denied to her and to her daughter.

And there was Sudhir. That Tyagi Boy. Glimpses of him sped past Sukanya. Sudhir in her grandparents' house on the day she wore the green sharara. Sudhir at Begum Samru's church, gazing at the marble altar, sunlight streaming down on him from the dome above. Sudhir at Gumbi's haldi, eating the leftover piece of sweet. Sudhir at the student protests, his face flushed, his fist raised. Sudhir waiting for her outside Puru's library. Sudhir at Bibi's terrace, raising his glass to her as the skies behind him crackled with thunder and lightning. Sudhir in the hospital bed, asking her to open the taweez. All of these images were there, but she couldn't think of him as a composite. What would it take, what would it need, and how long would it be before she could piece them all together into a story she could tell herself?

Bulandwada was there, the time-worn mohalla with

its old houses and even older ways of being. It was being wracked, battered, by time, by progress, by change. But it didn't seem to mind. I have raised your family, Sukanya, your father, his parents, and others of your kin before them, it seemed to say. I am glad to meet you, happy to invite you into my fold, but don't think I'll be gone just because you are. Like the clouds you look at with such fervour, I too am a shape-shifter. I have changed before. I will change again. The stories are all the same. Of love and acceptance. Of revenge and jealousy. Of envy and desire. Of rebellion and conformity. Only the people change. I will remain.

London was emerging from the clouds, with its medieval towers, baroque cathedrals and glass and steel buildings. This was the city that has raised her, this had been home. And where did you disappear to? it was asking of her. Everything has been on hold since you left. You must pick up the pieces of the life you abandoned so carelessly. Did you forget the way, come let me guide you back. Here is Angie, who has let you read her new comic books before she read them herself when you were both five, who has waited for you when you were held up in school, whose mother has baked you oatmeal and raisin cookies every Christmas. Here is the used-book store you have worked in the summers. You don't know it yet, but one day the sweet, papery smell of dusty old books will make you ache with homesickness for this place. Here is the house where your parents sit and watch TV in the evenings, *The Kumars at No.*

42, snow falling like powdery dust outside the window, the camel-print curtains left open. Home means many things, Sukanya. And you will keep running into them as you bumble through life. For now, home is a place where people know your name. Lalli, gudiya, bitiya, darling, sweetheart, mate. You have many names in many places. *There is no missing piece*. You are whole.

She turns away from the window, from the endless clouds and assesses the plane. The stewardess arrives, smiling but a little irate. It is a long flight, and people have placed many demands on her. She serves the meal, an insipid affair of mashed potatoes, bread and salad. Sukanya accepts the food in its plastic container, the little sachets of ketchup and mustard, the small packets of butter, the plastic fork and spoon wrapped in a paper napkin, unable to awaken her appetite.

'Aren't you going to eat? What are you thinking about so intently?' asks the voice from the next seat.

She looks at the face regarding her with such deep concern, and smiles. She takes the weathered hand that has reached out to stroke her hair into her own, the strength gone from it, and looks at the age spots sprinkled on the loose, bluish skin.

'Of course I will eat, Bade Papa,' she says. 'Just missing the food from Bulandwada, that's all. I can't wait to show you London.'

Bade Papa smiles. He cannot wait, either. They start eating as the plane continues its journey over the ancient kingdom of clouds.

RAISING READERS

Books Build Bright Futures

Dear Reader,

We hope you enjoyed reading this book and we'd love your attention for one more page, to share with you what's going on with children and books.

The number of children reading in their leisure time and for fun is in rapid decline. Young people have a lot of competition for their time, and a worryingly high number have only a few or no books at home.

If this is not a crisis already, it soon will be.

Studies have shown that reading for fun is the **single biggest predictor of a child's future success** – more than family circumstance, parents' educational background or income. It improves academic results, mental health, wealth, communication skills and ambition.

Our business works committedly to create books that are well-researched, engaging, and enduring, but here are some ways we can all raise more readers:

- Reading to children for just 10 minutes a day makes a difference
- Don't give up if children aren't regular readers – it's not just about the number of books they have or read but about encouraging interest and engagement
- Encourage them to listen to audiobooks
- Support schools and other libraries
- Give books as gifts

Thank you for reading: there's a lot more information about how to encourage children to read on our website.

www.raisingreaders.in